DEADBEAT DAD

DEADBEAT DAD

LILY ROCK MYSTERY
BOOK 5

BONNIE HARDY

Copyright © 2023 Bonnie Hardy

This is a work of fiction. Names, characters, places, and incidents either are the product of the author's imagination or are used fictitiously, and any resemblance of fictional characters to actual persons living or dead, business establishments, events, or locales is entirely coincidental.

All rights reserved. No part of this book may be used or reproduced in any manner without written permission from the author and publisher except in the case of brief quotations embodied in critical articles or reviews.

eBook ISBN: 978-1-954995-08-6

Paperback ISBN: 978-1-954995-09-3

Cover Design by Ebook Launch

Editing by Proof Positive

GET A FREE SHORT STORY

Join my VIP newsletter to get the latest news of Lily Rock along with contests, discounts, events, and giveaways! I'll also send you *Meadow's Hat*, a short story set before book one :).

Sign up on bonniehardywrites.com/newsletter

"Misery is easy. It's happiness you have to work at."

Ondine
Written and Directed by Neil Jordan

CHAPTER ONE

"To what do I owe this pleasure?" Arlo smiled at Olivia as he wiped the bar with his cloth.

"I'm meeting someone here, so I thought I'd hang out with you to catch up." She looked over her shoulder and then back to him. "I don't have to ask about business, the place is packed."

"It's been like this all summer. I thought the crowd would back off a little after Labor Day, but if anything more people showed up. Hold on a minute. Have to take this to the table over there." He held a tray with three beers and a bubbly soda.

Olivia watched his tall lanky frame move effortlessly through the crowd. He carried the tray aloft, stopping to speak to a couple. Then he moved on to the next group. Four young adults sat at a high-top table near the small stage. The man looked up as Arlo approached.

He must be asking for IDs, Olivia observed. Three of the four handed over their driver's license before he set the glasses on the table. *I've never seen those people before. Probably up from LA.*

Arlo returned with an empty tray at his side. With deft

efficiency, he slid the tray under the counter and then checked his iPad for the next order. He poured a flight of beer, four samples from the pub brewery, then checked his order again before putting the flight on the tray and hoisting it in the air.

After a few minutes Arlo returned, the empty tray under his arm. He polished a glass and looked at her with a smile. "The usual?" he asked, using his tongs to drop ice in the glass.

"Thanks." When he didn't keep talking, she realized he was looking over her head at the busy room filled with customers. She ducked to give him a better view. He reached for the hose to fill her glass with soda water. Pulling a lemon from under the bar, he gave a skillful squeeze, sliding the drink closer.

"Waiting for Mike?" He reached for another clean glass.

"He's been staying late at the construction site." She eyed the slice of lemon he'd balanced on the rim of her glass. "I'm actually here to meet up with a potential new percussionist for Sweet Four O'Clock."

At the mention of her band, Arlo nodded. "The other one didn't last too long."

She took a long sip. The liquid hit the back of her throat with a tingle. Olivia stopped drinking to explain. "We took on a drummer for our tour this summer. But she had another gig for fall so we're looking for someone new. A guy named Malone contacted me on Gig Masters. He said he'd meet me here at five to talk."

Arlo leaned over the bar. "Malone..." His face looked quizzical. "You don't mean Beats Malone, the old drummer for The Eclectics?"

"That's him." Olivia's eyes grew wide. "He's famous in certain music circles."

"He's well known to a lot of people, plays old-time music

and rock and roll. He got a mention in a recent percussion documentary on Netflix. I call that *really* famous."

Olivia grinned. "Am I supposed to be honored with his presence or something? Do we roll out a red carpet when he shows up and then stop everyone and make a big introduction? That kind of famous?"

"You gotta admit, it doesn't take a lot to be famous in Lily Rock. But I think we can forget about the red carpet. If he stays even a weekend, I'm so naming a beer after him, probably an IPA."

Olivia held up one finger to temporarily halt their conversation. She looked over his head at the bar clock on the wall. *It's a little past five.*

"He's late," she told Arlo. "I'm not impressed."

"He's a drummer. Being late goes with the territory," Arlo said with a smirk.

"Actually coming in late can be catastrophic for a drummer and the entire band. We depend on the percussionist to come in right on time." Olivia put the phone on the bar top. She took another sip of her soda water. "So do you think Beats is his nickname? I mean, he's a drummer and all."

Arlo reached under the counter again and refilled her glass. "I thought his name was weird the first time I heard it. But then I read an interview in *Rolling Stone*. Apparently Beats is his given name. His family comes from Switzerland and Beats is as common as naming your kid John."

Olivia's eyebrows raised. She checked her phone again. "Okay, I'm not an expert but culturally speaking, the Swiss are even more particular than the Germans about time, and if that's the case, where is our potential new drummer?"

Arlo didn't answer. He moved to the other end of the bar to take an order. Olivia sipped on her water, thinking about the phone call she'd received the day before.

"This is Olivia Greer," she'd answered.

"Saw your ad on Gig Masters," came a male voice. "Thought I'd call about your job. My name is Beats Malone. Heard of me?"

"I can't say that I have," she'd responded.

"You're in Lily Rock, right? I want to make sure I have the right band, Sweet Four O'Clock?"

"We rehearse here. Are you familiar with the town?"

"Yeah, I read up on it: a couple of hours from LA, in the mountains. Small-town vibe, something about a dog who's the mayor. I know a few people who live up there. I'm a percussionist, by the way. It said in the ad you were looking for one."

Once she realized he was a drummer, she'd dropped her guard. "Give me an idea about other bands you've played with." After a salvo of name dropping, they'd arranged for a meeting the next day.

Olivia glanced to her left and then to her right, waiting for Arlo to return. People stood at the bar, beer glasses in hand, chatting loudly. She felt people standing behind her as if ready to pounce on her chair when she stood up.

I wish Sage were here to meet Malone. Then the decision could be made by both of us. When I told her he was coming up to talk, she pulled away from the conversation so fast. I suppose she has a lot on her mind, what with...

Arlo called out, "I'm going to check on that table again." He glanced over her shoulder, his eyes narrowing. "Those kids drink fast." A ding from the kitchen cut through the sound of loud voices. Olivia saw four plates slide under the warming lights.

Arlo grabbed the plates, stacking them on his arm. "Food for the table over there," he told her as he hustled past. She watched as he placed the food in front of the young people and then reached back to grab a bottle of catsup off another couple's table.

When Arlo returned to the bar, his mouth was drawn in a tight-lipped expression. Olivia raised her eyebrows, waiting for him to explain. "They wanted me to speak to the people leaning on the wall waiting for their table." He raised his voice to explain further. "The boy said, 'They keep staring at us. It makes me feel uncomfortable.'" Arlo shook his head. "We got people waiting for seats because it's Friday night. I can't afford to turn away customers. My motto is: drink a beer, eat the food, and then go."

"So who is that group anyway?" Olivia asked.

"Three of them are siblings. I only know that because they live with their mother up by us. The fourth one may be the boy's girlfriend. I don't know that for certain." He slid his towel over the counter again. "They moved here six weeks ago. Cayenne keeps her eye out. I don't think she feels quite right about all those older kids living with their mother in a mountain cabin."

"Cayenne's intuition is kicking in again," Olivia agreed.

Before Arlo could say more, a loud bark pierced the crowd of voices, most likely coming from the parking lot downstairs. "Is that the mayor?" Olivia set her glass down.

"Sounds like him." When the barking continued, Arlo focused his gaze toward the railing. Every barstool at the long counter was filled with people drinking, the forest providing atmosphere from a distance. Those who liked the view of the trees came early to grab seats. Plus it was a good place to start up conversations with strangers.

The barking continued as the pub grew quieter, more and more people pausing to listen. One man shoved the shoulder of his companion, holding his finger over his lips.

"That is Mayor Maguire!" Olivia spoke loudly and then

stood up from her stool. She snatched her cell phone off the bar, slipping it into her pocket. She began to push past people standing in the way, heading toward the exit.

"Let me get this," Arlo shouted after her. "I don't want you going all hyper-sleuth on me. You're always getting in over your head."

Olivia paused. "Why don't we both go together to see why he's barking so ferociously?" She waited for Arlo to untie his apron and walk around the bar as people resumed their conversations.

"See anything?" Arlo asked as they passed people sitting on the rail looking over.

One man shook his head. "Whose dog is making all the racket?"

Arlo took Olivia's elbow. "It's not someone's dog, that's the mayor of Lily Rock you're talking about. He doesn't bark for no reason." Arlo made his way through the remaining crowd with Olivia close behind. When people began to follow them, Arlo turned around.

"Stay put. We'll figure this out. You just keep drinking." The crowd did not need a second invitation. Those who stood now sat back down as the voices grew louder in conversation.

Once outside, Olivia followed Arlo down the metal stairway. At the foot of the stairs, she stopped to listen. "I think M&M is over at the end of the parking lot near the woods." She followed Arlo as they made their way closer.

The barking grew louder as they passed parked vehicles and reached the area where the pavement ended and the woods began. "Stay behind me," Arlo insisted. "I'll go first and see what the commotion is about."

"Okay," she agreed.

"Hey, Mayor," he called out. The sound of his voice only made the dog bark louder.

DEADBEAT DAD

"It's me, M&M," Olivia shouted. As soon as Mayor Maguire caught sight of her, he jumped up and down and then stopped barking. His tail wagged, urging them forward. He turned his back on them, his head bowed, sniffing something on the ground.

The closer they got, the more her stomach tightened. Arriving at the same time, they flanked Mayor Maguire.

"I see now," Olivia said, her voice filled with concern.

A body lay on the ground, facedown in the dirt.

"This doesn't look good," Arlo said.

The body was awkwardly posed, with one arm folded underneath, blood oozing on the dirt from under his body.

Arlo grasped Mayor Maguire's collar with one hand and spoke in a calm voice. "Good dog," he said. Once he'd secured the dog, he stooped down to look more closely at the body. Olivia came up next to him.

"Looks like a male; he seems to be unconscious," Arlo stated flatly.

She felt her heart beat in her throat. "That's a lot of blood. Can you check his pulse?" Taking Mayor Maguire's collar, she moved him back so that Arlo could look more closely.

His fingers wrapped around the exposed wrist of the unconscious man. After a moment he dropped the hand and then backed away. "I can't feel a pulse. You'd better call 911."

Olivia let go of the mayor's collar to reach for her cell phone. Her hand trembled and her breaths came in short gasps. She tapped in the numbers. Mayor Maguire gave one sharp bark as if to hurry her along.

"We've got this, Mayor," she assured him.

The labradoodle lifted his head, round black eyes looking directly at her. He seemed to be considering her words as if seeing for himself whether she had the situation under control. Satisfied that she meant business, he nudged her knee with his nose.

Olivia patted his head with one hand as she spoke into her cell phone. "There's an emergency at the Lily Rock pub. We've found a body at the edge of the woods."

CHAPTER TWO

Emergency responders filled the parking lot. The body had already been lifted onto a gurney, which was then loaded into the back of an ambulance. Since the face of the victim was covered, Olivia suspected that time of death had already been called.

She'd been warned to stay away from the body by Officer Janis Jets, who was the first on the scene. Olivia watched as Janis spoke to Arlo, but she couldn't hear what they were saying. A shudder rushed up her spine remembering the blood oozing in the dirt. She looked up to see people lined up along the railing, drinking beer and staring at the commotion in the parking lot. *Janis must have told them not to come down.*

"Stay where you are," Officer Jets shouted to one man who'd eased his way from the stairway to get a closer view. He scurried back as the onlookers laughed and pointed.

Janis continued to shout. "Stop laughing. Listen carefully. I want a brief statement from all of you before you leave the pub." Her constabulary assistant, Brad May, stood next to Janis. At her announcement, he looked stricken. Jets turned to him and glared, offering a small pad of paper and a tiny pencil.

Olivia saw Janis's face contort with anger as she yelled at Brad. Finally he took the notepad from her hand. When she asked him another question, he shook his head no. She reached into her jacket and pulled out a pen, snatching the small pencil from his hand.

As Jets's former assistant, Olivia couldn't help but smirk. *Brad is out of his element right now. I'm going to ask her if she needs my help.* Pulling her shoulder bag closer to her side, she stepped over the yellow tape delineating the crime scene. Janis entered information into her iPad while Olivia watched.

"I might have known you'd be here," muttered Jets without turning around. "Your boyfriend is over there. Why don't you go and talk to him? I'm busy."

Olivia was surprised at the news. "I didn't see Michael."

Being a small town, Lily Rock often called on a group of volunteer first responders. "I was talking to Arlo when we heard Mayor Maguire barking," she explained to Jets.

"Silly mutt," muttered the officer. "On the one hand, he's always hanging around, but on the other hand, I think we got to the body much faster because of him. The doc narrowed down time of death right away; sometime between four and five o'clock."

"So he was murdered?"

"I am fairly certain he'd been wounded. I saw lots of blood. Probably a knife wound." Jets looked at her iPad, a smirk on her lips.

"Oh right, I didn't see that." Olivia felt her stomach clench. *What an awful way to go.*

Jets turned around to face Olivia. "Since you won't go away, why don't you tell me what happened. Spill. What you heard and saw as you approached the body. Spare no detail. Go ahead. Bore me."

"Oh." Olivia blinked. "Okay then, like I said we heard Mayor Maguire. When he didn't stop barking and got even louder, we both pushed through the crowd to make our way into the parking lot. I followed the sound of the mayor's barks to the far end of the parking lot, near the woods."

"Go on," she said, typing with one finger into her iPad.

"As soon as Arlo and I got closer, I could see a body. The mayor leaned over him, sniffing. Once Arlo got the mayor to stop barking, he checked on the body. Arlo tried to find a pulse. Right after that he told me to call 911."

Jets tapped some more. Then she closed her document. "That's pretty much what Arlo already told me. Now if I could only get the mayor to give me his account." Janis looked at Olivia.

"He doesn't know how to write," Olivia played along. Then she smiled. "He probably could tell us a lot about sniffing."

Jets shrugged.

Olivia sighed. Then she inhaled deeply, trying to clear her thoughts.

"So what I want to know is why were you at the pub this afternoon? You don't drink and you weren't with Michael. Just catching up with the local barkeep because you didn't have anything else to do?"

Olivia's eyes grew wide. "That's it! I forgot to tell you. I was supposed to meet up with a new percussion player. We arranged to get together at five o'clock. If that went well, he planned on sitting in with the band later this evening. Beats Malone, that's his name."

She took a deep breath, continuing to explain. "As soon as we found the body, I forgot all about Beats. He was late and..."

Janis's mouth drew a straight line. "Okay, Nancy Drew. You're the amateur sleuth here. Do you think the dead guy is the wannabe percussionist?"

"I've only seen him on social media. But I know somebody who's seen him in person who could identify him." She pivoted toward the stairway where Arlo was talking to Brad. Jets followed her glance.

"You mean Arlo, not my assistant, I assume?"

"I mean Arlo. He went to a few Eclectics concerts and followed Beats on social media, so he'd be more likely to know if that's his body."

"I've got this," Jets muttered. "Forget what I said earlier about looking for Mike. You stay here and wait."

As she walked away, Olivia did exactly the opposite. She looked for Michael in the sea of faces surrounding the crime scene. She saw him right away, standing tall and talking to another responder. He didn't hesitate to break up the conversation to stride across the lot, heading in her direction. Once he got close enough, she reached out to be enveloped in his arms.

Her face pressed against the warm flannel of his shirt as she buried her head in his chest. He spoke first. "I came as soon as they called out for first responders. Lots of traffic, or I'd have been here sooner." Michael's breath warmed her ear.

Her fear dissolved instantly, as it always did when he was near. She lifted her head and took a step back. He released her from his arms, looking down at her face.

"I was here to meet a new percussionist," she explained.

His face filled with concern. "I was up on the hill getting ready to break ground on the new house when I got the call."

"I know." She nodded. "You've been really busy up there, but at least I always know where to find you."

"I turn my back for a minute and you find another dead

body. Geez, Olivia. You are a handful."

"To know me is to love me." The corner of her mouth lifted, as if inviting him to agree.

"I do love you. Now then, why is Janis jabbering at Arlo?" He pointed over her head.

She turned to see Janis's mouth moving rapidly, then she raised her hand and snapped her fingers at a paramedic close by. Once he came closer, Janis shouted some orders. The paramedic nodded his agreement and then walked toward the ambulance. He opened the back doors. From where she stood, Olivia could see the gurney with the body. As the paramedics waited, Janis and Arlo walked toward the ambulance.

Arlo lowered his head to step inside. He leaned over the body. Olivia watched as a paramedic pulled back the blanket, exposing the victim's face. Arlo nodded. He looked again and spoke a word to Janis Jets. Only then did he step out of the vehicle. Even from a distance, Olivia saw that his face looked downcast. Jets stood to the side, continuing to poke at her iPad. Arlo caught sight of Michael and Olivia, making his way across the lot toward them.

"I think he's gonna tell us what's going on," muttered Michael.

Arlo came closer, his mouth looking grim. He stopped in front of them, his hand squeezing the back of his neck. "So Olivia, I don't think Beats Malone is gonna be your new drummer."

Olivia nodded, her heart thumping wildly. "Was that him, the dead body is Beats?"

"I recognized him immediately from his Instagram account. Now we know why he didn't show up for your meeting."

She felt Michael's arm reach around her shoulders. He pulled her closer to his side as Janis Jets came over to talk.

"Until we can find a family member, I'm going to assume Arlo is correct that this is the one and only Beats Malone. His wallet says the same. The doctor has yet to determine the exact cause of death, but it looks like a knife wound to me."

Jets glanced around the parking lot. "Once Brad gets all the statements, we'll let people go. That will help us match vehicles to their owners. Then we'll check the pub's surveillance for other clues."

"Most of the pub is covered with CCTV," Arlo added.

"There is closed circuit," Jets agreed. "But I suspect the camera doesn't go that far into the corner behind the pub. It's so close to the woods. I don't think we'll get anything, but we will certainly check it out."

Everyone nodded.

Jets turned to Olivia. "This isn't your first dead percussionist, now is it? A year ago that Franco guy got killed, and now Malone." Jets looked confused. "Isn't that in some movie, you know, about a series of dead drummers?"

"*Spinal Tap*," Arlo interjected. "The drummers in *Spinal Tap* keep dying."

"That's it," exclaimed Janis. "Just like *Spinal Tap*, you've got another dead drummer. What is it with you anyway?" She glared at Olivia. When she couldn't get a reply from her, Janis turned on her heel. Heading toward the pub, she shoved past people who stood on the steps, making her way up the stairs.

"I better get back to the bar," Arlo muttered. "Brad is supposed to take down everyone's phone number so they can be contacted if necessary." He sighed, then his face brightened. "The pub may become a tourist attraction over this. You know, the place the famous drummer, Beats Malone, met his end." With a shrug he turned away, leaving Michael and Olivia alone.

"How about we go home now," Michael suggested.

A quizzical look came over her face. "I'm ready to get out of here, but I wonder where Mayor Maguire went?"

Michael glanced toward the back of the lot and then turned to look beyond into the woods. "I think I see him over there," he said, pointing. Sure enough, the labradoodle stood at the edge of the forest, his tail waving above his body.

"Come on, M&M," Olivia yelled.

He bounded across the parking lot, stopping abruptly to sit in front of her boots. She smiled down at him.

"It's going to be dark soon," she began. He licked her hand. She inched her fingers to scratch behind his ear. "Why don't you come home with us tonight? There's been enough excitement for one day."

The dog looked at Michael, then back to Olivia.

"You can ride in the truck," Michael offered. "Olivia will follow us in her car."

The mayor nodded his furry head. He trotted away from Olivia to stand on Michael's right side by his knee. As Michael and the mayor took off toward the truck, Olivia pulled out her cell phone.

Her heart skipped a beat. *One missed text from Beats Malone.* She scrolled to her messages, feeling the need to read Beats's text again. Her hand trembled as she read the message.

Got held up. Will be a few minutes late. Been listening to your band on my phone. You rock.

Tears formed in Olivia's eyes. Her hand shook as she shoved the cell phone into her shoulder bag. *He really wanted to play in our band.*

She made her way across the lot to where she'd parked her car earlier. Unable to shake her sadness, she slid into the driver's seat, holding back tears. *Up until I came to Lily Rock, I'd never been involved with a murder. And now I'm right back into the thick of things.*

CHAPTER THREE

Early Monday morning Olivia stopped by Hello Age to hand in her official resignation. Sheila stood behind the desk, a big smile accompanying her rosy cheeks.

"Oh Olivia, it's so good to see you!"

Olivia handed over the envelope. "I'm sorry it's taken so long to visit, but the band started the summer tour."

Sheila smiled. "We miss you so much here. I know you had to go after the big turnover in the spring. But I'd hoped, as did many of the residents, that you would come back even if just to participate in karaoke night."

"I love karaoke night! Maybe Raleigh can come too."

Sheila's eyebrows raised. "I heard Raleigh moved down the hill a couple of weeks ago."

"I guess I still have some catching up to do," Olivia admitted.

Sheila looked at her more closely. "They call me nearly every week. I guess they still miss their granddad. Don't worry, their move was a good thing. The estate became final and Raleigh decided to live in Los Angeles. I'm happy for them. It's good for a young person to make friends with other young people, don't you think?"

"You're right. I'll send Raleigh a text just to let them know we're thinking of them." She glanced around the room. "Look at this place. Hello Age provides so many opportunities to be part of a thriving community. People need people, I guess."

Sheila reached under the counter. She held up a clipboard. "Now that you are no longer on staff, I will put you on a mailing list for all of the Hello Age community activities." She shoved the clipboard across the desk.

By the time Olivia drove away from the retirement community, an hour had passed. She took her time, stopping to chat with residents along the way. *I'll volunteer at Hello Age from now on. Even if I don't get paid, I still like hanging out with everyone.*

She drove out of the parking lot onto the main highway toward the Lily Rock Music Academy. *I'm a bit late. I hope Sage isn't too busy.* Since getting back from the summer World Music Festival, Olivia hadn't seen much of Sage at home. *I'm so happy we both agreed to have tea this morning.*

Once inside the academy administration building, she knocked lightly on Sage's closed door. "Come in," came the familiar voice.

Opening the door, she stuck her head in. "Sorry I'm late. Are you too busy for tea?" One look at Sage told her something was wrong. "Are you okay?"

Her face looked pale and her eyes bloodshot, as if she'd been crying. "I've had a bout of morning sickness," Sage explained.

"I'm so sorry. Can I get you something? Soda or crackers?"

Sage stood to her feet as Olivia pointed to the round protrusion where her sister's flat belly used to be. "I thought morning sickness happened in the first trimester."

Sage nodded. "It hits me again when I'm overtired."

"Let's sit down then," Olivia suggested. Once they were settled, Olivia knew she had to explain why Sweet Four O'Clock would not be hiring a new percussionist very soon. *Do I bring up finding the dead body of our potential percussionist to a pregnant woman?* She plunged in. "So I guess we won't be interviewing a new drummer."

"So I heard." Tears welled up in her sister's eyes. She wiped them away with the back of her hand. "I'm just more emotional these days."

"It was a shock, even for those of us who are not pregnant," Olivia admitted. "Have you been able to keep anything down today?"

"Just sips of water." Sage managed a smile.

"Why don't we take a short walk outside to the Curated Cuisine? We can grab tea and a muffin. A walk in the fresh air might help."

"Sounds good." Sage sniffed.

They walked side by side down the pathway to the student cafeteria. Olivia spoke first. "I bet Meadow was excited to see you after being away for a month."

"Not just excited. She unloaded two quilts and several knitted hats with matching gloves on me for the baby."

"You still don't want to know if it's a boy or girl?"

"That's why Mom is using a lot of gender-neutral colors for all of her crafts."

"So no gender reveal party?"

"Not if I can help it." Sage grinned. "I'm going to go old-school and be surprised when baby arrives."

"That sounds very mature. Have you thought any more about decorating a room for the nursery?"

"I'll tell you as soon as we sit down." Sage walked through the entry door and made a beeline to the beverage station.

She returned with a decaffeinated tea and a coffee for Olivia. Once they found a bench outside, Sage took a sip and then picked up the conversation. "So you and Michael, how's the house construction coming along? Will you be moving soon?"

"You're stuck with us for at least a year longer."

"I'm happy you'll be with me for the first few months anyway. You can bond with your new niece or nephew."

"That would be amazing." *I'll be an aunt. I never believed that would happen to me. Our small family is growing...*

She looked at her sister. "Do you think Meadow will give us a chance with the baby? I mean, she'll be using her super-grandma power and probably take over all aspects of the raising and sheltering."

Sage smiled. "I think Meadow will be a wonderful grandmother, but I'm the mom, don't forget. Baby is my responsibility."

Olivia clearly heard the word "my". *She's so protective. Why hasn't she told me about the baby's father...*

Olivia remembered that first conversation months ago.

"How was your hiking trip in Colorado?" she'd asked.

"The Rockies were amazing."

Sage left no room for further conversation after that. It wasn't until a month had passed that Olivia noticed Sage shifted from coffee to tea in the morning and then would excuse herself right away to use the bathroom. She'd return looking very pale.

It took three months of evasion and excuses until Sage finally admitted, "I'm pregnant."

"No way!" Olivia had felt relieved and very surprised. She'd assumed that Sage, having just turned forty, didn't want children. Olivia would always remember the hug they shared at the announcement of a baby.

"You're happy, right? You want the baby?" she'd asked right away.

"I am thrilled." Yet a slight catch in her voice led Olivia to believe otherwise. But even after admitting she was pregnant, Sage never mentioned baby's father.

Olivia had spoken to Michael about her concerns. "It's not uncommon to meet someone on spring break."

"I've only been around one woman who was pregnant, my ex-wife. After our son died from cancer, it became very painful for us to talk about him. At least until we decided to meet up once a year just to honor his memory. Things got better after that."

She reached over to touch his hand, knowing instinctively that no words would help with his loss.

Michael recovered quickly after her touch. "So our Sage is pregnant." He leaned back in his chair. "Does that mean I'll be an honorary uncle?"

"How about just an uncle, no honorary about it? Along with Meadow, we'll be the most important adult influence in baby's life, living right in the house, at least for the first year."

"I guess I'd better get moving with the construction then." Michael turned his hand over to envelop her fingers in his.

Sage's voice brought Olivia back to the present.

"So I was thinking, the huge walk-in closet in the main bedroom could be transformed into a small nursery. It would be close to my room but there's still a door to separate us when necessary. Baby could stay there for several months and then we could set up the office as a bedroom."

"Great idea," Olivia agreed. "Plus I don't use that office. It was Marla's and I've never felt comfortable there. Once you've gotten to know baby better, you can decorate the office with more detail."

Sage looked happy, her eyes bright with anticipation.

"Plus the oversized closet is plenty big enough for a crib, changing table, and rocking chair. Do you think we could take a look and figure out what to do with all the stuff that's in there now?"

"How about this coming weekend? I'll put the extra bookcases and chair on Offer. Someone will want them."

Sage nodded her agreement.

* * *

Wind brushed against the pine tree limbs, sending needles into the sky. They bounced off the front of her car as Olivia pulled into the driveway in front of her house. She kicked at a pine cone on her way to the front door.

"Hello, doggo," she greeted Mayor Maguire.

He'd spread out on the mat in front of the door, his chin resting on his paws.

"Mind getting up so that I can unlock the door?"

He rose reluctantly, and then as an afterthought, offered her a paw in greeting.

"Nice to see you too," she said.

She waited for the mayor to come inside before closing the door. Her cell phone pinged. She opened the text from Janis Jets.

Meet me at Thyme Out. Got more questions about our dead body. Now.

Olivia shoved her cell into her purse. "See you later, M&M," she called out, shutting the door with a thud.

Thyme Out hummed with activity. The smell of freshly ground coffee filled the air. After the morning rush, the glass display case held a few leftover cookies and two large brownies.

Cookie Kravitz stood behind the counter, impressive in

his white bakery apron. Gray hair swept back from his face, a mustache covered his full lips, and a goatee finished his look. Sharp blue eyes watched a child who looked into the display case.

"You like the ones with candies," suggested his mother.

"I don't want any chocolate," the child complained. "My teacher says it's bad for my long-range health journey."

Cookie shook his head and then raised his eyes to greet Olivia. She smiled back, pointing toward the open patio door. He nodded before reaching into the glass case. He pulled out a huge chocolate brownie with chocolate frosting and chocolate chips on top. "Here you go, kid," he said to the boy. "I guarantee when you eat this, you will no longer care about your long-range health journey."

The child eyed the enormous brownie with a look of awe. Olivia waved at Cookie as she passed, stepping onto the back patio where her eyes immediately sighted Officer Janis Jets hunched over the farthest table.

"Got your message," Olivia mumbled as she pulled out a chair to sit down with Janis. When she did not look up from her tablet, Olivia got back on her feet. "I'm going to order cookies before every one is gone. Want anything?"

Jets continued to read, holding up her empty mug of coffee. "Sure. Coffee of the day. Make it black."

Before Olivia moved, Cookie appeared at the table, a pot of coffee in his hand. He refilled Janis's mug. "There you go, sweetie. What can I get you, Olivia?"

"Six thyme shortbread cookies and another black coffee," she said immediately.

"Be right back." Cookie bent over to whisper in Janis's ear before he turned to go.

She giggled. "He's incorrigible," she said in a low growl. "I love that man!"

"So you've said," Olivia muttered.

Jets cleared her throat. "I want you to read the police report from yesterday. If everything is written as you remember, then I'll have you come to the constabulary to sign. At your earliest convenience, of course." Jets smirked.

Olivia read from Janis's iPad while Jets sipped coffee. When she was done, she handed it back. "I forgot to mention I had an appointment with the victim and was waiting for him when the murder occurred."

"Right, I'll put that in later. Anything else you have for me?"

Olivia felt defensive. "I'm not holding anything back, at least not deliberately."

"That would be a first," Jets said, turning back to her iPad.

Cookie arrived with a full mug of coffee for Olivia and a basket filled with thyme shortbread cookies.

"Oh yum." Olivia reached for the one on top.

"Would you ladies like anything else?" he asked.

"I do have a question." Janis gestured toward another table. Olivia followed her gaze to two people sitting across the outdoor patio. A young man and a woman sat in silence looking at their cell phones. "Are those two Lily Rock residents or tourists?" Janis asked.

Cookie rubbed his beard, looking out the side of his eye. "Those two come in here nearly every day. I think the female told me she moved to Lily Rock some six weeks ago. I assume she lives with the guy because he's always with her."

Olivia looked at the table again. "I've seen them before. They were with two other people at the pub Friday night. One of them asked Arlo to talk to some people who were waiting for their seat. I guess the guy was annoyed."

Jets nodded. "Just looking at them annoys me. I get a feeling of entitlement. Plus I keep an eye out for nearly everyone in this town, and I've been seeing those two around. Mostly at the library and the hardware store. I was just curious. But now that you say they were there Friday night, I have an excuse to get to know them better, to inquire about what they saw."

"Did Brad get everyone's contact information?"

"My assistant completed his task. Don't look so smug. He's working out okay. Better than when you had the job."

Olivia let the comment slide. "Arlo knows a little about them. They moved in next door to him. He said the guy and two other women are siblings who live with their mother up the hill. One girl must be a girlfriend."

Jets put down her coffee mug. "Is that so..."

"Arlo also said that Cayenne's been keeping her eye on the family. She's uneasy about them."

Jets's eyes widened. "So our Two-Spirit mystic has feelings about the new family. Okay then, maybe I should go chat them up." She turned to Cookie with a dazzling smile. "Get me the bill, garçon. I'm going to introduce myself to that couple over there, the ones chowing down on your famous cinnamon buns. See you later."

CHAPTER FOUR

Janis Jets strode toward the round table where the young couple sat. The woman disengaged from her cell phone first. She placed her elbows on the table, resting her chin on her hands. A hoodie hid her body, a pair of Ray-Ban sunglasses covered her eyes.

The young man across from her did not look up, eyes on his device. Decidedly unhip, he wore a Comic Con T-shirt frayed at the neck. His hair stuck out from a too small baseball cap, a beard struggling for recognition on his chin. Olivia watched as he shoved a piece of cinnamon roll in his mouth without looking up. Even from a distance she observed a certain awkwardness about his demeanor.

Janis stood by their table waiting. When the girl looked away and the man didn't look up, she thrust her hip to the right, her hand patting her back pocket. *She's reaching for her weapon...* Having closely observed the police officer for nearly two years, Olivia had become familiar with most of Janis's gestures. Watching more closely, she saw Janis pat the back of her blazer again. She *suspects something...*

Olivia felt impatient. *I want to hear their conversation.*

Look at me, getting all nosy again. Why do I keep doing this, butting my way into Janis's business? She wrapped her hand around the empty coffee mug. *I'll make my move as soon as they start talking.*

Jets finally cleared her throat. "Good morning," came her voice of authority.

Olivia dithered. *Do I move closer...or do I stay put...* She felt her legs tingle. She stood slowly so as not to attract attention. *I can't help myself.*

Olivia took that moment to move closer. Taking small steps, she edged across the patio to sit in an empty chair. Her back was toward the couple and Janis, but she could hear Jets clear her throat again.

Olivia closed her eyes to block out everything but the potential confrontation.

"You're new in town and I make it a habit to get to know people in Lily Rock," Jets finally explained.

"Go away," the female responded.

"Now is that any way to treat me, the senior officer of the constabulary?"

Oooh, look out, young couple. Olivia squirmed, knowing Jets would be very mad by now.

"We don't do small talk," came the girl's reply. "He has Asperger's," she added, as if that diagnosis explained everything.

"Is that so," Janis responded in a droll voice. "I've got a bad attitude, but that doesn't stop me from trying to be nice. What's your name?"

Olivia inhaled deeply.

"My name is Ashley Tennant. His name is Brandon Grey. What's yours?"

"Officer Janis Jets. I hear you live up on Hemstreet, right out of town."

"On the corner," Ashley said.

"You live there too?" asked Jets.

"Brandon and I share the basement. His sisters and mother live upstairs, not that it's any of your business."

"Everything is my business," commented Jets dryly. "Not that I'm really interested though. Don't get confused about that. I don't care about you personally. It's my job to keep close tabs on the residents of Lily Rock. You two are kind of dull-witted, if you ask me. Either that or you're doing a good job of pretending to be stupid."

Olivia inhaled quickly. *She's trying to provoke them.*

"You have no right to call us stupid. Come on, Brandon. Finish your roll and let's get going. I won't be disrespected by a small-town cop."

Olivia heard chairs scrape against cement. She took her purse off her shoulder to look inside for her cell phone, but mostly to hide her face should Brandon or Ashley look over and suspect she'd been listening. Then she turned in her chair slightly to get a better view.

As the couple stormed across the patio toward the door into the bakery, Janis Jets followed in hot pursuit. "Don't worry, I know where to find you. And by the way...welcome to Lily Rock." The last words were executed with so much tongue in cheek, Olivia was surprised that Janis didn't burst out laughing. She watched as Jets waved at the couple's backs Then Janis turned, raising her eyebrows at Olivia. *She knows I was listening in*

Janis walked over to Olivia. She pulled out a chair and flopped herself down. Olivia held back a smile. "Nice young couple," she commented dryly.

"Charming," muttered Jets. "I can't wait to get to know them better."

"I don't think the feeling is mutual."

Janis's jaw clenched. "My real beef is with you, Nancy Drew. I'm not going to bother asking why you keep listening in to other people's conversations. I know better than to try to get you to stop. So now I've decided to use your perverse character fault for good instead of evil. What's your take on Ashley and her silent partner named Brandon?"

"Ashley does most of the talking. I did notice that."

Jets smiled. "Happy to know your powers of deduction have not been lost working for the old folks up the hill."

"They're hiding something, that's what I think." Olivia spoke calmly, waiting for Janis to agree.

"This is where I have issues," Jets admitted. "On the one hand, I don't like people in general. I'm easily annoyed by human behavior with the exception of a few. So when someone is evasive, like Ashley, I assume she's guilty of something."

Jets continued her self-assessment. "I go out of my way to catch rude and annoying people. It's what I do. And when I catch them, I have a small party for myself. I dance. I sing. I drink. It's really quite something."

Boy, she's really showing me the inner Janis today.

Jets swallowed and added, "So over the years I have become very good at catching criminals. But here's the bite. Just because I think a person is a criminal, it doesn't mean they are."

"No dancing or celebrating just yet?"

Janis's eyes narrowed.

She's gonna chew me out again.

And then to Olivia's surprise, Jets burst out laughing. "You are very funny. You have excellent timing for the odd and witty joke."

"I've been told this before," Olivia admitted. "But coming from you I consider it high praise. Anyway, what's up with those two? I also have a gut feeling they're hiding something..."

"Two of us with the same gut feeling. Now that's not a coincidence," muttered Jets. "But for now we just watch and wait. They could be hiding something that has nothing to do with our dead body. Since catching a murderer is my first priority, I'll stay out of their business."

Janis knows how to prioritize. I'll give her that.

"So good to see you," Olivia said, standing up from her chair. "I'm going to check on Michael. He wants my opinion on the next phase of our new house."

"I heard you broke ground for the new construction."

"It was delayed because he was called to be a first responder Friday. But I think I can take a photo if I hurry. It's kind of a big deal, especially for him."

"See ya." Jets stood up too.

It wasn't until driving down Main Street that Olivia played the conversation over in her head. *If those two had only nodded and said hello, they may not have activated Janis's suspicions. If they have something to hide, why don't they at least pretend to be polite? I don't get it!*

At the top of the hill, Olivia parked in front of the construction site. Lily Rock, the town's namesake, shimmered in the distance. The full midday sun made the famous mountain's alabaster surface sparkle. Olivia stopped to look up and appreciate the view.

Michael picked the perfect lot for our new home. Lily Rock feels close enough to touch, like she's a giant mother protecting us from harm.

Olivia scrambled down the berm, her boots slipping in the dry dirt. Once she got to level ground she shaded her eyes with her hand, looking for Michael. *There he is.* He wore sunglasses, looking intently at an unfurled set of construction plans that he held in both hands. She walked closer as he raised his head.

"I thought I'd just drop in," she explained.

He removed his sunglasses, revealing his dark blue-gray eyes. Standing six feet tall, his broad shoulders filled out the soft flannel shirt. He rolled up his drafting plans, tucking them under one arm.

"Just in time." He leaned over to brush her lips with his. "We're going to do an official photo."

Olivia pulled out her cell phone. "*Architectural Digest* here we come." She followed him toward the site while Michael began to explain. "So over here will be the kitchen, and then behind that, the door to the deck, which faces..."

Olivia pretended to listen, but she had to admit she often tuned out. *He needs to process and I need to pay attention...kind of.*

"So what do you think?" Michael asked, looking down at her.

"I think you know what you're doing."

He nodded. "Good to have your support."

"So I had coffee with Janis," she said, changing the subject.

"Any news about the dead guy?"

"She didn't say anything, but she did introduce herself to two Lily Rock residents. The same two who were in the pub that night."

Michael looked over his shoulder at a construction guy who waited with his shovel. His glance came back to her. "I want to hear more, but would you mind if we took that photo first?"

"Not a problem," Olivia laughed. "Just point and I'll shoot."

* * *

DEADBEAT DAD

It wasn't until she was driving back on the main road that she realized she hadn't finished telling him about Ashley and Brandon, how they acted as if they were hiding something. *Oh well, we can catch up at dinner.* Steering the car into the next curve, she felt the warm air from the open window brush her hair back from her face. *I love this drive.*

Once she got home, Olivia made herself a cup of peppermint tea. She waited for the kettle to boil, standing at the kitchen sink to look out the window. *I'd better check my advertisement for a new drummer. Time to start interviewing. It would be good to get the jump on this before the rumors start. The music world is like their own small town. News, especially bad news, travels fast. No drummer will have us at this rate.*

Taking her mug of tea and her phone, she settled into a chair on the deck outside. With a tap she opened her Gig Master app. Eight people had responded to her ad for a new drummer. Scrolling and reading, she found the perfect candidate. *She already lives in Lily Rock, so it will be easy to meet.* Olivia sent a text. Before she could put her phone away, a response came back.

Would like to talk. Live in Lily Rock. Where can we meet?

Olivia texted back. 9 tomorrow morning. Do you know Thyme Out?

See you there.

Lifting the mug to her lips, she watched in the distance. A series of clouds drifted along the blue sky, partially covering Lily Rock. She inhaled deeply, appreciating the moment, except that her thoughts wouldn't let her relax.

CHAPTER FIVE

The following morning Olivia sat at Thyme Out, a mug of dark roast coffee in front of her. She contemplated the now familiar sense of uneasiness. *Anyone would feel off after discovering a dead body*, she rationalized to herself. *But this feeling is something different.*

A small line of people had formed in front of the bakery glass case. Cookie stood in the doorway leading to the kitchen, watching his employee handle customers. Olivia watched her too. She had blond hair wrapped in a bun at the nape of her neck, which emphasized her plump cheeks and the folds of a double chin. She greeted each new customer with a smile that sat on her lips as if it didn't belong.

Even from across the small indoor bakery, Olivia could see that the woman's smile did not connect with her eyes. Olivia raised her eyebrows at Cookie, who nodded in return. *I bet he's trying her out for Raleigh's old job.* She glanced at her phone. *I have ten minutes to get something to eat before my interview with the new drummer candidate.*

Leaving her jacket at the table, Olivia stood at the back of the line. She watched Cookie step in to help the new employee with the cash register. Within a matter of minutes, the people in line were served and it was Olivia's turn. Before the new employee could speak, Cookie intervened.

"I've got fresh thyme muffins in the back. Want one?"

"Yes, please."

He stepped through the doorway into the kitchen. Olivia took the moment to introduce herself. "I'm Olivia Greer," she said to the woman.

"I'm Bianca Grey." Her eyes looked cold and wary. "You a friend of Kravitz?"

"I am a friend," Olivia nodded and added, "of Cookie and his girlfriend."

"You mean Janis Jets?"

"The very one."

"She comes in several times a day." The woman nodded. "I figured she was the girlfriend."

"How long have you worked here?"

"Just since last Friday. The old employee gave notice."

Sensing the woman was looking for a reason to criticize the former employee, she interjected quickly. "Raleigh is also a friend."

Cookie arrived from the kitchen with a muffin on a plate. Bianca didn't respond to Olivia's comment. "Here you go." He placed it in front of Olivia, who bent over to smell the delicious aroma.

"Still warm. You're the best!" she told Cookie, picking up the plate. By the time she reached her table, the bell over the bakery entrance rang again. *Maybe that's my drummer...*

A quick glance filled her with surprise. *If I'm not mistaken, that's the same young woman who sat at the table in the pub. She looked younger from a distance. Now I can see she's pushing thirty.*

The woman stood in front of the door blocking the way of

another customer. Her eyes glanced over the room. Olivia raised her hand above her head to wave as the man behind her shoved his way past, heading toward the counter.

Olivia smiled as the woman came closer, nodding toward the empty chair. "You must be Bella."

"That's me." The woman shrugged off her coat and sat down. She looked at Olivia's coffee. "Is there any more of that?"

"You have to step up to the counter to place your order. I'll wait."

Bella looked over at the line in front of the counter. She rose and made her way toward the cash register instead of standing behind the last in line.

"I'll take a coffee with cream and sugar, and one of those big sugar cookies." Her voice sounded crisp, as if she were used to being waited on. Bianca turned her back on the next customer.

"Sure, honey," she said, reaching into the glass case for a cookie.

Cookie, observing from the doorway, stepped in. "She has to wait in line," he explained to his employee.

"But she's my daughter," explained Bianca.

"I don't care if she's the queen of England, she has to wait in line." He glared at Bella, who shrugged. "I'm not that hungry," she said in a clear voice. Making her way back to the table, she yanked out her chair. Sitting down she mumbled, "Small towns suck."

"If you say so." Olivia didn't want to argue, at least not just yet.

Giving herself a moment to brush aside an instant dislike of the woman, Olivia inhaled deeply. She slid her muffin to the center of the table. "You're welcome to have a bite of muffin. Once you taste it you may reconsider our small town and see it in a better light."

The woman shook her head.

"You play drums," Olivia opened the conversation.

"I've played since I was little."

"I was surprised to hear you live in Lily Rock. Is that full time, or are you part time?"

"Full time. We rented a cabin up on Hemstreet."

That confirms it. Arlo and Cayenne's neighbors next door.

Olivia took in Bella's face. Her gray eyes and perfectly plucked eyebrows accented her olive skin. The thin lips turned downward, which had already begun to form frown lines at the corners of her mouth. "I know you found my ad on Gig Masters, but have you ever heard Sweet Four O'Clock?" she asked Bella. "I guess I want to know why you think you'd fit in with our band."

Bella shrugged. "I don't have a lot of choice up here, do I? You are the best band I've heard since we moved. Caught your gig at the pub a few weeks ago. You're pretty good. Then when I saw the Gig Masters ad, I figured it was my chance."

Olivia sighed. *Maybe she's just finding her way in Lily Rock. I was like that once.*

"Okay then, why don't we arrange to have you come up to the music academy and sit in with us? Would this afternoon, say around five work for you? My sister, the fiddle player, is available and I'll call Paul, the bassist."

"I remember your sister. She's the pregnant one."

"Her baby is due next January." Olivia smiled. "We're all very excited."

Bella looked away from Olivia, as if offended by her happiness.

Olivia felt her gut clench. *Is she trying to be offensive...*

Olivia changed the subject to focus on Bella. "Did I hear you say the woman behind the counter is your mother?"

Instead of speaking, she reached to remove a chunk of the muffin, placing it in her mouth and then chewing. Finally she said, "She's my mother. What of it?"

"Nothing of it." Olivia smiled. "It's a small town and we make it a point to get to know new families, that's all."

"I bet," the woman said, glowering. "Your so-called hospitality is just another name for gossip."

Instead of disagreeing, Olivia chuckled. "You could say that." By now Cookie arrived at the table, carrying a carafe of coffee.

"Refill?" he asked her, ignoring Bella entirely.

"I'd like a cup of that," Bella insisted.

He took his time filling Olivia's mug. Once he'd placed the mug on the table he slowly turned to Bella. "We all like things. I'd like a pony on my birthday, for example. But in this bakery, you stand in line for the first order. After that I'm happy to refill your mug or bring another baked good with a bill."

Cookie's jaw had set, his eyes looked directly at Bella. *He's not going to let this go until she complies.* Bella looked across at Olivia, a look of expectancy in her eyes. *Does she think I'm going to intervene in this power struggle?*

Olivia took a sip from her mug, staying out of the exchange. Bella stood up from her chair. "Oh okay, have it your way. I'll stand in line." As she huffed away from the table, Cookie spoke in a voice loud enough for the entire bakery to hear. "I'm the boss in my own bakery. Better get used to it."

Olivia smirked. Then she whispered under her breath, "She wants to play percussion for Sweet Four O'Clock."

Surprise showed on his face. "Is that why you're talking to her?"

"She lives up here and it would be convenient when it

comes to rehearsals. Our other drummer lived down the hill and it could get complicated getting everyone together at the same time."

"That makes sense. Sometimes we have to compromise and train people. Maybe she's one of those. Raleigh was a bit rough at first."

"You miss them?"

Cookie smiled. "I do. I'm trying not to take it out on Bianca over there. She can't help it that she's not Raleigh."

Olivia nodded. "You're onto something. I've missed Dave for nearly a year. I deliberately didn't get to know his replacement. Maybe I need to give Bella a chance and stop being so critical."

"Why don't you see how she plays and then decide," suggested Cookie.

He'd left by the time Bella returned with a mug of coffee and two more muffins. "Here, I ate a lot of yours, have some of mine," she suggested, setting the plate in the middle of the table.

"I appreciate it." Olivia took a chunk of the muffin, setting it on her empty plate. "So we have a few more minutes. Why don't you tell me more about who you've drummed with."

As Bella began to speak, Olivia leaned back in her chair. Now that she was talking about herself, words spilled out of Bella's mouth. Olivia nodded, encouraging her to keep talking

* * *

By five o'clock, Sage and Olivia stood in the old Lily Rock Music Academy auditorium. The wood stage smelled of varnish and the old curtains of mildew. Paul had already pulled his bass out of the case. "So a new drummer is sitting in?"

"She's supposed to be here soon. How are you doing, Paul? I haven't seen you for a couple of weeks."

"I'm doing just fine. Good to be home and back with my family." He balanced the big instrument on his knee as he pulled out the end pin. "I've been praying for you since I heard about the dead body."

"You read about it in the news?"

"I have an app for Lily Rock news. Did you know the guy?"

"Beats Malone. A percussionist. I was waiting to meet him at the pub the same night."

Paul's eyes opened wide. "I just can't get over that we have another dead percussionist! What's up with that?"

"Just like *Spinal Tap*," commented Sage, holding her fiddle in one hand.

Paul nodded. "The movie. I saw that. Drummers dropped like flies." As if realizing what he'd said, he looked at Olivia. "You need to stay away from this dead guy's case. No more amateur detective for you. You've got Sage to worry about with her new baby on the way."

Olivia chuckled. "I know. Michael feels the same. I'm no longer working for the constabulary, so I won't be tempted like last year." They all turned toward a voice coming from the back of the auditorium.

"Is this the place?" Bella called out. She walked down the main aisle, looking left to right as if taking in the seating. "Do you perform here?"

"We rehearse here," Sage explained. "I'm Sage McCloud. This is Paul George, and you've met Olivia." She pointed to the drum kit at the back. "You'll have to set up and tune. We're ready when you are."

To Olivia's relief, Bella didn't make further comments about the auditorium. *She'll get into trouble with Sage if she starts making negative comments.* Bella made her way to the drum kit. She held a briefcase in her left hand, which she set on the wood flooring. She opened it and pulled out sticks. Olivia turned back around to give her a chance to set up.

As Sage and Paul talked about what to play, Olivia pulled out her autoharp from the gig bag. With a cell phone app, she adjusted the strings with the metal tuner. All the while she kept one eye on Bella, hoping she would not disappoint.

"Let's start with 'Circle'," Paul called out. It only took Sage a minute to raise the fiddle to her shoulder and begin to play. He plucked a bass line along with the turn. Olivia strummed and began to hum the familiar melody. Once Sage began to tap her foot, she launched into an improvised bridge and the groove opened up for all three.

Finally Olivia inhaled and began to sing. "Will the circle be unbroken." As her voice lifted she heard the drums. The beat was spot-on. She exhaled at the end of the phrase, appreciating the sound.

Bella may have a bad attitude, but she's a really good drummer.

CHAPTER SIX

Janis's text arrived early the next day.

Something you gotta sign. Get here soon as you can.

Olivia hurriedly dressed, running out of the house to drive into town. Once she'd parked and stood outside her car, she took a moment to stretch and admire the beauty of the morning before heading across the street. Inside the constabulary, she found Brad May behind the desk.

"It's hot in here," she told him, hoping to hide her irritation at seeing him in her old chair. *I used to have my own pass key to Janis's office. Now Brad has to let me in. So irritating.*

For the past several months Brad May had served as Janis Jets's new assistant. This morning he looked up from his computer, ignoring her comment about the heat. "Hey, Olivia."

"Janis wanted to see me," she said gruffly.

"Yep." He tossed a lock of his blonde hair out of his eye. "I'll let her know you're here."

Now I have to ask every time I want to see Janis. She took a deep breath, willing herself to be more reasonable.

DEADBEAT DAD

"You don't have to announce me. I love surprising her," Olivia said, walking to the glass door.

Brad wheeled his chair over to the security door. He slapped his ID card on the pad and the door slid open.

Passing through the entrance without further comment, she walked down the hallway to stand at Janis's door. Following three swift knocks, she stuck her head inside. Jets looked up, annoyance written on her face. "What do you want?"

"You summoned me," Olivia explained.

"Oh yeah, I did. I forgot. Get yourself some coffee and bring me a refill. I'll be ready for you by then."

Olivia placed two steaming hot mugs on the desk, then sat opposite Janis, who typed busily on her computer keyboard without looking up. Hands poised over the keyboard, her eyes narrowed.

"You wanted me to sign that paper?" Olivia prodded.

Jets shut the laptop and grabbed her coffee. Reaching under her desk, Olivia heard a drawer opening. Jets slid a paper toward her. "Here you go. Read it over to see if I missed anything. If not, go ahead and sign."

Olivia read her words, an account of her discovery of the dead body. She signed while Janis swiveled her chair back to the computer. "Done," Olivia announced, sliding the paper back to Janis.

"Okay that's good, but don't go yet. I have something I'd like you to look at." Jets waved her arm. "Come around to this side of the desk." She stood up, pointing to her chair. "You can sit here."

"This isn't some family video of you and Cookie making goo-goo eyes at each other, is it?" Olivia walked around the desk.

"Don't be ridiculous. We're not up for public displays."

That's what she says now, but what about that Christmas Card with them smooching on the front?

Olivia sat down and stared at the computer screen. Janis leaned over her shoulder, clicking a video which began to play. Olivia leaned forward, expecting to learn something, but feeling a little queasy. *What's she showing me now?*

An individual, whose face was hidden beneath a gray hoodie, held a skateboard under one arm. The camera came closer as they dropped the board to the pavement and pushed off. The skateboarder weaved in and out, where cars usually traveled in the middle of the street. The camera followed behind. Other than the sound of wheels hitting against the pavement, there was no sound.

With a kick, the board flipped over a curb. Fluidly managing the jump, the skateboarder caught the descending board with both feet, bending low, arms stretched in the air. Olivia held her breath as the skateboarder flew over a bench on their next jump. Then one hand reached out to grab the tail of the board before it landed on the other side.

The camera narrowed its focus to the feet of the skateboarder. Olivia looked at the worn sneaker. "I don't know what to call all of those tricks, but they're amazing," she said.

Whoever held the camera focused on the skater's body: the knees bent, one foot pushing, arms held at the side. Olivia blinked. *I feel like I'm looking at a secret video, the nightlife in Lily Rock after everyone is asleep.*

The lens pulled back to take in more of the environment. The skateboarder rode to the right but the camera did not follow this time. All she could see was an empty street, which could be any street in any small town. In the distance was the ambient clatter of wheels.

Then the camera shifted again. Now the skateboarder came back into the frame, this time speeding past the camera

DEADBEAT DAD

to execute a turn, accomplished so effortlessly that Olivia caught her breath in appreciation.

Jets spoke. "That move there is called a no comply. When a skater plants a foot on the ground and then pivots. They use it as a point of leverage to force the board against and over an obstacle."

Since when is Janis an expert on skateboarding?

Olivia checked the video. *Only a few more minutes.*

"This person is skating in downtown Lily Rock," she said aloud.

"Good eye, Nancy Drew. Now keep watching."

The camera pulled back again so that the skater was no longer in view. Main Street, with the constabulary on one side, along with the library looked deserted. The camera panned the park where the redwoods stood, no one on a bench, no one else present. Finally the video brushed past Thyme Out and Mother Earth, located on the other side of the park. It wasn't until the video stopped in front of Mother Earth that the skateboarder came back into the frame, sliding from the left.

I can't stop watching. It's the skater, not just the way they're dressed, but the speed and disregard for the town's boundaries. How they push and push as if they own the dark.

Janis leaned over her shoulder to shut down the video. "Okay, now mosey on back to your side of the desk and then you can tell me what you think about this video." She flicked her fingers as if to shoo Olivia away.

Once seated, the hair raised on Olivia's neck. She grasped her hands in her lap, willing herself to calm down.

Jets leaned over the desk. "So this was sent to me late yesterday. I have no idea who or why."

"It's ominous," Olivia said. "Kind of spooky the way the film feels benign at first, but as the camera takes in more of the environment, you realize the skater is doing all of that stuff right in our own town while the rest of us are sleeping."

"I think that's what the video is supposed to do. Scare me and make me focus at night on whatever might be coming next." Jets shook her head. "I kinda hoped you'd see it and convince me it was nothing more than a tourist having a whirl on a weekend vacation. But you feel it like I do." Jets sighed deeply.

"So you must have an idea who sent the video," Olivia said.

"I did some cursory checking, I'm not a tech person. I thought of calling in our local camera guy before I send it to someone in the department. If this is an easy fix, then I won't be too concerned. But if it's more, then I'd better get some experts in right away."

"Experts. Don't ask Thomas Seeker. He'll tell Meadow and you know what will happen after that."

Jets nodded in agreement. "Good call. You've saved me from myself on that one. I don't even want Brad to know, for what it's worth."

"Not even your assistant?" Olivia opened her eyes wide, using a pretend voice of innocence.

"He's gotten better with the secretarial stuff, but I saw you stare him down at the crime scene. Brad can't even remember to bring a pen with him and he's terrified of blood. Actually throws up at the smell. The sight sends him into spasms."

"Funny how you keep him on and fired me," muttered Olivia.

"Oh stop. We both know you were much better as my assistant. If it weren't for Michael..."

Jets reached for her coffee. After a sip, she scrunched her face. "Cold."

"I'll get us a warm-up," Olivia suggested. On the way to

the break room, she thought about the video. *I couldn't tell if the skater was a boy or a girl, adult or teen.* When she returned with mugs, she told Janis, "So it could be anybody. But do you think this video is related to the death of Beats Malone?"

Jets sighed. She looked at Olivia, not answering her question. Finally after a sip of her coffee, she said, "On the one hand, the video could have nothing to do with my investigation into Beats's murder. On the other hand? It may be pointing to why Beats was killed. I'm just not sure what the video means and that makes me very uneasy. I can't ignore the timing."

"Maybe that's the point... You're supposed to feel uneasy. It's the timing that intrigues me as well. A few days after a murder and then this distracting video."

The corner of Jets's mouth tightened. "You know outsiders underestimate small-town cops. I'm used to that happening and I think I'll use it to my advantage. How about just you and Mike, and then Cookie and I set up our own surveillance of Lily Rock at night? We can find a place to hang out and sip hot cocoa and see if we can catch our skateboarder in the act. What do you say?"

"When do we start? Michael and I can take the first watch."

"Ahh, isn't that adorable. You're already volunteering your partner without asking." *Sarcasm with a smile, a Janis Jets specialty.* "You can alert Mike and then ask him to meet with us on the Thyme Out back patio this afternoon." Jets sat up tall as if proud of herself. "Look at me. I just saved you a fight with Mike. Aren't I the best?"

"Michael would have been okay with me volunteering his services," Olivia said defensively.

Jets's arms dropped. "You say that now, but the next tiff you lovebirds have, it will come up as an issue. Trust me. I've had that relationship and it isn't pretty. Keep your powder clean and don't volunteer your man for anything you haven't talked over with him beforehand."

"Are you my mother?" Olivia glared at Janis.

"Absolutely not, I'm no one's mother. Just a cop who knows the score."

Olivia closed her lips. Reaching for Jets's empty mug, she stood up. "I'll take these to the break room," she muttered, walking out the office door. As she rinsed the mugs in the sink, she considered Janis's words. *She may be right. I'll test Michael first and see how he feels. Or better yet, I have time to drive up to the site.* She reached for her cell phone.

Have time for an early lunch? I'm buying.

A reply came before she could put her phone away.

Yes!

Olivia drove home, hoping to finish a few chores before packing a lunch and meeting Michael at the building site. She put dishes away and then pulled sliced turkey, lettuce, tomato, and Swiss cheese from the refrigerator.

As she assembled two sandwiches on whole wheat bread, her thoughts returned to the video. *It's interesting how one video can pose so many unknowns and in doing so, bring up so many unsettling emotions.*

By eleven o'clock she'd packed the lunch and climbed into her Ford. The curves on the road made driving fun now that they'd become second nature. Plus she had a chance to appreciate the view. In the distance oak tree leaves were turning to yellow, indicating the approach of fall. Olivia rolled down the window to feel the warm mountain air.

She turned her Ford onto the dirt road that led to the new home construction site. Two men, backs bent, measured and made marks in the dirt. Michael stood to the side, the construction plans in his hands. He looked up as Olivia drove closer.

Once parked, she slid the picnic hamper from the back seat. By that time, Michael had walked closer to the car and took the hamper from her hands. "Kinda heavy, what did you put in those sandwiches?" He laughed, pretending to drop the hamper.

"Don't you start. I've been told by a relationship expert that I must treat you with great respect, and I thought I'd begin by bringing lunch."

He looked down at her. "Is that so...and who is this expert?"

"None other than Janis Jets," Olivia said. "So where are we going to sit, so that I can volunteer you for another assignment?"

"Right over there." Michael pointed. "I had my guys make us a bench so that we can look at the construction. I figure you'll be bringing more lunches before we complete this project." He sat down, patting a space next to him.

"Let me tell you all about my morning. By the way, have you ever done any skateboarding?"

Michael's eyes grew wide. "Now I did not see that question coming. I've never set foot on a board with wheels. That would be my idea of inviting disaster."

CHAPTER SEVEN

When Olivia arrived at the bakery, Thyme Out's *Closed* sign was already visible in the window. Cookie stood at the counter. As soon as he saw her, he let her inside. "Hey there, looks like we have an assignment from the local sheriff." He pointed to a table outside where Janis and Michael already sat.

As she got closer, Michael rose to give her a big hug. She stepped back from his embrace, a smile on her face. "We've been summoned by the boss," she said.

He winked and said in her ear, "I only have one boss..."

Cookie arrived at the table. "I think we can get this party started."

Olivia sat next to Michael, keenly aware of the sound of clanking coming from the open window in the kitchen. She turned to Cookie. "Is your new employee still at work?"

"She's got a kitchen to clean up. Part of her job description. I get here very early in the morning to bake and I don't want to confront pans soaking in the sink."

"Makes him crabby," Jets commented.

"So what time do you get here in the morning?" Olivia asked.

Cookie yawned. "Sometimes as early as four o'clock. I have to give the yeast time to rise."

Janis shook her head. "Too early, just sayin'," she muttered.

Another thump and a clank came from the open window. "Is your new employee expressing her dissatisfaction?" Olivia asked Cookie.

He frowned. Before he could respond, Janis interrupted.

"Bakery chitchat aside, let's talk surveillance." Jets pulled out her iPad. "I'm sending information to each of you for your phones. Now is the time to ask questions."

Cookie took a deep breath. "In answer to your question," he leaned toward Olivia, "I had hoped the mother of three would be a tad bit more...motherly, for want of a better word. So long as I ignore her complaining, it will work out okay."

"Makes sense." Olivia nodded.

Michael's phone pinged. He glanced at the screen. Olivia's phone pinged next. A message titled Lily Rock Surveillance Team met her eyes. By now Cookie's head was bent over his phone as well.

Michael finished reading Janis's written instructions first. He reached out to tap her hand. "It's good to do this together. Sounds kind of dicey, sitting in town on top of a building in the dark hours of the morning."

Cookie smiled. "When you get off duty, you can come by for fresh coffee on your way home. Slip in the back gate, I'll leave it open for you."

"I know you three will get chilly and need lots of snacks, but I'd like to talk about the importance of our plan," grumbled Jets. "This is an assignment, not another opportunity to sip coffee and make small talk. But before I say anything more, do you have any questions?" She peered at each of them individually.

"Let me see if I got this right," Olivia began. "We sit on top of the mercantile building and watch for the skateboarder. We'll bring chairs and a pair of binoculars. It will be difficult to take photos in the dark."

"I have a couple of camp chairs at my place. I'll bring them," added Michael.

"Don't worry about photos. I want you to watch and wait. If you see something, then I'll put in a request for some pros to follow up. So far skateboarding at night in a public area is a minor misdemeanor, but only if property is destroyed. We don't have any Lily Rock rules for this, since we've never had a skateboarder sighting before." Jets shook her head. "Now let's get down to which day and what time..."

"Okay, no photos," repeated Olivia. "According to your memo, Michael and I are taking tonight and then Thursday. You guys will handle Wednesday and Friday."

"What time do we start—when the sun goes down?" Michael asked.

"Nah, you don't have to watch for that long. My video was stamped at 2 a.m. If you show up at midnight and stay until Cookie opens up the bakery around four o'clock, that should do it. Dress warm, you two. It gets chilly outside, even for this time of year."

Jets shut down her iPad. Olivia closed her document. She saw Cookie take Janis's hand under the table.

"We're not to tell anyone about this, right?" he asked.

Jets glared at him. "You should know about surveillance, what with your FBI background."

"Yes, ma'am. Got it!" His half smile made Olivia think he liked it when Janis took charge.

A clank from the kitchen drew Olivia's attention again. "She's a noisy dishwasher."

"I think she wants to go home; she's not my first passive-aggressive employee," Cookie said.

"Say more..." Olivia encouraged.

"I've noticed her dealing with customers. If she takes a dislike to someone, she ignores their requests. Yesterday a guy pointed to a blueberry muffin in the glass case. Instead of giving him that one, Bianca pretended she didn't hear him. She huffed and turned her back on the customer, walking into the kitchen. When she returned, she had a day-old blueberry muffin that I keep in back for Hello Age at no cost."

"The guy kept waiting?"

"That's what I'm saying. She went out of her way to grab a day-old one from the kitchen. He argued with her, but she ignored him. He started to walk away until I intervened.

"I called her on it, so she tossed it in the trash and got him a fresh one. The customer walked away shaking his head. I know I told her about the day-old goods, but she acted like I just made up a rule to give her grief. That's what I mean by passive-aggressive. She had me. She knew that I didn't want to explain again, especially in front of the customers."

"I see what you mean," admitted Olivia.

"So in her defense?" Janis Jets interrupted. "Correct me if I'm wrong, but Bianca lives with three of her own kids who failed to launch. The laundry and dishes alone must make a mother weep. That's enough to get on anyone's nerves, even a saint. No wonder she's so crabby."

Michael, who had remained silent for most of the conversation, broke in. "I haven't met anyone in the Grey family. Olivia says they just moved to Lily Rock recently."

"I spoke to one of them the other day. He was here with

his girlfriend. A surly piece of work, if you're asking my opinion," Jets said.

"Do you suppose they all live in the basement?" Olivia asked.

"That's enough to make me want to puke," Janis said.

"I met the older daughter yesterday." Olivia felt everyone look at her, wanting to hear more. "Her name is Bella and it turns out she plays drums."

"I was going to ask how the interview went," Cookie said, nodding. "I saw you two at the bakery yesterday. So she sat in with Sweet Four O'Clock?"

"I think we'll give her a trial period. She's planning on sitting in for the next couple of gigs in Lily Rock."

Olivia felt someone kick her foot. *Janis must be getting restless.*

Jets spoke out. "Okay then, you two better have an early dinner. Get a few hours' sleep and then meet me on top of the mercantile a little before midnight. The outdoor steps are on the east side. Park outside the village so we don't give away our clandestine activity. Got it?"

Olivia stood up first, followed by Michael. "We've got it," he said.

"Be sure to take note should anyone show up," Jets said.

Michael nodded as he and Olivia made their way through the bakery, the bell over the door chiming as they stepped outside. Olivia looked back over her shoulder. The lights to the kitchen had been turned off. *I guess the dishes are done.*

* * *

Around midnight Olivia and Michael stood on the mercantile's roof. She could see the outline of Lily Rock in the far distance. The streets were dark, the only illumination coming from the full moon. Olivia pulled her coat around her shoulders. Michael stood tall, his coat zipped to the neck, a baseball cap pulled over his head to keep away the chilly night air.

"It is getting colder. We're closing in on fall," he commented.

"Do you want some hot cocoa?" Olivia asked. She leaned over to unscrew a thermos they'd brought with them.

When Michael didn't turn around, she asked, "Everything okay?"

"Everything is just fine," he called over his shoulder. "I want to keep my eye on the street just in case."

She poured two Styrofoam cups, stepping closer to the rail. When she handed him the hot cocoa, he took it with a smile and turned his head back, viewing the town below. "Thanks for this," he said absentmindedly.

She snuggled next to him, her cup in a gloved hand. "Lily Rock is so quiet at night," she remarked. "It's my favorite time."

Michael took a sip of cocoa. He held the binoculars to his eyes. She heard a low chuckle. "Hey, look over there!" He pointed.

Michael handed her the binoculars. Olivia held them to her eyes, scanning the street and park below. She detected movement from behind one of the park benches. "Is someone crawling on the ground?" she asked.

"Look again. I think the mayor is doing some late-night surveillance on his own."

A bushy tail popped up from behind the bench. "He has a ball in his mouth and he's on the move." She watched the mayor toss a small ball in the air. He waited until it landed and then ran to fetch it himself. "He's like an only child with no one else to play with. Do you think he knows we're up here?"

"Mayor Maguire knows all," Michael said in a low voice. "We are merely the pawns in his doggie chess game, doing his bidding."

Olivia stifled a giggle. "If that's the case then he probably knows who sent that skateboarding video to the constabulary." Olivia set the binoculars on the railing. "I never knew this rooftop was accessible before."

Olivia finished her cocoa and sat down in the camp chair. "While you're watching, I'm going to close my eyes just for a minute." She yawned.

He turned from the rail. "See if you can get a little sleep. I've got this."

The next thing she knew, a hand was squeezing her shoulder, waking her from a deep sleep. "Time to go home." Michael kneeled next to her, smiling.

"Did you see the skateboarder?" She rubbed her tired eyes.

"No sign of anyone except the mayor. He stayed in the park all night. How about we get home so that I can get a couple hours of sleep before heading over to the construction site?"

Olivia stood. "Sounds good. Should we leave the chairs for Janis and Cookie's watch tonight?"

"Less to carry back to the car."

By the time they walked down the outdoor stairway and stood on the boardwalk, Mayor Maguire was waiting for them.

"Want a ride to our house?" Olivia scratched behind his ear.

"I see the light's on in the bakery. Do you want to stop in for coffee?" Michael asked.

Olivia shook her head. "I could use a couple of hours more sleep before coffee, if that's okay with you."

He laid his arm over her shoulders, pulling her closer to his side. "That's perfect. Sleep it is."

Mayor Maguire followed, keeping close to Olivia's right knee as they made their way to the truck. Once Michael opened the back door, the mayor jumped in. Olivia was next, settling into the passenger seat. By the time Michael sat behind the wheel, her eyes had closed.

CHAPTER EIGHT

Alone in the kitchen the next morning, Olivia looked out the window at her garden. She lifted a mug of coffee to her lips, appreciating the first taste of bitterness, a splash of orange lasting at the back of her tongue. *Michael's summer blend. Yum.*

Due to their late night and her sleeping in, she'd missed sharing coffee with Michael. Turning from the window, she surveyed the tidy kitchen. *I wonder if the kitchen in our new house will bring me the same sense of joy?*

She remembered the first time she'd stood in that kitchen. Grieving the unexpected loss of her friend Marla, Mayor Maguire had been there as she opened drawers and cupboards, trying to figure out where everything was in order to brew a cup of tea. Once she'd discovered she'd inherited the house, it had taken months to work through her loss, to make the house her home.

Olivia cut a slice of bread off a fresh loaf. She pulled the toaster out and plugged it in. Sliding the bread into the top slot, she pushed the lever down and then stood back. *I do love the smell of toasting sourdough.* A scratching at the back door made her smile. "Hold on, M&M. I'm coming," she called out.

As soon as she opened the door, he sauntered in, his mouth bulging at the sides. She leaned over. "Drop it," she commanded. Instead of obeying the command, he pulled his head back, giving her a side-eye. "Drop it!" she repeated. A green ball fell from the mayor's mouth, bouncing across the kitchen floor.

She picked it up with a grimace. "Ick, it's all wet." The mayor sat at her feet, looking up, his dark eyes hopeful. "I can't play now. I slept in and have to get going. Maybe this afternoon we can hang out."

The mayor's head drooped.

"If I didn't know any better, I'd think you understood every word I said." She patted his head. Holding the ball in her open palm, she said, "You can have the ball back to play by yourself. I know you can do it. I saw you in the park."

The mayor took it from her hand, racing through the kitchen into the great room.

Her toast popped. She walked closer, taking a knife from the drawer. Spreading butter over the crusty surface, she stood once again looking out of her kitchen window, savoring her first bite.

An hour later Olivia drove into town. Early lunch-goers were already lined up outside the Lily Rock diner. The streets, crowded with people meandering along, made Olivia smile. *Sometimes it's fun to be a tourist destination. I like the energy visitors bring.* She drove around the block three times before she found a space near the park.

Across the street Olivia caught a glimpse of Meadow through the library window. Since she no longer worked as Janis Jets's assistant, she made it a point to stop and chat with

Meadow; conveniently located next door, Meadow kept her fingers on the pulse of Lily Rock's constabulary.

Olivia walked through the library doors. "Hey, Meadow, how is the book world?"

The woman looked up, welcoming Olivia with a smile. "Well dear, funny you should ask. I'm missing a lot of books."

Her eyes narrowed as she waited for Olivia to share her indignation.

Knowing most Lily Rock residents respected Meadow's unspoken rule that library books should be taken out for no more than thirty days, Olivia felt a bit shocked. "Do you know who has them?"

Meadow gestured with her finger for Olivia to walk closer. "I know who has them but I'm hesitant to confront anyone, since they're new to town and all."

Olivia's eyes followed the direction of Meadow's nod, where the three Greys sat together on the overstuffed sofa in the middle of the library. All of their heads were bent over cell phones. "So it's one of them?" she asked.

Meadow whispered, "Not all of them, just the boy. He puts books under his jacket and walks out the door without checking them out."

"No way," Olivia said, incredulous. "I suppose you don't have tracking devices at the library, but then you've never needed them before."

"It would cost a pretty penny to put them in every book and up until now, we've not needed to enforce the overdue policy. Everyone in Lily Rock just checks them out and brings them back without a reminder. But now I can't say everyone."

Meadow sighed and continued. "Of course, there was that time in the seventies when I had to track down an *Old Yeller* book from a teen. He had it on his shelf at home and read it over and over and didn't want to give it up. So I bought him a paperback and he gave me the library copy and I've never had trouble with him again." Meadow shrugged. "Or anyone else until now."

Olivia glanced over her shoulder at the three family members. "Do you think he has one of your books? I can go and ask him if you'd like. That way you don't need to be the bad guy."

"I'm not a wimp," Meadow muttered. "But I would appreciate you intervening on behalf of the Friends of Lily Rock Library. I'll watch from here. Go and see what you can do."

Olivia turned from Meadow, heading toward the sofa in the reference section. She pulled her shoulders back to look more determined. None of the Greys looked up, even though she stood directly in front of them.

"Excuse me," she said in a firm voice.

The youngest broke first, glancing up toward her, a slight smile on her face. "Hello," she said.

Olivia felt immediately disarmed. The young woman's blue eyes looked so charming, as did her smile.

"Hello," she answered back. "I don't believe we've met."

"I'm Blair Grey," she said in a sweet low voice. "These are my siblings, my brother Brandon and sister Bella."

At the sound of her name, Bella looked up. "Oh hi. Didn't see you there," she said off-handedly.

Olivia glanced at the book resting under her phone. "Reading up on Gene Krupa, I see." She wanted to connect with the girl. The book with the faded cover was a biography of the famous drummer.

"Yep," she said, head ducking back to her phone. When Olivia didn't follow up with another comment, she looked up again. "What can I do for you?"

Olivia glanced at the boy. He reluctantly detached from his screen, his eyes focusing on her neck, not on her face. He just stared, saying nothing. Olivia pointed to his bulging jacket. "I think you may have picked up a lost library book. The librarian wanted me to grab it so she can check the catalog to see who checked it out last."

Brandon scowled.

"Give her the book." Bella nudged him with her elbow.

When he didn't reach into his jacket, she leaned over and took the book herself. "Here you go. He has Asperger's, you know, and doesn't understand about checking books out." Olivia took the book from her hand, noting the cover. It was a dog-eared coffee table book titled *This Old House*.

"Are you interested in renovating homes?" she asked him.

He didn't answer her question. Rising to his feet, his face looked impassive. *He's so much taller than his sisters. Over six feet.* Olivia took a step back. He shrugged and then stepped in front of her. Turning to the right, he disappeared into the reference stacks.

She turned back to Bella. "Thanks for the book. Meadow is always happy to help new people in Lily Rock. She'll tell you the library rules and help you check out books of interest. I'll tell her Brandon is reading about house renovations. She'll keep a lookout for him. Then the next time you come in, she'll have books ready."

"How quaint," murmured Bella. She turned to her sister. "Did you hear that, Blair? The librarian's name is Meadow and she helps people with books."

Blair giggled and Bella rolled her eyes. Their laughter grew louder until they doubled over, gasping with mirth.

Olivia felt the hair raise on her neck. *Wow, I've been mocked before, but never by two people so in sync.* "See you later," she mumbled, wanting nothing more than to get away from the two sisters.

Back at the desk, she slid the book over to Meadow.

Meadow's eyebrows raised.

"That family is a handful," Olivia whispered. "If I were you, I'd start asking the Friends of the Library to find some money to install trackers in hardcover books to keep track of the inventory."

"I think you're right," Meadow nodded. "That's long overdue."

Olivia observed Meadow's lips purse together.

"Thank you for helping me, Olivia. Did I hear the one girl say her brother has Asperger's?"

"That's the second time I've been told that Brandon Grey has Asperger's," Olivia admitted. "I've not heard him speak yet. The other time his girlfriend did all the talking, and this time his sister. But between us two? I think there's something else going on. I've known lots of people on the spectrum and none of them thought stealing was okay."

"I agree." Meadow nodded. "We may be optimistic in Lily Rock, but we aren't stupid. I suggest we keep an eye on that family, at least until they come to appreciate our ways."

"I hope they eventually will," she told the older woman. "Right now I'm heading next door. Do you want to come over to the house later for dinner? We can catch up."

"Will Sage be there too?" Meadow asked hopefully.

"I'll text her and find out. See you around six o'clock."

"I'll be there. And I'll bring a fresh loaf of bread and some strawberry jam."

"Yum," Olivia said. "I had a piece of your sourdough for breakfast."

She exited the library, turning left on the boardwalk. Walking into the constabulary, she felt a pang looking at Brad sitting in her old spot behind the desk. "Hey, Olivia," he drawled. "She's in the back."

"Thanks," she said, walking past him. This time he used his card quickly, the glass security door sweeping open in front of her. Heading down the hall, she glanced at the empty cells and then stopped in front of Janis Jets's office. The door was open.

"Came to report about last night," she said.

Janis nodded, her eyes locked onto the computer screen. Swiveling her chair, Olivia sat across from her on the opposite side of the desk.

"Good timing. Tell me everything about last night," Jets encouraged.

Olivia settled into the chair. "Not much happened. We saw Mayor Maguire playing with a tennis ball. The view is nice from on top of the mercantile. It was cold. Take a blanket with you for tonight."

"A blanket? Who do you think we are, a couple of old-timers on a night out? Cookie and I have withstood all kinds of bad weather, just the two of us under a full moon."

"Wasn't it you who told me to bring a jacket? I guess you've changed your mind, so bring your bikini tonight if that works." She sucked in her cheeks to keep from laughing at Janis's surprised face.

Janis glared and changed the subject. "Since you have nothing to report about a skateboarder, I have something for you." She turned her chair to the computer and clicked. "So we got the toxicology report back from the Malone murder. The only blood at the scene was his. He was stabbed with a kitchen knife, thin and very sharp. No weapon has been found at the scene."

"Doesn't give you much to go on."

"Beats was in excellent health for a guy in his fifties." Janis continued to scan the report. "But the best information might come from his cell phone. They can't unlock it yet, but the team is working on it. I suspect there will be a text or call log that give us important information. Maybe somebody he connected with right before he arrived in Lily Rock was the one who killed him."

"I forgot to tell you..." Olivia hesitated. "I may come up on that call log. He texted me on his way up the hill." She pulled out her cell phone, thumbed through her texts, stopping at the one Beats had sent her. "Here you go." She held out the phone for Janis to see.

Janis snatched the phone from her hand. She looked at it carefully. When she handed the phone back to Olivia, she shook her head. "Do you have any knowledge about why a guy like Beats Malone, a pretty famous drummer, would want to drive all the way from LA to Lily Rock to sit in on a band like Sweet Four O'Clock?"

Instead of taking offense, Olivia shook her head. "I do not. And I've asked myself the same question. At the time I was a bit surprised, but then I rationalized to myself that Sweet Four O'clock is finally getting some buzz and that's what attracted him."

Jets cleared her throat. "You don't have to defend your band. The next thing I know you'll be telling me some old autoharp anecdote. I don't have time for any of this. I just want to know, why did Beats Malone drive all the way up the hill to Lily Rock to sit in with a band that couldn't offer him fame or fortune? Just doesn't make sense."

Olivia decided to take no offense at Janis's disinterest in the band. "You're gonna be sorry," she told Jets. "When our band makes it big and they want to interview you about how you knew us *when*, you'll have nothing to say because you didn't listen to my autoharp stories."

Jets smirked. "I think I can handle the notoriety when the time comes. In the meanwhile, I'm not holding my breath. Want to have lunch?"

"Sure." Olivia nodded. "But I'll have to get my blanket from the car first. I might get a little chilly at the diner."

"You're a pain," Jets scoffed as she put her computer to sleep.

CHAPTER NINE

The next morning Olivia woke to a text from Janis Jets. *She's better than an alarm clock.*

Get in here ASAP.

Keep your panties on, she texted back.

It took a couple of hours to get her life organized. She had to make phone calls for the band and finish tidying up the kitchen. Finally after several calls, she arranged for a sound guy for the pub. Then she texted her bandmates to make sure they agreed on a rehearsal schedule. After that she posted on their Instagram account so their small but loyal fan base would know where to find them at the final summer concert.

And then she had to empty the dishwasher. Meadow had come for dinner the night before. She showed up with a loaf of sourdough still warm from the oven. Sage had arrived late from work. Along with Michael fresh from the construction site, the four of them had a wonderful time catching up.

Olivia had planned the meal carefully to include a vegetarian dish. She lit candles and filled water glasses for each person. Michael, freshly showered, helped set the table.

As Meadow, looking relaxed in her denim jumper and

crisp white shirt, eyed the casserole at the center of the table, Olivia explained, "A pumpkin lasagna."

After Meadow went back for a second helping, she asked for the recipe. "Such a rich flavor," she said, finishing the last bite.

Over the chocolate cake and vanilla ice cream, they caught up with Sage about her pregnancy. "So now that you're five months along," Michael said, eyeing her belly, "is everyone at the music academy patting your stomach?"

Sage laughed. "I really don't mind people's interest. They can pat, especially if they ask first."

"I know it will be a girl," Meadow said, nodding with confidence. "I brought up Sage without a man in the house." She paused to sniff. "It's good to have the father," she nodded to Michael, "but a mother can do it by herself." Then Meadow glanced across the table from Olivia to Michael. "Baby will have just enough people in her life."

"Hey, wait a minute," Michael interjected, his lips turning down. "I'm a man and since I plan on being very much a part of this baby's life, I think a boy would be in order. I could teach him to blend coffee and draw."

Olivia glanced at him quickly. *He's kind of emotional about the baby and such a big softy. I just love that about him.*

"I'm very excited about the baby," Olivia added. "Boy or girl works for me."

Meadow smiled benignly over the group as she lifted a piece of cake to her lips. Her confidence was obvious. Olivia's active mind immediately started to question. *I wonder if Meadow knows who the father is and just isn't saying...*

She felt Michael take her hand under the table. Sage spoke up in a soft but firm voice. "You're my family. You're all a baby could ever want, boy or girl."

Sage looked down at her plate. When she raised her eyes,

she caught Olivia staring at her. The look of sadness vanished, replaced by a smile. "I suspect baby will be musical..."

"No doubt about that," Michael said reassuringly. "And baby may be an architect."

"Or a librarian," Meadow added. Then she looked at her daughter. "Or whatever she wants to be. Babies bring so much possibility."

The sadness in Sage's face lingered in Olivia's mind as she brought herself back to the present. *Gotta get going this morning,* she reminded herself.

Olivia hurried through a shower and the last of the phone calls. She drove into town. Once parked, she sprinted across the street toward the constabulary.

Upon her entering, Brad looked up expectantly.

When he didn't automatically open the door leading to Janis's office, she stood in front of the glass tapping her foot.

"Hello to you, too," he muttered under his breath.

Olivia knew she was being unreasonable. But before she could apologize, he wheeled his desk chair over to slap his key card on the pad. The door opened.

She rushed through adding a hasty, "Thanks."

Down the hallway she stopped in front of Janis's open door.

"Come in," came Janis's voice.

"At your service, boss," Olivia said.

"Glad you could find time in your busy schedule to show up," muttered Jets. "Don't bother to sit down. I wanted to report about our surveillance last night."

"Did the skateboarder come back?"

"Not exactly. Not the skateboarder, but we did see unexpected activity in the park around 3 a.m."

The hair on Olivia's neck rose. "And..."

"The mayor of Lily Rock was playing fetch with the

youngest Grey. Blair is her name." Jets shook her head. "Who does that? Name all their kids with the same first letter?"

Olivia remembered the skateboarder wore a hoodie in the video. "Do you think she is our skateboarder?"

"I wondered the same thing. Once we came down from the roof, I spoke to her."

"What did she say, I mean why was she in the park so early?"

"Slow down, Nancy Drew. I asked all the right questions. Apparently Blair hangs out in the wee hours of the morning because she can't sleep. She's a bit of an introvert and she likes to throw the ball for Mayor Maguire."

Jets continued, "That dog has a mind of his own. He's indiscriminate when it comes to his playmates." She glared at Olivia.

"M&M is a good judge of character," Olivia objected.

"Could be," muttered Jets. "But then you're basing a personality assessment on who the dog likes. Most dogs will hang out with anyone willing to toss a ball back and forth."

"Oh right," Olivia grinned. "Sometimes I forget that. Even a dog who is mayor and known for being psychic may turn a blind eye and forgive personality faults if the person tosses a tennis ball."

"There's something else." Jets turned to her computer. "Step over here and see." She clicked to bring up a video. It looked exactly like the one she'd shown Olivia days ago.

"You already showed me that one."

"Pipe down, smarty pants. This is one I got around six this morning. It's the same but different." She clicked again.

The video opened up with the lone skateboarder just as it had previously. But this time instead of hearing the board clicking along the boardwalk, music had been added. A familiar tune that caused Olivia to smile. "I am an orphan on God's highway," came the voice of Gillian Welch.

"I know that song," she said immediately. "We cover that one in Sweet Four O'Clock. Gillian does it best though, she's amazing."

"Woo-hoo for Gillian. What I want to know is why add that song to the same video and why send it to me?"

"Have you been able to trace the IP address?"

"Not having any luck. The tech team put it on the back burner for other pressing matters. Can't say I blame them. Skateboarding videos aren't exactly important in crime solving."

"Skateboarders have a particular fan base, or so I've heard." Olivia looked closely at the screen. "They do spend a lot of money on shoes. Although your skateboarder isn't wearing Nikes or a particular brand." Olivia looked down at her scuffed cowboy boots.

Jets played the video again before closing it down, then stood up from the chair. "So you're on for tonight. Keep an eye out for the dog and what's her name...Blair. She doesn't look tall enough to be our skateboarder, but she may be the one behind the camera taking the video."

"Will do, boss," came Olivia's quick reply.

"Knock it off and get out of here," grumbled Jets. She flicked her fingers toward the door, abruptly ending the conversation.

Once outside the constabulary, Olivia looked through the library window for Meadow in her usual place behind the counter. *I'm going to pop in for a minute.* Once inside she recognized the youngest Grey girl talking to Meadow across the counter. She lingered back to listen to their conversation.

Meadow spoke in her official librarian's voice. "Your name on the application does not match your driver's license. For that matter, you also have an old address. I can't issue a library card to you with those discrepancies."

"I changed my name a few years ago when I turned twenty-one. I just didn't register it with the motor vehicle department. It's not rocket science. I only want to take out a book for my brother." Blair sounded exasperated.

"I cannot make an exception." Meadow lifted the card to look at it more closely. "It says here your last name is Malone. Why do you use Grey instead?"

"That's none of your business." Blair snatched the card from Meadow's grasp. When Meadow looked surprised, she shrugged. "I don't suppose it matters. It's not a secret. Our dad abandoned us years ago and we don't use his name. Does that make you happy? Grey is my mom's name. She's the only parent we have. My brother will keep stealing books or you can issue me a card and I'll check them out for him. Your choice."

Blair didn't wait for Meadow's response. Instead, she turned around as if to leave, colliding directly into Olivia.

"Get out of my way," she snarled, pushing past. *So much for the big blue eyes and innocent smile the other day.*

Olivia spoke quickly. "I couldn't help but overhear—your last name is Malone?"

Blair shook her head, glaring at Olivia. "You too? What's with this town? We don't use that name anymore." She headed toward the library exit.

Olivia stepped up to the counter. "You wouldn't think a name on a library card would cause so much anger."

Meadow shook her head. "There's something not right about those kids. I can't quite put my finger on the problem, but I may have inadvertently stepped into a family issue. I didn't mean to upset her."

"I know you didn't. Maybe she'll come back and apologize."

"Maybe," sighed Meadow, obviously unconvinced.

"We loved having you for dinner last night," Olivia said, changing the subject.

Meadow smiled. "It was a beautiful evening. I went home and journaled about our conversation so that I can tell the baby when she grows up. Every child wants to know they were greatly anticipated."

"You will be the perfect grandmother," Olivia told her. "I know Sage feels so much better with you at her side." Olivia flushed. *But who's the baby's father? Why can't I just be happy like Meadow and not care?*

It wasn't until Olivia sat behind the wheel of her car that she realized she'd missed something very important in the exchange between Meadow and Blair. *Wait a minute. If those three kids are all Malones, are they related to Beats?*

Instead of starting the engine, she picked up her phone to text Janis.

Call me. I was at the library with Meadow and we got info on the Greys that may be connected to your murder investigation.

Olivia waited but Janis didn't text back.

CHAPTER TEN

Michael sat down first, his back against the cushion. She slid in leaning her back into his chest. Once his arms wrapped around her, she rested her head under his chin. Snuggled onto the oversized lounger, they watched the sun dip behind the trees.

"I overheard a conversation in the library. So it turns out Blair is the daughter of Beats Malone." She felt him pull her closer.

He kissed her head. "Go on..." he encouraged her. She told him about Meadow and the library card, ending with, "I was shocked. Beats sounded like a terrible father."

"So the other two, Brandon and Bella, are also his kids?"

She felt his warm breath against her ear. "I suppose so. They all live together with their mother and use her name. So I'd assume that Bianca is Beats's ex-wife." Then she added, "When Arlo told me that Beats was famous, I looked at his social media. I couldn't find anything about a wife or kids; maybe he pays someone to manage his accounts. There are articles about his playing, but not about his personal life."

"Interesting." Michael nuzzled her ear with his warm lips.

"You don't sound that interested," she said.

"You're sitting in my lap and my hands are very close to your body, so I may be a bit distracted." He gave her ear a quick kiss.

She brought her knees up and then turned, lifting her body to sit astride on his middle. She leaned in for a kiss. "Am I to understand we can talk about Beats later?" he asked hopefully.

She kissed him again. "Stop talking," she said against his lips.

"Once again, you have read my mind."

* * *

Later that evening Michael poured himself an IPA. He handed Olivia a tall glass filled with ice and sparkling water. "I'll grill the wings if you want to make a salad," he offered.

She looked out the window over the sink and then took a sip. "It's warm enough, we can eat outside. I smell chicken. Are the wings in the refrigerator?"

"They're right here." Michael lifted the lid of a pot on the stove. "I boiled them first."

"Ew, who boils their chicken wings?"

"It's my secret preparation technique. Just wait until you taste them hot off the grill."

Michael removed each wing from the boiling water. Piled on a platter, he headed through the great room. The doorbell rang. "I'll see who that is," she told him, leaving her glass on the counter.

She peered through the peephole. Janis Jets stood with her hands on her hips. She glared at the door, so Olivia opened it quickly, gesturing for her to come inside. "You got my message?"

"I got your message all right. I stopped and talked to Meadow before coming over. She confirmed the incident, that Beats Malone may well be the father of those three young adults who call themselves Grey." Janis looked over Olivia's shoulder. "Do I smell the grill? I'm starving."

"Why don't you stay for dinner?"

"What about Cooks?"

"Give him a call. Michael has enough wings for an army. I hesitate to tell you but he boiled them first. Have you ever heard of doing that?"

"I don't care how the sausage is made," muttered Jets. She walked to the kitchen.

Olivia called out, "Get yourself a beer and meet us on the deck."

Outside she found Michael standing over the grill. "Cookie and Janis are joining us."

"Perfect timing," he said, lowering the lid. "I hope he hurries because this will only take a few minutes."

"How about we eat the wings as an appetizer? I'll make a salad; I'll also grab some paper plates." She gave him a peck on the cheek before heading into the house.

Janis leaned over Mayor Maguire. "I found him at the back door."

Olivia pointed to his bowl. "You can feed him dinner, the kibble's over there." She opened the refrigerator as she heard Janis dumping dog food into the mayor's bowl.

"There you go, doggie," Janis coaxed.

Olivia pulled lettuce and vegetables out of the drawer to lay them on the counter.

Janis spoke over her shoulder. "Cookie will be here any minute."

Mayor Maguire lifted his head, a growl coming from the back of his throat.

"That's probably Cookie," Olivia said. "Why don't you get the door while I prepare the lettuce?"

She heard a voice call from the great room, "Hey, Mike!"

When Janis didn't return, Olivia assumed they were talking on the deck. She rinsed the lettuce, letting it dry on a towel. Picking up her glass and the paper plates, she walked toward the deck. She found Cookie and Michael looking out toward Lily Rock, Janis sitting in a chair, her feet propped on the rail. Olivia put the plates on a nearby table and then pulled a chair closer to talk to Janis.

"So now what?" she asked.

"I suppose you mean the case. If all those people are related to my dead guy, then the circumstances have been turned upside down. At first, when no one claimed the body, I wondered if Beats had any family. We did some searching but didn't come up with any close connections. But now that you tell me all those Greys are also Malones, I have a lot of questions. Maybe they're trying to distance themselves because one of them is our murderer."

"That family sure acted like nothing had happened. I mean, they were at the pub when the body was discovered and not a peep about being the children of the deceased."

"It's just cold-blooded," muttered Jets.

Olivia sighed. "The problem is they were all in plain sight at the pub before we found the body. I don't think they could have done it."

"What about Brandon's girlfriend? What's her name again?"

"Ashley Tennant. She was at the table with the other three. I don't think anyone got up to use the restroom. You can confirm that with Arlo. He was keeping his eye on that table the entire time. Plus there's closed circuit in the pub. You can check that."

"We've looked at the CCTV," mumbled Jets.

"I'm going inside to get another beer. Anyone else need a drink refresh?" Cookie called out.

"Not for me, sweetie," Janis said.

"I'm good." Olivia shook the ice cubes in her glass.

When Cookie disappeared into the house, Michael raised the top of the grill. Olivia felt her stomach growl. *They don't look boiled now.* Slightly charred, the wings looked crispy and smelled delicious.

Michael lifted each one with his tongs, piling them on the platter. He stepped over to Janis, offering her the first wing.

"Hot," she said, dropping it back on the pile. "They look delicious. Let them cool off for a minute and I'll try again."

Michael set the wings on the table next to the paper plates. Then he pulled up another chair. "So to continue your conversation, from what I hear the Greys are not the Greys but the Malones."

"It does change things," came Janis's clipped voice.

Cookie walked from the house, a beer in his hand. He pulled paper napkins from his pocket, which he left on the table. Then he moved his chair closer. "Kind of makes our skateboard surveillance seem trivial. The murderer could be living right in that house next door to Cay and Arlo."

Olivia's stomach clenched. "The way you put that makes me feel nervous."

"Or the ex-wife may have done him in." Cookie took a long sip of his beer. "I don't have to remind you that ex-wives aren't all nice people."

"Bianca Grey was home making dinner for her family when Beats was murdered," Jets concluded. "I admit no one was in the house to confirm her alibi, but she probably didn't do it."

"Why are you so convinced it's not Bianca?" Olivia asked.

Jets took the last sip of beer and put down the empty bottle. "There's a good chance Beats may have been paying her spousal support. I don't think she wanted that source of income to end. We'll delve into her bank accounts and see if I'm right."

"He paid twenty years after the divorce?" Olivia's eyebrows raised.

"They had four kids together and she didn't remarry. It's quite possible," Janis said.

Cookie nodded. "Makes sense. My ex didn't remarry because she wanted me to keep paying. Some women are like that."

"Don't worry," Jets said, "I'll call Bianca in for another chat at the constabulary to ask about spousal support. I can get a warrant to search her house after that interview."

Olivia looked over at Michael. "It's time to dig into those wings. Since we're still doing the skateboard surveillance..." She looked at Janis for confirmation.

"I would appreciate it if you would do it tonight. I'm not sure what the skateboarding video has to do with the Malone murder investigation, but it was sent at the same time and the skateboarder could be one of those kids."

Michael rose to his feet, disappearing into the house. He returned with another beer for himself and Janis, Mayor Maguire at his heels.

"Come here, M&M," Olivia called. The dog trotted to her chair. He turned his body around and then lay at her feet, resting his chin on her shoes.

Janis took a sip of beer from the bottle Michael offered her. "So let me get this straight. Blair told you at the library that Beats abandoned his family. Is that right?"

"That's what she said."

"So I can get the tech guys to take a deeper dive into Beats

Malone's history. We did a cursory look right after we found the body. As I said, most of his personal info had been scrubbed. But if we go in through the kids' names and his ex-wife's, maybe we can find out something that will lead us back to Lily Rock and his death."

"Do you think Lily Rock has something to do with why Beats was killed?"

Jets shook her head. "I have to check but I doubt it's possible. I mean, what could our little town have to do with any of this? The whole Grey clan only moved here a few weeks ago. And Beats was coming up for a Sweet Four O'Clock audition, not necessarily to live."

"How about Beats's cell phone? Were you able to tap into that?"

"The team is still trying to unlock his passcode," admitted Jets. "Once we have that, it will be a full-on investigation, even if I have to arrest everyone in the family and question them separately."

Olivia heard the determination in Janis's voice. "I want to help," she finally said, expecting to be turned down but unable to stop from offering.

Janis cleared her throat but made no invitation.

Olivia felt a flicker of hope. *She didn't say no right away.*

Michael interrupted, "Help, as in listening to the interviews? You're not going undercover like that time at the music academy."

She heard the concern in his voice. But she waited for Janis to respond to her question. When Jets said nothing, Olivia sighed. Sitting back in her seat, she closed her eyes, opening them quickly when Janis finally spoke.

"I could use your help."

Olivia sat up, her eyes wide open. "You could?"

"You have a knack. People open up to you. I could use that

with the Grey kids. I say *kids* even though they are adults. But they act like some kind of clan, talking for each other and hanging out together. Their behavior is unnerving and I could use your help."

This was the first time Olivia had heard Janis Jets acknowledge that she was useful. Every other occasion, Jets chided and made fun of her interest in solving crimes. But this time it was different.

"Let me know what time you want me tomorrow and I'll be there. Should I bring my amateur sleuth gear? You know, a Sherlock Holmes hat and a magnifying glass?"

Jets snickered. "Don't make me regret my decision, Nancy Drew. When I hear from Bianca Grey, I'll let you know." She looked toward the table. "I think it's time to dive into those wings before you and Mike have to get ready for the stakeout."

Michael rose to his feet. He grabbed the platter, piled high with crispy wings, and offered them to Janis.

"I'll get the salad." Olivia stood from her chair.

Janis looked at Olivia and then reached for a wing.

Olivia walked into the house. Once in the kitchen, she felt a tingle up her spine. *I'm back. Janis needs me.*

CHAPTER ELEVEN

Olivia snuggled into her covers, shutting her eyes to the glare of the morning sun shining through the curtains. After a long night of surveillance, she'd fallen into a deep sleep, exhausted from keeping alert. "Go away, sun," she muttered, turning over to plant her face into her pillow. Yet her thoughts traveled back to the night before.

She sat in her chair as Michael stood, watching from the rooftop. He was quiet, barely moving and not turning around to talk to her. When he spoke she had to struggle to pay attention.

"So Janis had a word with me last night...when you were in the kitchen."

Olivia got up and stood next to him at the rail. Without making eye contact, they both stared at the park. The only movement she detected was an owl that swooped from one branch to the next.

"She told me," he continued, "that you were upset when you got fired."

"I thought you knew that," Olivia said.

"I knew you were upset, but I didn't realize the extent. She said even Brad noticed you were angry when you came to the constabulary. You're not a rude person by nature."

"True," she said, nodding her head. "I'm very pleasant for the most part."

Michael chuckled. "Right. Anyway, Janis values your interviewing skills, and I may have been overly protective."

"Janis values my inner detective, the one she calls Nancy Drew," Olivia commented dryly.

"Your what?"

"People fascinate me. I've always been that way."

"You fascinate me, that's all I know. And I don't want to stand in the way of you being you."

"Does that mean you won't interfere when Janis and I work together?"

Michael sighed. "She's not going to hire you as a constabulary assistant. She thinks you're more of an administrator."

Olivia felt surprised. "She's never said that to me."

"She doesn't want to get between us." Michael placed his hands on her shoulders, turning her body to face him. "That's why she hired Brad. You are overqualified as an administrative assistant. Brad can be trained. He doesn't have, let's say, your natural inclination to be curious and help people."

Olivia felt both mad and happy. *It's good to be seen but not to be treated like a child.*

Michael leaned closer to look at her face. Then he placed another hand on her shoulder. "It must be exasperating being talked about like this. You're not a child and I'm sorry I treated you like one. I was scared and I overreacted. Can you forgive me?"

"I have forgiven you," Olivia admitted. "I know I've been rude to Brad so I'll work on that."

Michael kissed her forehead. "Why don't we leave it at

this? Janis relies on your help. It's between you two. I'll stay out of the way and not interfere anymore."

She'd felt satisfied that night, which carried over to the morning. *At least we got that out of the way.*

She opened one eye. The sunshine played against the window.

Half an hour later Olivia stepped into the kitchen showered and dressed. She found Sage sitting at the kitchen table, looking pale, with circles under her eyes. "It's Friday, shouldn't you be at work?" Olivia asked. She walked to the coffeepot to pour herself a full mug. "Can I make you some tea?"

When Sage didn't answer she turned around. Her sister's face was buried in her arms. "Honey, you feeling okay? Is it the baby?"

Sage raised her head, her eyes red from crying. "I called in sick today. The first time since I got pregnant. I figured I could take a day off and get ready for our gig at the pub tonight."

Alarmed, Olivia asked, "Do you want to cancel the engagement? Maybe you're just overtired..."

"I am having trouble sleeping." Her eyes welled with tears.

"Do I need to call Meadow so that she can come over and fuss?"

Sage shook her head. "I'm not that desperate. How about an herbal mint tea? It might calm my stomach."

"Consider it done. We can sit and chat while I fix you some toast. Does that sound good?"

"Jam, no butter," Sage said. "I'm going to the bathroom. Be right back."

By the time she returned, she'd combed her long hair into a braid that hung down her back. Her face looked less puffy, though still quite pale.

Olivia had put a piece of toast with strawberry jam on the table, alongside a mug of tea. Sage sat down and then bent her head over the mug to inhale. "Smells so good and it does calm my stomach. Thank you."

Olivia watched her take a small bite of toast and then a sip of tea. When Sage put down the toast, Olivia pointed. "Finish that one up. I can make you another. I've heard that pregnant women need to eat more frequently, like every two hours."

Sage obediently picked up the toast and took another bite. "When I forget to eat, the nausea gets worse. Pretty soon I'm unable to keep anything down and then I forget to drink. I guess I'm not good at being pregnant."

"Since I've never been 'with child'," Olivia used her hands to make air quotes, "I'm not an expert. But I've known other women who say fatigue can disrupt an entire day. It's important to get lots of sleep. What does your doctor say?"

Sage finished the last bite of toast before answering. "I can't get ahold of him. The nurses give me information but it feels so impersonal. I'm thinking of hiring a doula, at least that's what Meadow wants me to do."

Olivia felt relieved. *I'm happy Meadow didn't appoint herself as a doula.* "Okay then, let's work on that this weekend. I'll help you find someone in Lily Rock."

Sage ran her finger over the crumbs on her plate. Then she looked up.

Olivia said, "I'm going to make another piece of toast. Do you want one? And how about an egg? I can scramble for both of us."

"I'll do the toast." Sage stood, walking toward the toaster. Olivia stood to reach out and give her a hug. She held her sister close, feeling the baby bump between them. "You know you can tell me anything, right?"

Sage nodded, her face against Olivia's shoulder. "I know. I was going to talk to you a few days ago, but then you found another dead body, and I just didn't have the energy for the conversation."

Olivia released her from the hug, taking a step backward. "My crime-solving behavior has been on everyone's minds lately. This may not be the best topic while you're pregnant. We can chat about other things like decorating the nursery and moving furniture out of the office."

Rubbing her sleeve across her eyes, Sage nodded. "I'm getting more excited about decorating the nursery. It makes having a baby feel very real."

"Decorating will be a welcome topic of conversation." Olivia patted her shoulder. "But for now, let's get some more food in your belly."

After their breakfast, Olivia sent Sage away for a shower. She took the time to plump pillows on the sofa and open the door to the outside to let in the warm breeze. When she heard Sage moving around the bedroom she called out, "I think you should hang out here for the rest of the day. Change of scenery may do you good."

Sage emerged with her hair wrapped in a towel on top of her head. She'd dressed in soft pants and an oversized shirt. "I'm glad I called in to work," she told Olivia with a grin. "Thanks for putting the mother into mothering."

"You're welcome."

Sage made her way to the sofa, settling into the pillows. She'd brought a book to read. Olivia continued moving around, making sure to be quiet. When she looked back, she saw that Sage had stretched out her legs on the sofa and closed her eyes. The book lay open on her chest. Olivia reached for a blanket. She gave it a shake and then placed it over Sage, tucking the sides close to her body. *I'll go into town and see Janis. By the time I get back, I'll make her lunch.*

It wasn't until Olivia opened the door of the constabulary that she determined to greet Brad.

"How are you doing?" she said immediately upon entering. "Sorry I was so crabby with you the other day."

"That's okay. I was surprised, that's all. Janis told me not to worry and to grow a pair." He sighed.

Olivia gave him a thumbs-up. "We're good then?"

"Yep," he said, reaching into a drawer in his desk. "Janis gave me this. Here's a key card for the security door. You can tap it on the pad or punch in the code for it to open."

"I remember." Olivia took it from his hand.

He swiveled to face his computer as she made her way past the desk to tap the pad. The door immediately swished open. She walked into the hallway, putting the card into her back pocket.

She found Janis Jets in interview room one. Janis stood in the far corner staring at her cell phone. She didn't look up. "Glad you could make it," she said, still staring at the phone.

Two chairs had been placed on opposite sides of the conference table. "Bianca Grey is supposed to be here by now." Janis clicked her phone and placed it on the table. "Sit there," she said, pointing.

Olivia obeyed, shoving her purse under the chair. She folded her hands in her lap and waited for further instructions.

Finally Janis sat opposite her. "Bianca did not think it necessary to comply with my request to come down to the station." She shifted in her seat. "After a bit of persuasion she said she'd come, but I'm thinking she may change her mind again. We'll see. In the meantime I want you to put on that sincere face. Bring your best good-cop routine. Let's crack this investigation wide open. I know Bianca is hiding more than she's saying."

"Maybe not," commented Olivia. "Maybe Bianca is just doing her best with three adult children who seem to be unemployed and living under her roof."

"That may be," Jets stated flatly. "But what about this? Do you think Brandon's girlfriend may be the culprit?"

"Ashley lives with the rest of the them in Bianca's house. She's like one of the family."

Jets nodded. "Right. The biggest case of failure to launch I've ever seen. It's one thing to have a young adult staying with you while they get some money saved for their own place."

"Or if they need parental support for some other reason, should that be necessary," added Olivia.

"But the whole bunch of them…it's like they can't exist without each other. Though I wonder how Ashley Tennant got involved. She must really love that Brandon."

Janis's cell phone rang. She listened and then spoke. "Okay. Send her in." She put the phone back on the table. "Looks like Bianca showed up. I'll meet her in the hallway and chat her up a bit. Why don't you make a fresh pot of coffee? It will give me time to ask a few questions as a warmup."

Olivia stood to make her way through the open doorway. On the way down the hall she could hear Janis greet Bianca.

"Hello, Ms. Grey. Thank you for coming in today. It must be your lunch break."

"This better not take long," came the woman's impatient reply.

"It will take as long as it takes. Thyme Out can get along without you for a bit. We could call your employer and explain…"

"Your boyfriend, you mean," muttered the woman.

The conversation between Janis and Bianca grew distant as Olivia walked into the break room. She rinsed the pot and began to measure new grounds into the filter.

Then she remembered, *I have to tell Sage where I am.* She pulled out her phone to text. At the constabulary. Be home soon. Eat more toast. She selected an emoji blowing kisses and then hit Send.

When Sage didn't respond, Olivia smiled to herself. *I hope she's still sleeping. That's the best thing for her right now. Maybe I'll put on a pot of soup for the weekend when I get home.*

The aroma of coffee filled the air. Olivia watched as the last bit of water dripped into the pot. When it finished, she nodded. *That should give Janis enough time with Bianca.* The interview room door stood open. She stuck her head in to announce, "Anyone want coffee?"

"I do," came Jets's immediate reply.

Bianca glared. "I drink plenty of coffee at work."

"Okay then, I'll bring a bottle of water and two mugs." Olivia spun around, moving briskly down the hallway back toward the break room. *Bianca's going to be a tough one.*

CHAPTER TWELVE

Olivia returned with two mugs and an unopened water bottle tucked under her arm. She placed the mugs on the table and the bottle in front of Bianca Grey, who scowled and muttered, "Can't even get me a glass..."

A retort lay in her mouth, but she closed her lips in time. Olivia inhaled and sat down next to Janis Jets. She crossed one leg over the other under the table, settling herself into the chair, the defensive words she wanted to utter sliding back down her throat. *Bianca triggered me.*

That was close. Spatting about a glass of water could have derailed this interview. Olivia took a closer look at Bianca as Janis Jets opened her iPad.

She'd worn a red leather jacket, her professionally manicured nails matching the shade of the jacket. Blond hair had been recently bleached and coiffed, a thick mane of bangs dangling over her forehead, which she pushed back with her hand. The silence in the room felt thick.

Olivia waited for Janis to speak. Jets looked at her iPad, offering no hope for conversation. Finally Bianca Grey gave in. "If you don't explain to me why I'm here, then I'll just go." She pushed her chair back as if to emphasize her point.

Jets closed her iPad. "I told you on the phone, new information about the murder of Beats Malone has come to our attention." Then her voice shifted from mild to forceful.

"Remain seated."

Bianca complied, a sullen expression on her face.

Jets continued, "Of course, you're well aware that you held back important evidence: that you are Beats's ex-wife and that you are the mother of his three children."

"He abandoned us when they were small. As their only parent I had quite a difficult situation, but I managed all by myself," she said.

The back of Olivia's neck tingled. *Under other circumstances I would empathize with this story. But in this case, she's so self-righteous, I want to disagree.*

"I see," Jets said, maintaining a dispassionate voice. "How long have you been divorced?"

"We've been separated for nearly twenty years. The divorce was final somewhere in that time, I don't remember exactly." Bianca flipped her bangs out of her eyes with a manicured forefinger.

"Okay, let's cut the nonsense," Jets said. "Beats Malone is your ex. You have three children by him. Where were you last Friday between five and six o'clock?"

"I was at home making dinner for my family," she replied calmly. "No one can tell you otherwise."

"You'd be surprised," Jets said calmly. "Every guilty person I interview seems to think they have the perfect alibi and are invisible. It turns out someone always sees you. There's a person or a camera that catches people. Unless you have a cloak of invisibility..." Jets's eyebrows shot up. She watched Bianca as if she hoped she'd catch the joke.

Olivia suppressed a giggle.

Bianca's face remained impassive. Jets looked over at Olivia. Her left eye narrowed a fraction, making her wonder. *Does she want me to say something...*

Olivia cleared her throat. "Was someone with you that night to corroborate your alibi?"

"My children were at the pub. They texted me and I texted back. That's enough corroboration."

"Don't play dumb with me, Bianca," Jets said firmly. "You can be anywhere and text."

She opened her blue eyes, looking innocent. "I didn't kill my ex. I don't even know how he died. It could have been one of his girlfriends, you know, a woman he picked up on a tour."

Jets's eyes narrowed. "So he played around? Your ex?"

"He was on the road most of our married life, of course he played around." She bit her bottom lip as if wanting to say more, but then she closed her mouth.

Janis cleared her throat, checking her iPad. "Beats Malone died of a stab wound," she told her. "They found a deep incision right under his ribs, which pierced his heart."

A smug smile came to Bianca's face. "How fitting. He broke my heart and the hearts of his children. What goes around comes around."

"Is there any financial gain after his death? Did he leave an insurance policy for the kids?"

"He's been a poor provider for our family all along. I don't think he ever took out an insurance policy. He never makes his payments. A real deadbeat dad."

"We also found a cell phone in his pocket," Jets said, eyeing Bianca carefully.

Did her eye just quiver? That's the first time I've sensed any break in her confidence.

Janis's statement hung in the air. Bianca stared to the right as if she were searching for words. She finally muttered, "His cell phone is none of my business. Like I told you, we haven't seen or spoken to him for years."

"Did you tell me that?" Jets asked.

"I'm telling you now," she insisted. "None of us, my kids included, have anything to do with deadbeat Malone."

Jets leaned forward, her elbows on the table. "Well, Bianca, that's kind of funny. You see, we're pretty certain that Beats Malone paid spousal and child support to you for years. And that he never missed a payment."

Bianca's body grew rigid. "You don't know anything about me or my family. He kept all of his big earnings to himself over the years. He only paid what the court ordered and nothing more."

"I see," Jets said, as if she didn't see at all. She stood abruptly. "Thanks for coming in. You can go back to work and I'll be in touch."

Bianca stood from her chair. "I'm not going to drop in every time you have a question about a man who means nothing to me. You'll have to contact my attorney from here on out. Here's his information." She shoved the business card across the table toward Jets.

"Olivia will show you out; have a nice day."

She huffed and then walked around the table toward the door. Olivia stood to follow her out. Once in the hallway, Bianca hissed over her shoulder, "Get away from me. I don't require an escort." She exited through the back door. Olivia heard traffic noise from the alley before the door shut with a clunk.

Janis Jets sat at the interview table when she returned.

"I don't think I was at all helpful," Olivia apologized. "She gave me a bad vibe from the moment I saw her."

Jets nodded toward the chair. "Actually you did a good

job. You kept quiet and didn't let her take charge of the conversation with some unrelated bit of nonsense. She also gave away much more than she intended to."

"How's that?" Olivia sat down.

"She told us she was at home at the time of Beats's death. I don't think she knows her neighbors can be asked for verification. I mean, Arlo and Cay live right next door."

"But Arlo was at work. I was talking to him and waiting for Beats."

"But Cayenne wasn't at the pub, now was she..."

Olivia nodded. "No, she wasn't. In fact, Arlo told me that Cay thought the Grey family was a bit, you know, off. That's the way Cay describes people who make her feel uncomfortable," added Olivia.

"Here's the plan," Jets said. "I'm going to talk to Cay this evening. I'll look into Bianca's alibi. My gut tells me she's lying about some part of that being-at-home-cooking-dinner scenario. I don't know why she'd lie. It may have nothing to do with Beats's death."

"If she was cooking dinner, she failed to tell her kids," Olivia added dryly. "They were eating burgers and fries and drinking beer at the pub that night."

Jets nodded. "Interesting. I'll confirm it with Arlo and talk to Cay. Afterward I'll give you a call."

Olivia asked one more question. "Are you and Cookie doing surveillance this evening?"

"We're on. It may be the last night. I'm not sure my plan warrants losing sleep since no one has shown up, so it feels like a lost cause."

"Do you think the skateboarder may be one of those Grey kids?"

"That's exactly what I think. But until I have proof, I'm at a loss." Jets flicked her hand at Olivia. "Get out of here now, I have work to do."

Once outside the constabulary, Olivia inhaled deeply to clear her thoughts. *I'd better get home and check on Sage. If she's still sleeping I can make some calls to sub out the fiddle player for our gig. I don't think Arlo will mind, and it would give Sage a much-needed rest.*

Olivia leaned against the building and scrolled through her contacts. She found two possibilities and then hesitated. *Sage might be feeling better. I'll go home and talk to her instead.*

Olivia didn't want to wake Sage, so she opened the front door quietly. A voice called from the great room.

"Back already?" Sage's head appeared over the back of the sofa. Her hair had fallen around her shoulders in soft waves, her eyes no longer looked red and puffy.

"Hey there, did you sleep the whole time I was away?"

Sage yawned. "I sure did."

Olivia sat in a chair opposite her sister. "How is your tummy...ready for a little more food?"

"I'm hungry for the first time all week," Sage admitted. "I think I can fix something for myself though, you don't have to."

Olivia felt relieved. "I pulled up a couple of people to sub for you tonight. I can give them a call if you say so. It might be a good idea to take a night off."

"Oh no," Sage exclaimed. "I'm on for tonight. Really, the nap helped so much. I feel more myself."

"Okay then, how about I make you a grilled cheese and you get dressed?"

Sage stood up from the sofa, the blanket falling to the floor. "I'll meet you on the deck. The fresh air will be good for me."

"I'll have the food ready."

As Sage headed to her room, Olivia turned toward the kitchen. Alone with her thoughts, she considered the earlier interview and Bianca's information about her marriage with Beats.

I bet that's why the family sticks together so closely. They've always had each other. Probably afraid to move away from their mother and maybe they stay to protect her. You just never know about people...

She flipped the grilled cheese sandwich onto a clean plate. Grabbing napkins, she walked into the great room and through the doorway to the deck. Sage sat with her feet up on the rail looking out toward Lily Rock. "Here you go," Olivia said. When she walked around the chair to face her sister, Sage wiped the back of her hand over her eyes. *She's been crying again.*

"Thanks," Sage mumbled, reaching for the plate.

"Is there something you want to tell me?" Olivia asked quietly.

"No, I'm fine." She picked up half the sandwich. "I'm just so emotional all the time, probably hormones."

Olivia patted her on the shoulder. "I'll leave you to it then. Let me know if I can get you anything else."

Sage nodded, taking a bite of sandwich.

Olivia walked back into the house. *I may do some calling around for that doula. I think she needs support from someone knowledgeable.* Olivia sat at the kitchen table, scrolling on her phone to search out possibilities. Janis Jets's name appeared on her screen as an incoming call.

"Yes?"

"I got it," claimed Jets when she answered.

"Got what?"

"A court order signed by the Riverside judge. I can search the Greys' house for evidence."

"Really? You didn't tell me you were going to do that earlier."

"I didn't want to say anything until I knew for sure. The search warrant is right here in my hand."

"When are you going to their house?"

"I want Bianca to think my investigation is over since our chat. She'll let her guard down and then whammy, guess who's standing on her doorstep ready to come inside early Saturday morning. You want to come along?"

"Of course I do." Olivia didn't hesitate.

"Okay then. See you at the pub for your gig tonight. Cooks and I will do the last surveillance after that. Then I'll text you Saturday morning for the details concerning the warrant. I have forty-eight hours to execute, so that should work out."

"Okay, boss."

"Stop it!" The cell clicked off.

CHAPTER THIRTEEN

Olivia stood in front of the mirror in the pub's restroom. Even over the roar of the hand dryer on the wall, she heard loud voices from the bar. She waved her hands in the air and then reached behind her head to brush the hair up on her neck. Her curls fell back down in disarray.

She looked down at her feet. Her performance boots looked worn but well cared for, scuffs shined away with a recent polish and elbow grease. The crocheted vest over the thin off-white dress skimmed her slim body. Fluffing the skirt away from her boots, she took a deep breath.

All set, she told herself. She grabbed her autoharp off the counter, tucking it under her arm. Shoving the door open, she made her way past boxes stacked against both walls. Voices from the bar grew louder as she approached the door that opened to the stage.

"And now it's time to welcome Sweet Four O'Clock," came Arlo's introduction, quickly drowned out by cheers and applause. She had to turn sideways to ease her way forward past people standing on the sidelines. Olivia was the last of the band to wave and greet the crowd. She took one step closer to the audience, only inches away from high-top tables.

As the cheering subsided, she scanned the band. Sage balanced her fiddle on her shoulder. Paul held his upright bass, while Bella looked small sitting behind the drum kit. Olivia nodded her head at each one, taking a second glance at Bella Grey.

The girl did not smile or connect with her eyes. Olivia followed her gaze.

The Grey family. They'd pulled bar stools to the side of the stage where they sat with their backs supported by the wall. Blair was closest to the band, only a couple of feet away from the drums. Bianca sat in the middle still wearing her red leather jacket. Brandon leaned toward Ashley, who seemed to be speaking into his ear. Blair looked detached, staring into the distance.

Olivia pried her eyes away. *It's as if they are connected with an invisible cord, which makes them feel like one person.* She shook her head to clear her mind and turned to Sage, who smiled and nodded at the crowd.

Olivia tugged at the brim of her leather hat. Her finger edged up to touch the customary feather she wore for decoration. She waved again at the crowd and then seated herself on the stool.

Filled with the combination of excitement and confidence, she felt her excitement course through her body. Ready to make music, her quiet self had been replaced by the seasoned performer, the person she'd become over the years. Her other persona. "Hello, Lily Rock," she said into the microphone.

The small crowd cheered. "Okay, so we're not Coachella, but we've still got groove." Her words were followed by Sage tapping her foot on the stage. She raised her fiddle higher on her shoulder, tucking it under her chin. With a nod, Sage kicked off the first song as the crowd cheered appreciation.

* * *

After their set all four performers stood at the front of the stage, bowing together. To Olivia's surprise, Bella had lost her detached attitude. She didn't even look at her family but grinned at the crowd, holding her sticks in the air. *She's enjoying herself.*

Olivia glanced to the side where the Greys sat. Bianca grimaced. Brandon and Ashley glared, while Blair leaned over to speak to her mother. None of them clapped for Bella or Sweet Four O'Clock.

What's that about...

Olivia gave a final wave to the appreciative crowd, stepping down to make her way past the Grey family. Once she left the stage the others followed, all except Bella, who lingered behind to speak to her sister.

Inside the restroom Sage pulled on Olivia's arm. "Bella did okay. But did you see her family?"

Olivia nodded. "They seemed almost hostile, as if Bella had broken some secret family pact. I don't get it," commented Olivia. She reached under the counter for her autoharp gig bag. "I'd like to ask Bella to sit in again, but I'm afraid her family's opinion may undermine her joining us."

Sage started to speak and then bit her bottom lip. "I agree," was all she said.

Once Olivia left the restroom, she found Michael waiting for her by the pub kitchen. She stood next to him as he finished a conversation with Arlo.

"The pub is doing great," Michael said.

"Crowded tonight because of the local band." Arlo smiled

at Olivia. "It's cool to hear you now that you're back from the summer tour."

"Thanks," she said. Before she could say more, loud voices came from the stage area, one voice rising above the rest.

"Mom never said you could play with that band."

Olivia walked forward, looking around the corner. Blair stood in front of Bella, her voice escalating. "We don't want you to do anything that reminds us of Deadbeat." She shoved her sister away with both hands. Bella raised her hand behind her head as if to slap Blair. Her eyes caught sight of Olivia.

"And you can mind your own business," the girl shouted, dropping her arm.

Olivia stood her ground. Bella had turned away and started walking into the hallway toward the restroom. Olivia felt Michael's hand on her shoulder. "Let it go," he told her. "A family squabble that you don't want to get involved in."

She leaned closer to him. "The Grey family doesn't want Bella to play with Sweet Four O'Clock. At least that's what Blair was saying before she shoved her sister."

"I only caught part of the drama," he admitted. "Let them go," he said again. "Why don't we say our goodbyes and head home."

"Good idea." Olivia looked over her shoulder and then back. "I want to say goodbye to Sage. Can you give me a minute?" Her eye caught sight of Sage standing at the bar chatting to a guy she didn't recognize.

Sage laughed at something the man said. He leaned in to whisper in her ear. She laughed some more. Olivia walked closer. "We're heading home," she told her sister. The man looked up and smiled.

Sage turned around. "I was just talking to Jeff. I'll see you soon."

Olivia smiled back at the man named Jeff. When she didn't leave, Sage introduced her friend.

"This is my sister, Olivia Greer." Sage turned to the man. "And this is Jeff Grossman. I met him in the spring in Colorado. A fellow hiker."

Olivia took in his clean-cut jaw and button-up blue shirt. "Nice to meet you," she said. She leaned over to give Sage a quick kiss on the cheek. "See you at home."

Olivia caught sight of Michael. He stood near the exit with his arms folded over his chest. As soon as he saw her looking at him, he grinned. They walked out the door shoulder to shoulder. Once down the stairs, he took her hand in his.

"Great job tonight. The drummer wasn't bad. Pretty surprising since she's so young. What do you and Sage think?"

"I thought she loosened up and was pretty good. Until I heard her sister tear into her. Since when does a girl in her twenties need her sister's permission to play in a band..."

Olivia shook her head and continued. "I can't imagine living with my mother at that age. I was out on my own as soon as I could put the money together. There's something to be said about getting your own place." She kept talking.

"Did I tell you they call their dad Deadbeat? You'd think they'd stop now that he's actually...dead."

"It gives harsh and demeaning a whole new look," Michael muttered.

"I didn't know my father, but I can say one thing about Mona. Whenever I said a bad word about him, she'd call me out every time. She'd say, 'He may not be around, but you had a father and it's important to speak respectfully.'"

Michael stopped walking. He put his hand on Olivia's shoulder, turning her around to face him. "I can see this Grey family has gotten under your skin."

"More than I realized," Olivia agreed. "I thought we had a drummer, but I wonder if Bella can stand up to her sister—or her mother for that matter. And I'm starting to think one of those kids may have had something to do with Beats's murder. They just hated him. I hear the anger and resentment clearly between Bella and Blair when they talk about their dad."

On the short drive back home, Olivia felt unsettled.

Michael squeezed her hand. "The moon is full. Why don't we head up to the lot and I can show you this week's progress? We poured the slab so you can get a feeling for the space before we begin framing."

"That's a great idea," she said. "I need to get out of my head and I'd love to see the place in the moonlight."

He curled his fingers around hers.

Olivia looked out her window as he drove leisurely over the winding roads. From one curve to the next, the moon lit the way. Michael pulled off the main highway, taking the gravel driveway down the slope toward the construction site. Once he stopped, Olivia opened the door. By the time she closed it, he'd made his way around the truck to stand next to her.

Michael pointed toward Lily Rock, illuminated by the moon. "A spectacular view," he said.

She wrapped her arm around his waist. "I can't believe how clear it is tonight." They both stood, not speaking, staring out toward the mountain range at the shimmering legacy of their small town.

"I'll show you what we've accomplished since you were last here." Michael took her hand as they ambled together down the pathway.

"So that's the foundation..."

"Right. When it cures we'll drill for the posts. Then the

inspector will sign off and we can take the next step. The framing will be done quickly."

He pointed to the right. "That's where the main bedroom will be. The great room and atrium in the center, and the kitchen to the left."

"And behind our bedroom?"

"Will be our bathroom. The design feature is a wall of windows overlooking Lily Rock. Of course you can use the shades for privacy," he added quickly. "Sometimes people walk back in the woods."

"I forgot about that shower! It's been a while since I looked at the plans."

"Every day brings us closer. That's why I want you to watch each step for the next several months, to be a part of our new house. Plus if you see something that you don't like, now's the time to say so. I can fix it. But the further we get into the construction, changing course becomes more difficult."

"You really love this process, don't you?"

He thought for a moment. "To create something as important as a home for the person I love most in the world, well that's just the best thing I could possibly be doing." He looked at her. "Don't hold back any of your thoughts about this house. No matter how I react, just know I like to solve problems. We're going to have a place we can call our own, that's what matters to me."

Wrapping his arm around her shoulders, he pulled her closer. "How are you feeling now that the performance is over? Ready to go home and get a good night's sleep?"

"I'm ready to go home," she said, deliberately ignoring the part about sleep.

CHAPTER FOURTEEN

It was nine o'clock on Saturday morning when Janis Jets brandished her search warrant in Brandon Grey's face. "Where's your mom?" she asked brusquely.

"At work," he mumbled.

Janis brushed past him into the house. "I can call and make certain of that, you know." She stood in the middle of the room looking around. "You might as well leave that door open. My team is coming in a minute. Just sit down over there," she pointed to a sofa, "and watch how a crackerjack small-town police force works."

Brandon stepped away from the door. Olivia followed Janis into the house. *This place feels claustrophobic.* Furniture crowded the small living area. Plates with bits of food lay on nearly every flat surface. Glasses with smudges had been left on the stair treads.

Clothes, abandoned over the backs of furniture, brought her mother's admonition to mind. *Don't put it down; put it away.* Two laundry baskets had been tipped over near the kitchen table, as if people had rifled through them looking for something clean to wear.

"I want to see that warrant," came a shrill voice from the stairway. Bella Grey, still in her pajamas, hurried down the stairs and straight at Janis. Before Jets could stop her, the paper had been snatched from her hand.

Olivia inhaled. *This isn't going to go well.*

Jets allowed the girl to read. Bella looked like a child who'd woken suddenly from a nap. Her tangled mass of hair hung over her eyes.

She shook the warrant in Janis's face. "I can just tear this up right now. You'll have to get another one, won't you..." As her fingers tore the corner off the paper. A slow smile come over Janis's face. She reached for her iPad.

"Do what you need to do. I have the electronic copy right here. And by the way, your petty schoolgirl antics don't work with me. That paper you are threatening to destroy is a warrant from the Riverside County court. It's an official document, not a love note from your high school boyfriend."

Janis made no attempt to retrieve the notice. She spoke again. "This whole family is off the rails. Every time I talk to one of you, a big drama unfolds. You distort the facts."

Bella tore the paper in half.

Jets sighed. In a calm voice she continued, "Like most entitled people, you disregard everyone else's opinion because you think yours is the only valid one. That's not going to work. I know I'm the boss. Get the hell out of my way before I arrest you for interfering with the course of justice."

Olivia watched as the scraps of paper floated to the soiled carpet. A slow smile came over Janis's face. She turned back to Bella. "In case you don't know, that particular crime comes with jail time. So why don't you get a bowl of cereal and sit down next to your brother while I get to work?"

"You can't treat my sister like that," came a wail from the hallway. Blair, tresses piled on top of her head, stood barefoot wearing cotton shorts and a thin T-shirt. "Just because our father was murdered, you don't get to pick on us. He never even knew us. He didn't care about any of his family. Why are you being so mean, just because you can't solve his murder?"

Jets scratched her head. "What's your name again?"

"Blair." The girl's bottom lip began to tremble. "And I'm upset, so just stop what you're doing and go away. I know my mom has to be present for you to search our house."

"You know that?" Janis sounded surprised. "How old is he?" She pointed to Brandon.

"I'm thirty-one," he commented quickly.

"I'm twenty-eight," Bella added.

"And you?" she stared at Blair.

"I'm twenty-five." Tears formed in her eyes. "I don't know why that matters."

"I can search a house so long as an adult is present. All of you are legal adults. Unless you have any other legitimate objections, I will proceed."

"You're on some kind of power trip," Bella spat. Without saying more, she moved closer to the sofa and sat down. Then as if suddenly becoming aware, she looked toward Olivia. "Why are you here?"

"She's my consultant." Jets glanced toward the open front door. Olivia heard car doors slam. "That will be my crew," Janis announced. "Olivia, stay with them while I have a look around."

I don't want to babysit this bunch. By now all three Grey siblings sat side by side. Olivia looked at a nearby chair, clothes piled on top. They smelled like old perspiration, as if they hadn't been washed in weeks. She bundled them in her arms, dropping them in a laundry basket nearby.

The sisters stared at their cell phones. Brandon's eyes scrutinized Olivia, from her shoes to her chest to the top of her face. "I saw you at the pub last night," he said in a low mumble. "And the night Deadbeat was found murdered."

"I saw you, too, that night. I was talking to Arlo at the bar," Olivia admitted. "Actually I was waiting for your dad. We were in negotiations about him joining our band."

"Loser," commented Bella.

"He's not our dad," Blair added in a snide voice. "He's a sperm donor."

Olivia felt her chest tighten, recoiling from the girl's bitter remark.

Bella interrupted. "Mom set us straight when we were children. She's the only parent we need. She treats us respectfully."

They unanimously discount their father. She looked at Brandon.

"Did you get ahold of your mother this morning?"

"I texted my mom," he said. "But her boss won't let her leave."

Blair's eyes widened. "He can't hold her against her will."

"She needs the job," muttered Bella. Her eyes flashed at Olivia. "You have no idea what it's like to raise three children on your own with no support. My mom has to take menial jobs just to feed us. She could have been an attorney but she couldn't afford tuition."

"Your mom could have gotten a scholarship," Olivia said brightly. "Lots of divorced women go back to school and get a better education."

Bella's face flushed red. Then a voice came from upstairs.

"Hey, knock it off down there. I can't concentrate. Just be quiet, all of you."

Olivia's phone pinged with a text from Janis.

I hear everything you say. Stop trying to reason with them.

DEADBEAT DAD

Olivia texted back. Find the knife yet?

Kitchen is next, came Jets's reply.

Olivia looked up from her phone at the siblings. Finally she blurted out, "Do any of you skateboard?"

Brandon looked up immediately. "Why do you care?"

"I was just wondering. I saw a video the other day and the skater was in downtown Lily Rock at night."

"A video?" He squirmed and then added, "No one here skateboards. Our mom thought that was dangerous, so we never got into it."

Olivia scanned Brandon's face. *Was it my imagination, or did he flinch when I said the word skateboard...* "Okay, not you guys then, but I was also wondering..."

Brandon's head dropped to look at his phone, as if to end the conversation.

Olivia didn't give up. "How come you didn't talk before? Your girlfriend, Ashley, did all the talking for you." Olivia made the pretense of looking around the living room. "And I was told she lived at the house. Where's Ashley?"

"She's not one of us," Blair stated flatly.

"She only stays here some of the time," Bella quickly added.

"She's around somewhere," mumbled Brandon.

Before Olivia could ask more questions, she heard Janis's boots clomping down the stairs. Jets stood in the living room looking glum. " I didn't find anything unusual upstairs."

When no one said anything, she added, "One more place and I'll be done here." She took steps toward the kitchen.

"Need any help?" Olivia called out. *Please need my help. I am so done with these three.*

Before Janis could reply, a low moan, as if someone were in pain, caught her attention. Olivia quickly turned away from Janis, seeking the source of the sound. She looked from one Grey to the next. Moans came from the back of their throats as each stared straight ahead.

"Stop that," she cried.

The nonverbal primordial sound continued. *They're giving me the creeps.*

Then the moans intensified, as a high-pitched *eek* came from Blair. Still staring ahead as if not seeing Olivia, they wailed together. Olivia put her hands over her ears.

Bella began rocking back and forth. Olivia felt disoriented. *How can I get them to stop this...*

Finally Jets thundered from the kitchen. "What's going on in here?" She stepped into the living room. "Playing crazy won't stop this search. Just knock it off!"

Blair stopped first. She smiled sweetly at Jets. "It's just something we do. We've always done that when people annoy us. Ever since we were little, we'd just, you know, communicate with our voices but no words. We get each other. That's why no one can come between us."

Brandon stopped the throat noise, leaving Bella's voice continuing alone. Now she hummed a non-melody singsong tune, rocking back and forth. She smiled at Janis Jets as if taunting her.

"Aren't you three something else," commented Janis dryly. "So close and yet so crazy."

Olivia dropped her hands and watched with fascination as Janis took charge.

"Do any of you have a job?" Jets asked matter-of-factly. "You act like people with too much time on your hands."

Bella glared. She looked at Brandon and Blair, who picked up their cell phones to stare at their screens.

"We work from home," Bella finally explained.

"All with your own computers, I assume?"

"That's right," answered Blair.

"Computers that I can take with me to the constabulary as evidence," Jets added, a gleam in her eye.

Now all three chins lifted, eyes glaring.

Olivia stood from the chair. "Are we done here?"

Jets's eyes narrowed, then she nodded. "We're almost done."

Olivia felt the tension in the room.

Jets looked at her iPad. She read and then cleared her throat. "So my guy outside found a shed out back. He says," Janis looked down at her iPad and then up again, "that your girlfriend Ashley was out there, all by herself." Olivia watched the three siblings' shocked faces. *Looks like you lost control of the narrative, kids.*

"I'm going to have a word with Ashley before I go." Jets turned toward the front door, shouting over her shoulder, "Olivia, come with me."

Olivia followed Janis outside. She hurried to catch up. "A shed?" she asked.

"They found Ashley in the shed." Jets walked faster. "There was a small bed inside. It looked like she'd been in there for some time."

"My guys took down her information while I was looking in the kitchen for the weapon." Jets looked directly at Olivia. "But that's not all." Jets walked closer to her truck. She reached into the flat bed, pulling out a board with four wheels.

"A skateboard," Olivia said aloud. "Do you suppose that's the one from the video?"

Jets nodded. "I'll have to look at it again, but I think this is the same board. The wheels are pretty distinctive." She rolled one with her finger, then spoke again. "According to her own statement, Ashley Tennant has no living relatives."

"No mother, brother, sister...or father?"

"Nope," Jets said, stopping to think. "It seems she's just an orphan on God's highway."

Olivia stared at Janis, who stared back. Olivia was the first to speak. "Just like the song on the anonymous video..."

"So we have the skateboard and the link to the song. I'm thinking that's an important connection with Ashley and maybe the Grey family. I'm going to ask her to come down to the constabulary for an informal interview.

"I know she's hiding something. Hopefully she won't resist and refuse to come." Janis held her crossed fingers for Olivia to see.

CHAPTER FIFTEEN

Olivia arrived home later that morning. Her stomach rumbled as she walked into the house. *I need a cup of coffee after all of that business at the Greys'.*

She put down her purse, hearing voices coming from the kitchen.

"More coffee?" Sage's voice asked.

"Absolutely," came the gruff male response.

Olivia stopped in her tracks. *A couple drinking coffee mid-morning could only mean one thing. He spent the night.* She turned toward the door, sliding her purse from the table. *I'll give them privacy. Drive to Thyme Out for coffee.*

She parked in front of the bakery. *Sage is probably with that guy named Jeff. If she met him on her hiking trip last spring, he may be the baby daddy. I don't want to spook her by interrupting what sounded like a potential reconnection. Wait until I tell Michael. Our niece or nephew may have a real live father sitting in the kitchen!*

Once inside the bakery, Olivia looked around for an empty table. One round table with two chairs stood empty in the corner of the room. It was being wiped down by none other than Bianca Grey. Olivia could not see her face. *Okay, one more Grey to go.* She stepped closer as Bianca shoved the cleaning cloth in her apron pocket. "Is this seat taken?" Olivia asked.

Bianca glared at her. She bit her lower lip, her face growing sullen. "It's yours," she growled under her breath, moving away from the table.

Olivia put her sweater on the back of a chair to mark the table as taken. She wandered up to the bakery counter to place her order. Cookie stood with long tongs in his hand, a smile on his face. "I hear you had a busy morning," he commented. "I'll get the coffee of the day while you pick out a muffin."

"I'd like the summer solstice blend," she commented.

"I figured as much. Michael nailed that one. People have been coming in just to buy their own packaged coffee after tasting it here."

As Cookie poured, Olivia looked around for Bianca. When she didn't see her, she whispered to Cookie, "So we didn't find the weapon."

"Janis told me." He glanced nervously around. "Why don't you go back to your table and I'll meet you there."

She nodded. "How about the blueberry muffin?"

With the long tongs, he lifted it to a clean plate. She handed him money, taking her plate and mug of coffee.

Back at her table, she sat in her chair so that her back was to the corner and her eyes could scan the room, keeping a lookout for Bianca Grey.

After the last bite of muffin, Cookie arrived at her table. He held the coffee carafe. "Here's a refill." Once her mug was full, he added, "Be right back." She sipped and savored the hint of orange in the blend, then inhaled deeply.

Cookie arrived as promised. He'd brought his own coffee

in a mug prominently displaying the Thyme Out logo. After sitting opposite her, he leaned over the table. "So I kept Bianca here while Janis did her search. Of course, she chewed me out. I reminded her that she's not in charge of my bakery and that she could be replaced with an employee with a better attitude. Since she didn't want to lose the job, she huffed away. I won." Cookie smiled over his mug of coffee. "Then Janis called to say the search was over. Bianca got a call a minute later. I assume it was from one of her offspring."

"Did her mood change after the call?"

"It's hard to tell. She's a surly one on the best of days. I mean, she walks around here like she's too good for the job. I might have fired her the first week except I felt kind of sorry for her, with all those grown kids living at home."

"She told you that whole story about her ex abandoning his family, and how he's a deadbeat dad?"

"She tells it to anyone who will listen," muttered Cookie.

"I guess she never found another suitor."

"Not that I can see. It's as if possessing those kids is her entire life."

Olivia sighed. "That is sad. I can see why you might have felt sorry for her. If I hadn't just spent the last hour in the company of her terrible children, I might feel sorry for her too."

"It was that bad?"

"Awful, they even have a sound they make together, like a hive of bees. It's well rehearsed and eerie. They kind of moan and wail. Very weird."

"The way you describe it sounds very *Lord of the Flies*."

"Or in their case, Queen of the Bees."

"That would be Bianca."

"Yep, she's the queen and all of her offspring with the B

names are in her hive." Olivia looked up. "She's behind the counter."

"Thanks for the report. Oddly, none of my customers seem to care about her attitude."

"A tribute to your coffee and baked goods." Olivia smiled at him.

"Bianca has a crabby waitress vibe. It's kind of a thing. Maybe no one expects her to be nice."

"They have you for their nice needs," Olivia commented dryly.

"Damn, Olivia. Michael is lucky. You do cheer me up." Cookie smiled at her. The corner of his mouth twitched. "But then my Janis, she's something else. I guess Mike and I are both lucky."

As if conjured by the mention of her name, the bell over the bakery door rang and Janis Jets stepped into the cafe. Her glance took in the room, her eyes stopping on Cookie and Olivia. She made a straight path to their table. "What are you two talking about?"

"You," commented Olivia, taking a sip of coffee.

Cookie stood up. "Here you go, sweetie, take my chair. I have to check on my employee."

Jets sat down. Olivia watched as her fingers reached for Cookie's thigh, giving him a pinch. He grinned and then turned to go.

Jets focused her full attention on Olivia. "So what did you learn from those overgrown brats?"

"I was just talking to Cookie about them," she admitted.

"So spill." Jets rested her hands on the table, setting her bright gaze on Olivia.

"They couldn't stop complaining about their father. So far as I could tell, they had no remorse or sadness over his death."

"Yah, yah, yah, I heard that. But did they say anything about Ashley Tennant in the shed out back?"

Olivia shook her head. "I tried to bring her into the conversation by asking Brandon why he was suddenly talking, since she did all the talking before."

"And..."

"He just brushed me off."

Jets looked thoughtful. "I thought the house would reveal more. If not the weapon, at least something that would point the way for the investigation. It's been just over a week and we really have no evidence, just a bunch of circumstantial iffy gut feelings. With no weapon, I'm forced to believe his family had nothing to do with his death."

Olivia shrugged. "I'm not a psychologist, but I wonder why Bianca was making dinner for a family that was eating dinner in the pub?" When Jets didn't respond, Olivia spoke again. "By the way, all of those Greys are in their twenties, except Brandon, who's thirty-one. Something feels off."

"On the one hand, it's okay for kids to live with their parents if they need help making financial ends meet. I did that a few times. My mom made me feel welcome and I helped her out with rent. But eventually I moved out." Janis shrugged. "But on the other hand, three children under one roof with no job...makes me wonder what's going on."

"It's the numbers," Olivia agreed. "One child at home maybe. But three? So let's get back to Ashley. Do you think she's the one who sent the video to the constabulary?"

Jets paused to think. Then she said, "The way they flew through the air on that board. Every time I watch that video I admire the sense of defiance that goes with skateboarding on public property. Especially when everyone else is asleep. That got me too. I think Ashley is our skateboarder."

"The person on the video is an athlete and an artist. Performance art," concluded Olivia.

"She's pretty magnificent, I must admit. She's got moves." Jets nodded in appreciation, and admiration shone in her eyes. "I assume someone in the Grey family took the video, probably Brandon. He'd be my first guess. On the one hand, we can ask who, but on the other hand, what about the why? Why would a person send that video to the constabulary?"

"I've been wondering the same thing." Olivia noted Jets's set jaw. *She's really hit a dead end with the investigation. That has to be infuriating to such a good cop.*

"Maybe Ashley sent the video and it was a cry for help," Olivia suggested. "You know, like on YouTube where they say 'Blink twice if you're being held captive.' That might have been her blink twice moment..."

Jets's eyes widened. "That's not a bad line of inquiry. We did find her all alone in a shed out back."

Olivia took a deep breath. "Ashley may have been asking for your help by sending the video. Without a family of her own, she may be confused about the Greys."

Jets looked thoughtful. "So on the one hand, Ashley may be a suspect for Malone's murder. Though I have to say, I don't know why she'd kill Beats, and she had an alibi in the pub. But on the other hand, Ashley may be caught in a situation where she's being emotionally abused, and she doesn't know where to turn for help. I did leave her a message to call me." Jets picked up her phone from the table, glancing at the screen. "She hasn't called back yet."

Janis nervously stared at her phone. "I want that girl to call!" Then she texted and put the phone down. "I alerted Brad. He can keep trying to get ahold of her. It's time for me to wrap up this gabfest and get back to work. I'll drive around the neighborhood and keep an eye out. Maybe I can ask a few neighbors if they've seen anything suspicious at the Grey house."

"Cayenne," Olivia said instantly. "Arlo told me she'd been worried about the family even before we found Beats."

"You already mentioned that, Nancy Drew." Jets looked at her phone again. "If we hurry, we can catch Cay at home before she heads to work." Jets stood up from the table.

"Does 'we' mean me too?" Olivia asked.

"I'll drive the truck. Hurry up," muttered Jets.

CHAPTER SIXTEEN

Arlo answered the door.

"Came to see Cayenne," Jets mumbled, pushing past him. Olivia smiled apologetically.

"Howdy-do to you too," he said, a slight smile at the corner of his mouth.

"Hey." Olivia patted his arm.

"Is this about the Malone investigation?"

"Yes, it is."

"Cay's been watching the Grey house all morning. She's outside on the deck." He nodded to the half-open sliding glass door where Janis had pulled up a chair next to Cay.

"I'll join them," she told Arlo.

"Ladies first." He gestured with his hand.

Shoving the glass door closed behind her, Olivia stepped onto the worn redwood deck. She didn't interrupt the conversation.

"So Olivia told me that Arlo said you felt uncomfortable with your new neighbors."

Cayenne nodded.

Pulling up a chair for herself, Olivia sat and listened.

DEADBEAT DAD

"Tell me if I'm wrong," Cayenne said in her quiet voice. "But someone, who told someone, who told somebody else, may not be the most reliable evidence."

"That's why I'm here!" exclaimed Jets. "I want to get it from the horse's mouth."

Cayenne looked amused. "I am not a horse, nor am I a magical Native American."

Olivia repressed a laugh. Wearing black jeans and a black T-shirt with the pub logo, Cay appeared quite ordinary.

"Oh come on, Cay. Don't give me that magical Native American stuff. You got gifts. You gotta give me that," muttered Jets.

"I am Two-Spirit. I hear words people do not speak aloud or even admit to themselves. So does she. Why don't you ask her?" Cayenne nodded in Olivia's direction.

Olivia shook her head vehemently. "I have no idea what you're talking about."

"Your intuitive skills are not as finessed, but you have them," Cayenne said. "Like right now you know the answer to Janis's question. It's more about Ashley and less about the Greys."

Olivia's eyes flew open. "I did mention that earlier to Janis. That I'm concerned about Ashley."

"Enough of this mumbo jumbo," Jets said in her most commanding voice. "I want to ask what you're 'feeling' about the family next door." Jets used her fingers to air quote the word "feeling."

"Which of my neighbors interests you the most?" Cayenne asked.

"Okay, you set me up. I'm interested in the one who isn't a Grey. Ashley Tennant, for one. We found her in that shed behind the house just a few hours ago. I don't know if she's being held captive or just lives out there to maintain privacy.

Either way, there's circumstantial evidence that she may know who killed Beats."

"Ashley wants to belong," Cayenne said.

"Okay, what does that mean exactly?"

"That Ashley will do nearly anything to be part of a family," Cayenne explained. "She lives in the shed and in the house, depending on the mother's mood. That is my observation."

"So Bianca kicked her out. Is that why she was hiding in the shed?"

"She would not choose to isolate herself. I've heard Bianca argue with Ashley. I assume she was told to leave the house." Cayenne turned to Olivia with a knowing smile.

Olivia felt her chest expand, followed by warmth and then a sudden sense of loss. *Whenever I'm around Cayenne, I feel everything more intensely.* She said, "If Ashley is searching to belong, she may be attracted to the Grey family."

Jets's eyes widened. "You mean the Grey family is like a cult. And Ashley may be a new recruit."

Cayenne looked over the railing to the property where the Grey family lived. Surrounded by a chain-link fence, the two-story house looked rundown. Paint had peeled off the siding by the front door. Missing shingles exposed black tarp underneath on the A-frame roof. Behind the main house was the shed, surrounded by trees. Firewood had been piled against the nearby fence. Toward the back of the lot, a lime-green vintage VW Beetle was parked.

Olivia shook her head. "From this perspective, the Grey property looks..."

"Unkempt," Cayenne finished her sentence. "That is exactly what I thought. They moved into a clean and well cared-for property. Within two weeks the paint started peeling. Then shingles started falling off the roof. There's no reasonable explanation." Cay scratched her head. "Oh, and that car arrived recently. In the woods over there." She pointed.

"That's an old VW," remarked Jets. "Could be worth some money to the right person."

"The people in the house act afraid," stated Cayenne. "And very angry."

"They were very angry at Beats Malone," Olivia agreed.

"You mean the dead man," Cayenne confirmed.

Olivia explained, "You may not know, but Beats was the ex-husband of Bianca, and the children's father."

"I understand," Cayenne commented. "And that would explain a lot." She didn't say more.

Jets leaned forward. "Is there anything else you've noticed about your neighbors that would help me understand them better?"

Cayenne sat quietly, taking a minute as Jets fidgeted in her chair. Olivia looked beyond the railing to the house below. *I wonder if Cayenne sits out here not just to observe, but to wrap her mind around the family because she's worried what might happen next...*

Cayenne broke the silence. "You are right to be concerned about the situation, especially for Ashley Tennant. She's vulnerable and may act out. That is all I can tell you that you don't already know."

Jets sighed. "You're not very helpful. I thought Two-Spirits had all the answers. I already knew something was off before our visit today. I need more than that. Plus I think Ashley is a wannabe Grey. She's not the problem. Those kids and that mother make me suspicious."

Cayenne's eyes twinkled. "Like I told you, I am not magical."

Jets stood up, and then sat down again. "I forgot to ask. On the day Beats was killed, were you out here looking at the house? And if you were, did you see Bianca?"

Cayenne considered the question carefully. "I was here and I did see Bianca. The children were not here. I did step away for a couple of hours for a work emergency. One of my houses had a plumbing leak."

"Can you narrow down the time?" Jets opened her iPad.

"My cleaner called around 3:30. I left right away. I didn't get back until well after seven o'clock."

Jets nodded. "So then you can't provide an alibi for Bianca being at home from four to six o'clock last Friday..." Looking exasperated, Jets closed the screen on her tablet. "I'll be going now." She turned to Olivia. "You are welcome to stay and chitchat and do your intuitive thing. I have work to do."

"I have to get going too."

Cayenne nodded a goodbye.

Janis and Olivia left together, using the side stairway.

As Janis got behind the driver's seat of the truck, Olivia looked back. Cayenne sat in silent repose, her eyes on the Grey house. *She's like a bird that watches from afar. Silent. Intense. Ready to fly from her perch if needed.*

Olivia buckled her seat belt while Jets checked her phone. "Ashley's coming in to the constabulary." She dropped her phone on the console, shoved her key into the ignition, and shifted into drive. Pushing her foot on the accelerator, the truck sped away. Olivia grabbed the door handle as Janis continued driving at breakneck speed back to town.

Jets parked behind the constabulary. "Go through the back," she said, hopping out from behind the driver's seat. Olivia swung her legs around to step onto the pavement. She slammed the door behind her, rushing to the back entrance.

Jets followed her inside. Down the hall and into her office, she barked, "Sit there, I'll check with Brad." The door closed behind her.

Once seated, Olivia looked at Janis's computer. Her screen saver showed a photo of Lily Rock. She inhaled deeply and then heard a scratch from behind. Getting up, she opened the door and found Mayor Maguire sitting in the hallway. He yelped with excitement.

"Hey, Mayor."

Once in the office, he made a beeline for her purse that she'd left on the floor next to her chair. As the mayor began to sniff, she heard voices coming from down the hall near the break room.

"What do you mean, Ashley has already come and gone? I told you to keep her here. What happened?"

"She was in a big hurry," came Brad's response. "You didn't tell me to arrest her or anything so I didn't know how to make her stay."

"How about an excuse?" Jets demanded. "Use your imagination, flirt with her, or ask her out. I can't believe you let her go."

Done sniffing her purse, Mayor Maguire walked around the desk. His tail waved at Olivia as he investigated Janis's chair. By the time he'd made his way back around the desk, the arguing had stopped.

"I see he found you," Jets said. She stood in the doorway. "He's been hanging out with Brad all morning. I suppose you heard what happened..."

"Ashley left," Olivia said, reaching to pat the mayor's head. She scratched behind his ears, waiting for Janis to say something more.

"I want to look at the pub's closed circuit camera view of the night in question."

Olivia's head jerked up. "You haven't looked at that already?"

"We looked where the body was found, but we didn't check out the inside view of the tap room and the kitchen and back hall. I want to see those."

"Are the Greys still your first suspects?"

"Oh yeah, I haven't changed my mind about that. But I'm wondering if those three kids and Ashley actually sat at the table the entire time in question."

"I didn't see them move."

"Neither did Arlo," muttered Jets. "But come on, it was really crowded and your back was to the table. You were waiting for someone to show up, so you might have been distracted. Plus Arlo had his hands full with all of the customers."

"That's true. We might have missed something."

"So I'm going to spend the next couple of hours looking at all of the CCTV inside the pub tapes."

Olivia stood to leave. "I'm done for now?"

"You are dismissed," Jets said dryly. "But take the mutt with you. Brad doesn't need any more excuses to not do his job."

"Don't forget I need a ride home," Olivia added. "You drove me."

"Get out of here, would you? Call your boyfriend if you need a ride. You've got the dog. You two take a hike."

Olivia didn't bother to argue. When Janis turned to her computer, Olivia left the office, followed by Mayor Maguire. The two headed down the hall to the back exit. Once on the boardwalk, Olivia paused. Mayor Maguire took the opportunity to bound across the street. He trotted into the park, disappearing behind one of the redwoods.

She called after him, "M&M, wait for me!" She hurried

across the road. Once inside the park, she saw his tail disappear around the trunk of a giant sequoia. She called out again, "Mayor Maguire!" *I'm not supposed to walk under the trees.*

Signs with clear orders had been posted every three feet along the rail. *Foot Traffic Not Allowed*, the signs insisted. The Lily Rock town council made the decision to fence off the trees a few years ago, when the trees began dropping needles and dying away.

"Mayor Maguire," she called again. His nose peeked out from around the trunk of the largest sequoia. He yipped, begging her to follow.

"I can't come to you," she cried in earnest.

By now people had stopped to watch. "I'll get the doggie," cried a small boy. His mother snatched his hand. "Oh no you don't. It's against the rules. We'll get cited."

Olivia knew the woman spoke the truth. Just last week one of the town council Old Rockers handed two people a yellow slip, which required them to attend a video production titled "Save the Trees" at the town meeting hall. Refusal to show up would result in an official citation from the constabulary, along with a sizable fine.

Neither visitor nor resident wanted to take the time to watch a boring rendition narrated by a local arborist, an expert on native flora and fauna and giant sequoias. So most people made it a point to obey the rules.

The mother took the child's hand and walked away. This time Mayor Maguire trotted back to the sanctioned walkway. He leaped over the rail fencing, coming to sit in front of Olivia.

"You silly mutt," she said, leaning over to pat his head. "What were you doing behind that tree?" Olivia looked past the dog to where he'd stood in the grove. "Is there something you want me to see?"

He'd brought her important clues before—once he'd arrived with a boot in his mouth, resulting in an arrest. She reached for her phone to text Janis Jets.

M&M found something buried behind the big sequoia.

Jets replied: So what?

Remember that time he found the boot???

The next thing she saw was Jets running across the street toward the park. "Get out of the way," she demanded. The crowd parted on command as Janis, hand at the back of her blazer, pushed her way toward Olivia. She pointed to the dog. "He's right there."

"He was over there before." Olivia pointed toward the wooded area.

Jets took two steps and leaped over the railing, walking closer to the sequoias.

"Look, Mommy, she's breaking the rule!" claimed a small girl who held an ice cream in one hand.

"Shush, dear. She's a police officer."

"Why do they get to break the rules?"

The mother sighed with exasperation. "Just lick your ice cream and watch."

Jets approached the sequoia, placing her hand against the rough bark. She disappeared around the back. When she returned, she held a plastic bag in her hand. She walked toward Olivia, a look of satisfaction on her face.

She leaped over the railing that faced the main road. Dashing between cars, she made her way to the boardwalk and then disappeared into the front entrance of the constabulary.

Olivia sighed. "Come on, M&M. She's not going to answer our questions right now. I guess we're on a need-to-know basis." The dog's tongue hung out one side of his mouth in a half grin.

"But then you already know what she found." Olivia shrugged. "If we hurry we can get home for your early dinner. No more side trips. Let's go."

Mayor Maguire stepped up to her right knee. His tail waved in the air as they walked toward the main road together.

CHAPTER SEVENTEEN

On Saturdays Lily Rock attracted day visitors to several popular hiking trails. For some reason they were always in a hurry, so Olivia kept to the dirt beside the road for her own safety as cars and trucks whisked past.

Mayor Maguire trotted alongside, making the occasional dash into the nearby woods to chase squirrels and do dog business. He caught up with her later, settling in next to her left knee.

Perspiration formed on Olivia's face as the road grew steeper. Deep in thought, she watched the mayor dash away once again. She waved, wiping her hand across her forehead. *He's having a great day.*

Olivia paused to take a breath. Close to the road an old oak tree offered some shade. In the distance she heard distinct sputtering. Shading her eyes from the sun with her hand, she saw a lime-green VW Beetle coming up the road. It moved more slowly than the usual traffic, a line of tailgaters trailing behind. *I bet that's from the 1960s.* The driver behind the wheel looked familiar.

One of the Grey sisters sat in the driver's seat. *Is it Bella or*

Blair? She closed her eyes for a moment to block out the sun, trying to remember both the girls sitting on the sofa only a day ago.

Bella's hair is darker and her skin more olive-toned. Olivia opened her eyes just as the VW Beetle chugged past. *It's Blair with the blond hair like her mother's.* At that moment, Blair glanced to the side of the road, where she saw Olivia. Her hand lifted as if to say hello. Before Olivia could wave back, she realized, *That girl is flipping me off. Not that we're exactly friends.* She shook pine needles from both shoes and then turned to continue her hike up the road.

The VW tailpipe spit out noxious gas, causing Olivia to cough. One car behind the VW beeped to get around. They finally pulled out and passed the slow car. Then a truck honked loudly. The driver yelled at the top of his voice, "Pull over, you idiot." Olivia appreciated his sentiment.

She looked to her right when a familiar bark caught her attention. Mayor Maguire came bounding out of the woods, skidding to a halt by her feet. With a quick skip he matched Olivia's stride, turning his neck to watch the traffic. The VW made a *putt putt* sound followed by a sighing noise before it came to a complete stop.

Mayor Maguire called out a bark of recognition, running ahead of Olivia. She heard brakes squealing as car after car came to a sudden stop behind the Beetle. *Lucky no one has rear-ended another car.*

Blair flung open the driver's side door. She ran around the back, as other drivers stuck their heads out their windows yelling, "What are you doing?"

Olivia kept her eyes focused on the girl, who opened the passenger-side door. To Olivia's horror, Mayor Maguire jumped in. Blair closed the door as the mayor's head poked out the side window and the car sputtered away.

So you get a ride and I have to keep walking. Thanks a lot, M&M! She dragged her purse across her shoulder, lengthening her stride. *I'm nearly home.*

By the time Olivia reached her doorstep, she was sweaty and annoyed. *The next time, I'll drive instead of Janis. Then she can walk back.* She reached for her keys. Once the front door was open, cool air hit her face. *Phew. Glad to be home. Sage must have left by now. I'm going to get a glass of cold water.*

Michael sat at the kitchen table, an iced tea in front of him. Olivia's bad mood instantly vanished. "I'm so happy to see you," she said immediately, reaching over to lift his glass of tea to take a sip.

He watched her drink, an amused smile crossing his face. "So you've been on a run?" he asked.

"I went with Janis this morning and she drove back to town but then ditched me."

"Why didn't you call? I'd have given you a ride."

"I would have except I caught M&M digging behind the park's giant sequoia. He found something buried in the dirt, so I called Janis. She retrieved the item and by that time I figured you'd be busy, so I walked home."

"So where's the mayor?"

"That's the annoying part." Olivia took another sip of his tea. "He ditched me to hop in a car on the roadway, a lime-green VW Beetle."

Michael stood up and took the glass from her hand. "Why don't I pour you another glass and refill my own? Then we can sit on the deck and talk about the mayor's poor taste in driving companions."

She reached to give him a hug around the waist. He stopped, his hand suspended with the glass. Leaning over, he kissed her head. "I like sweaty Olivia," he mumbled in her ear.

She pulled her hands away. "I'm glad somebody does. See you outside."

Once they were seated, their feet propped on the railing and a table with the two iced teas between them, Michael cleared his throat. "So what exactly did the mayor dig up from behind the sequoia?"

"At first it looked like a rock in a plastic bag," Olivia said. "But then he held it in his mouth and I saw something sticking out both sides."

"He's a good one for stick gathering," commented Michael dryly.

"But why would a stick be encased in plastic?"

"Never mind a stick. Maybe it's Meadow's Labor Day hat," Michael chuckled. "Remember last year when he buried that monstrosity to save us all from having to pretend we liked it?"

"It wasn't Meadow's hat," Olivia laughed. "But I do remember our relief. Meadow was convinced that hat made a statement, only she didn't realize that we all thought it made her look like a lunatic."

Michael reached out to take her hand. "Look at us sharing Lily Rock memories. Pretty soon we'll be invited to join the Old Rockers. Who would have thought we'd be this couple two years ago?" She felt the warmth of his grasp travel up her arm.

"Not I," she admitted. "I had no intention of ever returning to Lily Rock again, let alone being with you."

The chairs were close enough for him to lay her hand on his thigh. He left his hand over hers, inhaling deeply as he stared through the woods to the Lily Rock formation on the horizon. "We were destined to be together," he said.

She turned her head to look at him." I don't think I've ever heard you use language like that before. Destined?"

"Yep, I'm a new man. I believe in all that stuff now,

because I've experienced Olivia Greer. She's mysterious and deep. It must have been my destiny."

"Mysterious and deep...more like confused and constantly overthinking."

Michael sighed, picking up her hand to move it to his chest. "Sometimes we don't see ourselves clearly," he commented. "But I see you, never forget that."

Olivia touched his cheek and then reached for her iced tea. He took his drink as they both sipped in silence. Once he put down his glass, he asked, "So what was in the plastic bag anyway?"

"That's what I want to know." An exasperated sigh escaped her lips. "Since I didn't want to take the chance of being sent to an Old Rocker Save The Trees class, I texted Janis. She came right over. I couldn't see what she was doing because the trunk of the tree is so enormous. But it looked like she dug up the bag where M&M dropped it. I saw her shove it into her coat pocket. And then..."

"She just walked away?" Michael's eyes grew wide. "She didn't tell you what was in the bag?"

Olivia reached into her back pocket for her cell phone. She looked at her messages. "Janis has not texted since then," she announced, turning off the screen, leaving it on her knee.

Michael shook his head. "What do you think was in the bag? I know you have an opinion."

"A knife," she said without hesitation.

"So you think Mayor Maguire buried a knife at the foot of the sequoia?"

Olivia thought for a moment. "I don't know if he did the burying. I think the mayor may have been the one to find the knife."

"Why didn't he bring it to you?" Michael asked.

"It may have been like Meadow's hat. Maybe M&M was saving someone from themselves."

"So the dog could be protecting someone who owns that knife?"

Olivia shrugged. "That's all I can think of. But now Janis has it at the constabulary, so that leaves us out of the loop."

"We could interrogate the mayor." Michael smiled at his own suggestion.

"Except he hitched a ride with that VW and Blair Grey," Olivia muttered.

"Isn't she the one who played fetch with him that night we were on surveillance? Sounds like the mayor and Blair have a thing."

"Oh, I hope not," Olivia objected. "Don't let that smooth skin and the blond hair fool you. She's not what she seems."

"How's that?"

"Blair's a nasty piece of work." Olivia explained how Blair had flipped her off from her car.

"That's pretty hostile," admitted Michael.

"And she's the one who started all that throat noise when they sat on the sofa. It's like she's the youngest but an instigator."

Olivia felt her phone buzz. She plucked the phone from her knee to check her caller ID. "It's Janis," she mouthed to Michael.

"Yes," she answered.

"It's me," came a clipped voice.

"I know."

"Come on, you sound mad. You're not mad. Admit it. You needed the fresh air to blow the stink off."

"I can't believe you said that. I haven't heard that expression for years. For your information, Michael says my sweat smells intoxicating."

"He did not!"

"Maybe not intoxicating, but he acted like he was turned on when I came in the door."

"Stop!" Janis began to cough. "I threw up in my throat a little," she explained, still fake coughing.

"What do you want?" Olivia demanded.

"It's not what I want. It's what you want. To know about what was in the plastic bag."

"Not another boot?"

"A knife. A really good knife. I couldn't see anything on it, but I sent it immediately to the lab. Tomorrow is Sunday so they probably won't get me results until Monday, but I think that's my murder weapon. I can just feel it."

Olivia didn't respond right away. "Didn't you look for that knife when you were searching the Grey house?"

"In the house, I was looking for a weapon. That's why I wanted you to keep the kids busy on the sofa, so they wouldn't interrupt me."

"But you didn't find a knife," Olivia said.

"Not in the house. But the knife in the plastic bag, it looked like one of those that comes in a set..."

"I know the kind. My mother had a wooden block on the counter with knives. We never used them because we rarely ate meat. But they were sharp. She kept them out of my reach as a child, that kind of sharp."

"So the Greys had a set of six knives, all tucked up in a wooden block on the counter. I have a description from the coroner about the weapon that most likely killed Malone. Any of the knives would have done the job. I did take the knives away in an evidence bag. I wanted the lab to test them for traces of blood. But now I have not six but seven knives, all identical. Pretty intriguing."

"Who has seven knives in a set?" Olivia asked.

"Exactly," agreed Jets.

Olivia glanced over to Michael, who stood at the rail looking toward the sunset. "Anything else you want to tell me?"

"I'm done here. I have a hot date with Cooks. It's Saturday and we have plans."

Olivia continued to stare at Michael. "I have plans too, and they don't include talking to you on the phone. Bye."

She stood up, walking closer to Michael. "Time for a shower before we figure out dinner?"

He wrapped his arm around her shoulders. "A bath would be nice. Want company?"

"You're reading my mind. It must be destiny," she teased, setting her phone on the table. She lifted her lips to Michael and gave him a long kiss.

CHAPTER EIGHTEEN

Michael snuggled next to Olivia in bed. He whispered in her ear, "See you at Thyme Out in about an hour?"

She rolled over, ducking her head under the pillow. "If you insist," she said sleepily.

He ran his finger over her arm. "I'm going to talk to Cookie about the new fall coffee blend. We'll be done by ten or so. I'll set aside your favorite blueberry muffin." His voice assumed a more coaxing tone. "And a few shortbread cookies for later."

"I'll be there," came her muffled reply. He patted the pillow over her head as his goodbye.

Once he'd showered and gone, Olivia shoved the pillow away. She rolled over on her back to stare at the ceiling. *It feels like a lazy Sunday, so I'll wear my softest jeans and a T-shirt. Maybe I'll break open that moisturizer I've been saving.* She sighed. As if the effort of thinking was too much, her eyelids began to droop.

Half an hour later she awakened with a start. *Yikes, I'm supposed to meet him in thirty minutes!* Olivia popped out of bed, lifting her T-shirt over her head in one move.

After a shower she blotted her hair with a towel and then

hastily dried her body. Stepping back into the bedroom she looked into a drawer and pulled out her favorite jeans and a green T-shirt.

A bit of moisturizer and a comb through her hair finished the morning ritual. *Not exactly the leisurely morning I planned, but the extra sleep sure felt good.* Once she finished dressing, she headed up the stairs taking two at a time.

To her surprise Sage sat at the kitchen table sipping tea. *She's getting the morning I wanted,* Olivia grumbled to herself. Reaching for the coffee carafe, she spoke first. "You had an overnight visitor."

Sage looked up. "I did. You met him at the pub. Jeff is a good guy."

"I heard you yesterday morning but gave you some space. How are you feeling today?"

"I feel," Sage paused for a moment as if searching for the perfect word, "content."

"Oh, that's a good feeling," Olivia said, amusement in her voice.

"It's not what you think," Sage added. "We didn't, you know, do anything. But we did talk and laugh. It felt good."

"I see," said Olivia, not sure she saw at all. *I want to ask if Jeff is the baby's father. I'm afraid she'll think that I'm being too nosy. Better keep my mouth shut.*

"I'm supposed to meet Michael at Thyme Out in..." Olivia clicked on her phone, "ten minutes ago." She shoved the phone in her back pocket, giving Sage a small wave.

Once behind the wheel of her Ford, she texted Michael.

A little late. Be there shortly.

She started the car, making her way to the main road toward Thyme Out.

* * *

Once inside the bakery, she walked through the cafe and out the back door to the patio. The late August sun felt dry and warm. Michael and Cookie sat at the far corner closest to the alley exit, under the shade of a pine tree. Only one other table held customers: Bella and Blair, who leaned close together. Olivia ignored them as she walked past.

"Sorry I'm late," she said, sitting down in the empty chair.

"No worries." Michael patted her hand. "We were just talking about the Grey women over there. They've been whispering nonstop."

"More like children," Olivia muttered, still annoyed that Blair had given her the middle finger the day before.

Cookie chuckled. "When you live with your parents, you are for all intents and purposes a child. Plus they don't seem to have a job and they dress like teenagers."

When she heard Cookie echo her own thoughts, Olivia felt a wave of guilt. "Maybe I'm being unfair. Maybe they have financial concerns or emotional issues, things that other people aren't aware of..."

Cookie just laughed. "You go ahead and think those kids are diamonds in the rough, but I work with their mother and I can assure you that's not the case. She's a difficult human being and her bees don't stray far from the hive. I'll get you some coffee."

He pushed his chair back. Olivia watched as Cookie stopped to ask Bella and Blair a question. They did not look up. He smacked the table with his hand and walked away. Once Cookie's back disappeared inside the cafe, the girls began to giggle.

Taking in the entire incident, Olivia shook her head. "Cookie may be right. They are not diamonds in the rough. They don't even bother to be polite or act decently."

Michael raised an eyebrow, his head nodding slightly

toward Bella and Blair. *He's listening to their conversation.* The sisters' voices volleyed back and forth, raising in intensity.

"You are such a brat. Why didn't you tell me Deadbeat gave you that ugly car? I'll never sit in it again."

"We needed a car—and I'm not a brat. You only wish he'd given you something. It was easy. I just texted him and asked and Deadbeat dropped it off."

"No one was supposed to talk to him. That was our agreement. Wait until Mom finds out," Blair threatened.

"Wait until Mom finds out what?" came the distinct voice of Bianca Grey. Olivia turned her head for a better view. Bianca wore her Thyme Out apron. She stood next to the table glaring at her daughters.

"I told you Mom would be angry," Blair said with a tone of triumph.

"You have no right to be mad at me," claimed Bella. "You got money from Deadbeat. He told me you texted him and that he'd use PayPal to help out with your bills."

"That's none of your business," snapped Blair.

Bianca interrupted. "It is my business though. You broke our agreement. No one is supposed to talk to your father. He's no longer paying child support. His custodial rights ended as soon as he stopped paying."

Bianca continued chiding her daughter. "If you can afford to fill a car with gas, you can pay rent. I don't ask that much. I suppose now that Deadbeat is gone, you'll have to get a real job."

"She can wait tables or work at a bakery," Blair suggested in a saccharine voice.

Bianca spit back, "You're not too old to slap, young lady."

Ignoring her mother's threat, she kept talking. "Both of you are pathetic. I can make more than twice what you make every week."

"By being a social media consultant?" came her mother's scornful retort. "Not a real job if you ask me. A real job is raising three children all alone while their father gigs and has affairs."

"I can get a job any time I want to," Blair said angrily.

The sound of hand meeting skin met Olivia's ears.

"Ouch, you hit me," cried Blair.

"You provoked me," Bianca responded.

Olivia turned fully around to see Bianca and Blair standing nose to nose, squaring off for a fight.

Michael had heard enough. "Call Janis right now."

Blair leaned forward, hovering in her mother's face. She reached up and yanked Bianca's blond hair, forcing her mother's head to jerk forward.

Bianca raised her hands and shoved Blair. Off balance, the girl fell to the ground, small strands of her mother's hair gripped in her fingers. Bianca leaped on her daughter, her hands at her neck.

Michael bent over and pulled on Bianca's shoulders. Wrenching her hands from Blair's neck, he pulled her to her feet.

Olivia texted Janis Jets.

Come to Thyme Out. Back patio. Beehive emergency.

Michael held Bianca. "Stop right now. Calm down." Bianca struggled against his firm grasp. Blair rolled over, screaming aloud, "You tried to kill me!"

A piercing scream came from Bianca as she struggled. "You've betrayed me!"

Olivia dialed Jets.

"What?" came the crisp voice.

"The Grey family is having a knock-down drag-out fight at Thyme Out. Didn't you read my text?"

"I don't jump every time you text me," growled Jets.

Olivia paused. In that moment her eyes rested on Bella, who looked away, seemingly detached from the fight between her mother and sister. *She causes trouble and then backs off while other people take punches.*

Olivia spoke into the phone. "Mother and daughter are rolling on the patio bricks. You don't want to miss this."

"It's my lucky day," announced Janis. "Be right there."

Michael released his strong hold on Bianca. To Olivia's relief, she didn't fling herself at Blair. She rubbed her hand over her arm as Michael reached for Blair's elbow, yanking her to her feet. "You need to calm down," he repeated.

Once Blair stood, Bianca took a step forward. Michael continued with a calm voice. "Take your family problems home."

"You can't lecture me. Get out of my way," Blair cried. She pushed past Michael. At that moment, Cookie returned, blocking her way. She tried to get around him but he just grinned.

"Not gonna happen," he said quietly. "Go back to the table and sit down. Officer Jets may be in an arresting mood."

Blairs's eyes grew wide. "Which one of you called the cops? Just because we had a little disagreement..."

"I did not call the cops," admitted Cookie. "But one of my customers did and that's good enough for me."

At that moment the bell over the front entrance jingled. Cookie smiled at Bianca and her daughters. "I suspect that's Officer Janis Jets right now. She'll work out your disagreement and most likely address how you have disturbed my peace." He glared at Bianca. "In case you don't realize, no one does that—disturb my peace—without paying a price."

Cookie stepped aside with a smile as Janis Jets strode from inside the cafe to the patio. It only took a moment for her to take charge. "You sit down," she told Bianca. "And you," she pointed to Blair, "plop yourself next to her. I've heard you are causing trouble." All three women sat at the table as if making a point not to look at each other.

Jets set her briefcase on the table. "While you three cool your heels, I will take notes from a few witnesses inside. After that I'll get back to you." She opened her briefcase to take out an iPad.

Bella stood up. Janis glared at her. "I said sit down." One glance at Cookie told Olivia that he was enjoying Janis taking charge. He crossed his arms over his chest, slight amusement in his eyes.

Jets pivoted, then strutted past Cookie as she stepped inside the cafe. Michael came a step closer to Olivia. He leaned to whisper, "How about another cup of coffee while we watch our town constable in action?"

Olivia pointed to her chair. "I'm going to sit over there. And by the way, what happened to the promised blueberry muffin?"

Cookie overheard. "I've got a muffin and coffee," he told them. "Be right back."

When Cookie returned, Bella and Blair sat in silence. Only Bianca looked nervous. She restlessly crossed and uncrossed her right leg then the left.

Janis Jets returned to the patio, a grim smile on her face.

"So here's the deal," she said matter-of-factly. "After chatting with some of the inside customers, I have five witnesses who are ready to press charges about you two disturbing the peace." She looked at Cookie.

"Nice job," he said with a smile.

"Thank you." She cleared her throat to continue. "I'm going to write up a citation for all three of you, and I'm going to take those cell phones into my custody."

Blair snatched her phone away from the table. "You can't have my phone," she exclaimed.

"You have no right to search my personal belongings," Bella stated, reaching for her phone that lay on the table. "I wasn't fighting. I'm not disturbing the peace."

"I'm arresting those two," commented Jets. She turned to Bella. "And taking you in as a witness." Holding her flat hand out toward Bianca. "You can come along easy, or I'll charge you right now and put you in a cell for questioning. What's it gonna be?"

Bianca's face contorted with rage. She didn't speak at first, but then blurted out, "I'll come along with you."

"Okay then," Jets nodded. "Good choice."

She continued in a firm voice, "Right now I want all three of you to march yourselves to the constabulary. You're going to give me your phone passwords so that I can access the information on those phones. Should that go smoothly, I may not charge you; if you don't cooperate, I most surely will."

Bianca's eyes filled with tears. "I can sue you for this!"

Jets nodded. "As my mother would say, 'Easier said than done.' You may have to contact an attorney from jail if you keep obstructing justice." She swept her hand over the three women at the table. "All of you have done nothing but deny your relationship with Beats Malone. Let's not forget you were his closest relatives and that you are all suspects in my murder investigation."

Olivia watched as the three looked back and forth at each other. Finally Bella stood first, followed by Blair, then Bianca.

"We'll come with you," offered Michael in a cheery voice.

Olivia drank her last sip of coffee as Janis Jets escorted the Grey women through the bakery.

CHAPTER NINETEEN

As the back of Janis Jets disappeared through the constabulary security door, Olivia pulled on Michael's hand. "Stop for a second," she said in a low voice.

Surprise showed on his face. When the door slid closed, she said, "What about Brandon and Ashley? Maybe we could go look for her while the rest of them are busy with Janis..."

"You're worried about her?"

"I am concerned and curious about Brandon and Ashley. The three women are so mouthy."

Michael needed no more convincing. "Okay then, while Janis is interrogating the women, let's check out the rest of the family."

They exited through the front door.

Outside on the boardwalk they waited for traffic to pass and then crossed the street. Olivia suggested, "We can leave my car and take the truck. Let's do a stakeout by the Greys' house."

"Good idea." Michael held the passenger door of his truck as she hopped inside.

Once she'd fastened her seat belt, he put the key into the ignition. "Is it still surveillance if it's our idea?"

Olivia laughed. "I think Janis would approve. Plus there's a good chance no one from the Grey clan recognizes your truck."

They drove out of town and up the hill in silence. "That's their house." Olivia pointed to the chain-link fence around the property.

"Right next to Cay and Arlo." Michael pulled to the side of the road. He twisted the key from the ignition. "All of them in one house," he commented.

"They're a clan. Like something out of a story about the Hatfields and McCoys. It's hard to believe they come from a big city like Los Angeles."

"Not that there's anything wrong with that, only I'm curious why they stick together so closely."

"I know what you mean." Her eyes focused past Michael through the window on the driver's side. Olivia pointed to the shed behind the house in the back. "That's where Ashley was when Janis did her search."

Michael nodded. "And they found her with a skateboard."

"Uh-huh, Janis figures she's the one who sent the video to the constabulary. She's really good at skateboarding."

"I tried it once and nearly broke my leg." Michael turned back to the window. "It doesn't look like anyone is around."

Her cell pinged.

Where did you go? A text from Janis.

She texted back: We're staking out the Grey house looking for Brandon and Ashley.

Good idea came his text.

Did you get what you wanted from the women? Olivia texted back.

I released Bianca first. Still have the other two.

Olivia looked back at the house. She texted back.

Should we knock on the door?

No!

Olivia put her phone in her purse. "Janis doesn't want us to knock."

Michael looked at his phone. "It's been nearly an hour since we left the constabulary. I don't take orders from her." He opened his door and hopped out. Olivia did the same on her side. He came around from the back and they stood together, staring across the road.

Michael led the way. The first obstacle was the lock on the chain-link fence. He gave it a shake and it came open in his hand. He shoved the gate open, and Olivia went through first. They both stopped.

An anguished wail erupted from behind the house. Olivia broke into a run; Michael followed behind. At the front porch, Olivia stopped first. The wailing continued, louder now that they'd come closer. Her heart beat wildly in her chest. *Is that an animal or a human being...*

Sounds interrupted with gasps convinced her: *That's human!* Michael held his arm out to the side. "Stay here," he told her.

She bent over to catch her breath. The sobs made her heart wrench. Michael gestured with his hand. Olivia moved toward him. Only to stop at what she found.

Ashley Tennant bent over a body, holding her skateboard in her arm. Blood dripped off the front. Olivia watched as Ashley wiped her hand off on her jeans.

Her eyes drifted to the ground. Bianca Grey lay in the dirt, blood matting the hair at the back of her head. Her head was turned to the side, eyes open, staring blankly.

Ashley looked at Michael, then at Olivia. Her eyes were wild, face contorted. "I did it," she wailed. "I killed her."

Michael took a step closer. He reached out to touch Ashley's arm, but she yanked it back. Words tumbled from her lips. "She came to the shed. Into my room. I ran out the door. She kept yelling at me. I wanted her to stop. So I..."

Ashley looked at the skateboard in her hands. "I made her stop yelling." Her voice grew calmer. Her head hung down, hair hiding her face.

He stepped away from her to look closer at the body on the ground. Kneeling, he placed fingers against Bianca's wrist. Shaking his head, he laid two fingers near her jaw. "No pulse," he announced.

"I'll call the emergency service and the constabulary." Olivia tapped her pockets, searching for her cell. "I don't have my phone," she called out.

"Use mine," Ashley offered. Olivia drew closer. "On the ground."

Olivia picked up the phone as Michael stood to his feet. "Ashley, I'm not an attorney, but I'd suggest that you remain calm and stop talking. Tell Olivia your phone ID and she'll make that call."

"Six eight nine two," she said, "the same as all the Greys. We have the same code."

Olivia held the phone and blinked. Unlike the other Greys who had the latest iPhone, Ashley had an old model that looked like a burner. There were no apps on the screen. She punched in 911, watching Ashley as she waited. The girl's head hung down. She stood motionless, her back to the body.

After finishing the report to the emergency operator, Olivia called the constabulary. "Brad, this is Olivia. Send Janis to the Greys' house. There's been another death."

Ashley stood in one spot, her back still to the body.

Michael walked closer to Olivia. "How did Bianca get back here so fast?" he whispered in her ear.

"And why didn't we see her?" Olivia looked past the shed where the chain-link fence encircled the property and saw the break in the fence first. "Look over there," she said, pointing to the far corner of the lot.

"So Bianca came in that way? Oh yeah, I see the VW. She must have driven home as soon as Janis released her."

"She must have," agreed Olivia. "But that doesn't explain why she didn't just go back to work or come in the front way."

"Maybe she saw us parked across the street?"

Before they could speculate further, Olivia heard a siren's wail. "The ambulance is nearly here," she said.

"Janis won't be far behind," muttered Michael.

Within minutes they heard the clear voice of Janis Jets giving orders. "You get in the house. You go preserve the crime scene. I'll be out back talking to my witnesses."

Olivia watched Janis walk determinedly around the side of the house and straight to the body. Bending over, Janis checked Bianca's pulse.

Within minutes paramedics hurried past. "Your call," Janis said, standing up straight. Her eyes drifted to the skateboard and back to Ashley, who seemed glued to the spot.

"Anyone witness the murder?" asked Jets.

"Not me," Michael said quickly.

"Me neither," Olivia chimed in.

Ashley just shrugged, using the toe of her sneaker to make a mark in the dirt.

Good, she stopped confessing. The girl has a strong survival instinct.

* * *

By the time the paramedics removed the body, Janis Jets had arrested Ashley Tennant. "You have the right to remain silent," she cautioned the girl, nodding for one of her team to take her away. Janis finally spoke to Olivia and Michael.

"Did you see what happened?" she asked in a dry voice.

"We were in the truck, watching from across the street," Michael explained.

"We got impatient so we left the car to knock on the door. Then we heard a scream so we ran back here," offered Olivia.

Jets glared and shook her head. "You just can't help yourself. I gave you clear orders." She flipped open her iPad, biting her bottom lip. She tapped in a few notes and then closed the page. "I'll interview her back at the constabulary. On the one hand, I want to hear your take, but on the other hand? I think I'd better listen to the most obvious suspect. We'll take some DNA and have a look at the weapon."

"Death by skateboard," Olivia said.

"Looks that way." Jets glanced at her phone. "I released Bianca only an hour ago. She was as hostile as ever." Jet shook her head. "And now she's dead."

Michael nodded toward the shed where two police had left the door open.

"Yeah, I know," muttered Jets. "Ashley slept in that hole for some reason. Not good enough to hang out with the family? I don't get these people."

Jets stopped, her jaw clenching. "Have you seen Brandon? He isn't answering his cell phone, at least that's what the women told me at the constabulary when I asked."

Olivia looked at Michael. He spoke for them both. "We didn't see Brandon."

"We barely saw Bianca. She came from the back." Olivia pointed to the break in the fence where the VW had been left.

"Okay then, I'll have to tell the next of kin about the death. Not looking forward to that." Jets paused. "My assistant can track down Brandon." Jets held her hand to her head. "Lots of work tonight, just sayin'. See you two later." She moved away to join her team, who searched the shed.

It wasn't until they sat back in the truck that Olivia remembered, "I have a funny feeling about Ashley's cell phone. It looked pretty old."

"She doesn't seem to have a source of income," commented Michael, "which will be really bad because she needs an attorney double quick."

"None of them appear to have a job," Olivia agreed. "Except Bianca did, but not a great source of income as a waitress at Thyme Out."

"Not to feed four young adults," agreed Michael.

Olivia shook her head. "Do you suppose Beats gave them money? When they were arguing earlier, I overheard about the VW. Beats drove the car up the hill for them to have."

"So one of them had contact with their dad."

"Both girls texted him. Blair admitted that he put money in her account when she asked." Olivia sat back in her seat.

Michael popped the key into the ignition. "Doesn't sound like the behavior of a deadbeat to me." The engine turned over. "I know this sounds callus, but I need to shift my own gears and do something normal. Let's stop by the market and pick up some chicken wings for dinner."

Olivia nodded. She rolled down her window to let a fresh breeze come in. "It's hard to hold Ashley's pain and my own life in my head. Such extremes make me wonder not who killed Beats Malone, but why?"

By the time they got home, they found Sage sitting in the kitchen. She was laughing, her phone in hand. She waved and then said, "Michael and Olivia are back. Talk to you later?"

Ending the call, she asked, "What's for dinner?"

When Olivia didn't answer, she looked at Michael. "Anything wrong?" He reached into the shopping bag, pulling out a large package of chicken wings.

"We have food," he explained first. "But we've had a difficult afternoon. Did you know Bianca Grey?"

Sage's face grew white. Her eyes widened. "I knew her name," she said slowly. "She was the ex-wife of Beats Malone."

She sounds upset. Before Olivia could stop Michael, he explained.

"We found Bianca's body at her house, outside actually. It looks like her son's girlfriend may have killed her."

Sage's hand flew over her mouth. Her eyes fluttered. Then her body swayed, only to crumple. Falling away from the chair, her head hit the side of the table. Her body lay in a heap on the floor.

"I think she's fainted!" cried Olivia. She rushed to Sage. Kneeling next to her sister, she touched her face. Sage's eyelids fluttered.

"Sage," she called softly. Olivia inched her hand under her sister's head. She could feel a bump where she'd hit the table. "We need to call the ambulance," she told Michael.

"I'm on it," he said.

He held his phone when Sage's weak voice said, "It's okay, I'm fine."

"You don't look fine. You fainted and then bumped your head. We're going to call an ambulance," Olivia insisted.

"Oh, please don't," she said. "Give me a minute and get me some ice. I'm fine, really I am." She struggled to sit up. Her hand reached for the bump on the back of her head.

Michael put down his phone. He stepped next to Olivia with a frozen bag of peas. "Here, try this."

Sage placed it on the back of her head, holding it in place with one hand.

"Michael didn't mean to shock you," Olivia said quietly.

"Don't worry, honey. Everything shocks me these days. My heart beats wildly for no apparent reason. I feel lightheaded and tired. Then I feel great the next minute. I can't help myself. It must be the pregnancy hormones, at least that's what my doctor said."

Her mouth trembled as she tried to smile at Olivia. "I think I'm okay, but no more dead people talk."

"Agreed." Olivia was happy to see the color return to Sage's face.

"Okay then," came Michael's response. "I know some of my barbecued chicken wings along with grilled veggies will help. You two sit there and I'll get to chopping the onions."

"Ugh," Sage said. "I can't stand the smell of onions right now. Maybe in a few more months..."

Olivia patted her shoulder. *Pregnancy must be harder than I ever imagined.*

CHAPTER TWENTY

Olivia woke up with a start. Michael lay next to her, gently snoring. She eased her way out of bed, turning to unplug her cell phone. A quick glance showed a missed call. She hoped it was Sage's doctor getting back to her.

Another look at sleeping Michael made her smile. She tiptoed away from the bed. After brushing her teeth, Olivia slipped on jeans and a tank top. She piled her hair on top of her head and then washed her face.

She made her way down the hall. *Start the washing machine.* She stepped inside the laundry room and closed the door so as not to disturb Michael. Tight muscles in her back protested when she bent over to sort the dark and light items. Two pods and the lid went down. She used the timer so the load would start in another hour.

Once in the kitchen she sat down at the table and returned the doctor's call. To her surprise, he picked up right away. "This is Luis Martinez," came a deep voice.

"This is Olivia Greer. I left a message last night."

"Ah yes, Ms. Greer. You are Sage McCloud's sister?"

"I am."

"I had a chance to review my notes. Sage saw me a month ago. She's in her twentieth week of pregnancy. You said she fainted?"

"She fainted and then bumped the back of her head on the table. I wanted to call an ambulance, but she objected. So I got your number from her and wondered if you could advise me."

"Is she stable now?"

"I stayed up with her for several hours, insisting that she keep a bag of frozen peas on her head. She did not go to work."

She heard him chuckle. "I don't know your sister that well. May I assume she didn't appreciate your administrations?"

"You may." She felt herself relax. "I feel bad for letting her convince me not to call the paramedics and honestly, for not calling you right away."

"You have every right to question that decision," he commented.

Not gonna let me off the hook, is he...

He continued, "I think it may be time to put a specific plan in place, should Miss McCloud have any more problems. Please bring her in today at ten o'clock."

Olivia sighed. *I haven't been there since Doc left.* "You want me to sit in on the appointment?"

"I think that would be the best possible situation. I've been suggesting that your sister take some time off of work. So far she's paid no attention to my advice."

"I know how that feels," Olivia admitted.

"The two of us may be able to team up. Let's strike now right after her fainting incident. I'll check out her vital signs and hopefully by then she'll be weak with gratitude and putty in our hands." He chuckled.

"That would be a miracle. Sage has strong opinions. Goodbye, Dr. Martinez."

"See you soon, Ms. Greer."

Olivia went to the kitchen counter and filled the carafe with water. Michael appeared in the doorway.

"I can finish that up," he offered.

"Look at you sleeping in." She grinned at him.

He came closer to kiss the top of her head and then busied himself making coffee. By the time he pulled out a chair at the kitchen table, the aroma of freshly ground beans filled the air. He sat down first.

She brought two mugs to the table. Leaning over, she kissed him on the cheek before sitting down. "Heading to the construction site after this?"

"We're getting ready to frame," he said, nodding. "A very exciting time. Want to have lunch up at the site on Friday? I can take you through everything. There may be a few decisions that require your attention."

"Sounds good." She took a sip. "You want to know why I'm up so early?"

"Actually I figured you'd be worried about Sage."

"Got it in one," she ruefully admitted. "I've been spending so much time hanging out with Janis, I've neglected my sister."

"Why would you think that?"

"I finally put together that every time I tell her a story about the investigation, she gets upset. I kept ignoring the obvious until yesterday when she passed out. It really scared me. And then I talked to the doctor this morning, and he said he wants her to take off work."

"Did he say why?"

"I don't think he can tell me that. It's something Sage will have to reveal, but she's been so touchy about everything."

"Including not telling us about the father..."

"Of her baby," Olivia finished his sentence. "I felt this way with my ex-boyfriend. It's like walking on eggshells. I'm afraid to bring up the subject because I don't want to upset her further."

"So let's put this in perspective," Michael said in his calmest voice. "Don was an alcoholic who lied to get his way. Sage is your sister who doesn't want to reveal the baby's father. Two different situations." He stood from the table, returning with the coffee. He poured a full mug for each of them and returned the carafe before sitting back down.

"You're right," Olivia admitted. "Sage is not Don."

"Our job is to keep as calm as possible."

"And that's why I've decided to chart a new course."

Michael looked at her with interest.

"I'm giving up as an amateur sleuth to take care of my sister. I've already made an appointment with the doctor and I'm going with her as an extra set of ears."

"You think it's possible to stay out of the investigation with Janis?" He looked skeptical.

"I am going to do my best!" Olivia answered, sounding more confident than she felt.

"So you got an appointment with the doc. What's his name again?"

Olivia explained. "Dr. Luis Martinez. He exudes confidence and I felt better after talking to him." Her voice grew quiet. She felt her mouth quiver in a rush of emotion.

"You liked the doc?"

"I just realized what may be part of Sage's problem. The new Lily Rock doctor sounds a lot like the old Lily Rock doctor. He even took over the same office."

"You mean old Doc Callahan?"

"Sage may be comparing Doc Callahan with Doc Martinez." Olivia and Michael stared at each other. She felt a shiver down her spine. "You don't suppose the new doc is the father of Sage's baby?"

"We don't know for sure. We don't know when she first met Martinez. I do know that would be a big whopper of a secret, which could make Sage feel nervous."

Olivia put her mug on the table.

"Now that you mention it, we have no idea what is making Sage withhold the name of baby's father."

"We can agree on that." Michael nodded. "And I have to get showered and off to work." He rose from the table, taking both their mugs to the sink.

"I'll put them in the dishwasher," she offered.

He stepped over to kiss her on the head. "Keep me posted on the doctor's appointment. I'm in this with you and Sage. You know that, right?"

"I do." She reached for her phone. "And now that I'm a caregiver, I'm going to get organized with food and all possible ways of pampering Sage. I'm even going to call Meadow for advice."

* * *

Right before ten o'clock, Olivia and Sage waited in the office of Dr. Luis Martinez. His receptionist sat behind the desk, typing on a computer keyboard. Taking in the room, Olivia couldn't help but remember that first time she'd visited Lily Rock. That day a handsome stranger dropped her off at the doctor's office after a near fatal car accident.

"It's weird being here without seeing Doc," commented Sage.

Olivia patted her sister's hand. "I was just thinking the same thing. Get a load of her." Olivia gestured with her head toward the receptionist. "She's like the opposite of Skye."

The receptionist looked barely twenty, thin and angular, her dark hair held up in a high ponytail. Long artificial nails tapped at the keyboard. The intensity of the red polish contrasted with her pale white skin.

"I know," Sage agreed. "Good ol' Skye. She was as much a part of my childhood as Doc. With everything that happened, I still miss them both."

"I know, honey." Olivia patted her hand again. "But you like the new doctor, right? He sounded nice on the phone."

Sage looked down at her folded hands. "He's okay except that he wanted me to take time off of work."

Olivia feigned surprise. "Did he...you never mentioned that to me. What was his reasoning?"

Sage sighed. "My blood pressure was a little high last month."

"Why didn't you tell me?" Remembering her conversation with Michael about keeping calm at all costs, she made an effort not to sound alarmed.

"Because you had enough on your mind after that big arrest up at Hello Age. Plus there's your new house construction. Plus I thought it would get better. I did tell Meadow," she added.

Olivia felt a tug of guilt. *If she told her mom, at least she had someone to talk to.* "What did Meadow have to say about the blood pressure?"

Sage started to giggle. "You know what she said."

Olivia grinned. "She has a tea that will remedy the problem!"

As Sage nodded, Olivia looked at her more closely. "You look much better this morning."

"I have to admit, a day off of work let me sleep in and I do feel better. I'm so sorry for passing out like that last night. You and Michael probably thought the worst, that I'd lose the baby or something."

"I am concerned about you," Olivia admitted. "So is

Michael. We've talked and decided to keep a closer eye on you. In fact, while we're waiting for baby's arrival, have you considered hiring someone to take over your job at the academy?"

"I may need someone more after the baby comes," said Sage. "I was hoping to keep all of my sick days and use them then."

"Don't you have maternity leave?"

"Six weeks, that's it." Sage sighed, patting her belly.

At that moment the door opened, revealing a tall man dressed in a crisp doctor's coat, a stethoscope wrapped around his neck. When he smiled, a row of beautiful white teeth gleamed under his perfectly trimmed mustache. Gray eyes twinkled as he drew closer to Sage. He reached out his hand. "Good to see you, Ms. McCloud," came his melodious voice, the one Olivia remembered hearing over the phone earlier.

He held Sage's hand in his, looking into her eyes. She did not pull back. Finally he turned his eyes away and dropped her hand. A blush rose up her sister's neck.

It's got to be him, the baby daddy. Wait until I tell Michael.

The doctor turned and offered his hand to Olivia. "You must be Ms. Greer, Sage's sister. I am happy you could come to the appointment today. Why don't you wait here while I take Sage's vitals and do a quick exam? Then we can call you back to my office and the three of us can discuss a plan for the remainder of her pregnancy." His confident warm voice made Olivia feel that all would be well.

Unlike with Sage, he dropped her hand quickly. Sage stood to her feet, following him toward the inner doorway. He waited as she walked through first. He followed her, closing the door behind him.

Olivia took a quick breath, and then looked at her phone. *Boy, is he handsome and sexy! That full head of hair and those deep penetrating eyes. And I think he really likes Sage, at least it felt that way. He didn't stare at me and hold my hand. I wonder where they met and how they got together...*

"Excuse me," came a voice from the desk. The receptionist stood to hand Olivia a clipboard. "Please fill out this information for the doctor. As Ms. McCloud's next of kin, we'd like to keep your contact information on file."

Olivia took the clipboard from the girl and sat back down. As soon as she was done filling out the information, the door to the waiting room opened. Dr. Martinez smiled. "It's time to come back to my office," he said.

A shiver ran up her spine. *Why does everything he says sound like an invitation to his bed?* She left the clipboard on the receptionist's desk to follow the doctor through the doorway.

CHAPTER TWENTY-ONE

Sage and Olivia sat across from the doctor, the executive desk separating them.

"Your blood pressure is slightly elevated." The doctor's solemn eyes looked soulfully at Sage. Olivia reached out to squeeze her sister's hand.

"But she doesn't have to worry..." Olivia's eyes pleaded with the doctor.

"As long as she takes care of herself, we can keep baby in utero," he said with authority. He laid three business cards in front of them. "I am going to do some more tests and then I recommend that you engage one of these three women as a pregnancy and delivery doula. I've worked with all of them to great success." He pointed to the wall behind his desk where photos had been tastefully arranged. "And here is my evidence."

Mothers with smiling babies stared back at them. A few of the photos included a father, most often with a dazed look on his face. Olivia reached across to take the business cards. "I can help with this," she said, putting them in her pocket for safekeeping.

"I hope to go back to work tomorrow," Sage said. "They're expecting me."

Dr. Martinez's face turned grave. He looked at Sage. "I would prefer that you not return to work. If you can possibly manage, ride out the remainder of your pregnancy sleeping and eating healthfully at home, looking more like a bowl of dough rising in the warm kitchen than a frantic head of a music academy putting out fires."

Sage laughed. "A bowl of dough? That's exactly how I feel. Good one!"

The doctor leaned back, looking pleased with himself. He'd brought a laugh from his patient. *He seems to have a more than impersonal interest in Sage. Or is he like this with all of the expectant mothers?*

On the way home, the sisters discussed a plan for the rest of Sage's pregnancy. Convinced that she'd made the right decision, Olivia pushed aside thoughts of the Malone investigation, focusing on her sister instead.

* * *

Early the next morning Olivia stood in the kitchen, considering the day in front of her. She glanced at her cell phone on the counter. Janis Jets's name lit up on her screen. Instead of answering she explained in her head, *You can wait, Officer Jets. You're the one who tells me to stay out of your business, so now I will. Find your own murderer, I have a mother and baby to pay attention to.*

Olivia picked up the phone, turned it facedown, and placed it back on the counter. Where to begin...

An hour later she took a cup of peppermint and raspberry tea and walked toward Sage's closed bedroom door. She gently knocked with her free hand.

"Come in," came a sleepy voice.

Sage sat on the edge of her bed staring out the large window.

"I can't get used to the idea that I'm not going to work," she said.

Olivia stood near, holding out the cup of tea.

"Is that for me?"

"I brought you herbal tea." She placed the mug on the bedside table. Sitting on the edge of the bed beside Sage, she looked out the window. "When you called the academy board, did they give you a lot of trouble about a leave of absence?"

"We talked about using my accumulated sick leave. I suppose when that's used up, we'll have another conversation." Sage reached for the tea. "This smells amazing. Peppermint is so soothing for nausea."

"I looked up teas for pregnant women," Olivia said. "Peppermint and raspberry are both on the accepted list."

Sage held the cup to her nose and inhaled. "So soothing," she said as she took a sip.

"They may extend your paid leave once Meadow gets ahold of them. She's still on the academy board of directors."

"She'll try, but I decided not to worry." Sage patted her belly. "I have other things to do, as a big puffy mound of dough."

Olivia grinned. "I like Dr. Martinez. He's so confident."

"And sexy," Sage added. "I may look like a lump of dough, but that doesn't mean I'm completely in mommy mode. I think he appreciates pregnant women."

Uh-huh, just what I thought. I wonder where they met earlier...

"As your new caregiver, I'd like to go to the grocery and pick up some food for today and tomorrow. What sounds good to you?"

Olivia stood up and walked across the room to grab a paper and pencil. When she turned back around, Sage sat with her back against the headboard. Olivia sat in a small overstuffed chair nearby.

"How about some soup?" Sage asked.

"I'll make chicken soup, or would you prefer tomato?"

"As soon as you bring me chicken, I'll want tomato. So how about both?" Sage grinned.

"Chicken and ingredients for both soups, on the list. Then I'll get a piece of fish, which Michael can grill. And I'll bring home fresh vegetables." Olivia stood up. "I almost forgot. Have you had any luck calling the doulas?"

"I already have a doula," Sage said brightly. "I pick you. I don't need anyone else in the house so long as you're here."

Olivia felt oddly pleased. "I don't mind a bit. It will give us time to think about refreshing the space for the nursery." A sense of peace came over her at the thought of preparing for the new family member. "And I could use a break from obsessing about Janis Jets's business. Even Michael thinks me staying home is a great idea."

"At least he knows where to find you." Sage nodded.

Feeling the easy conversation between them, Olivia felt tempted to ask Sage more about her feelings. *Should I ask her about the baby's father now?*

Propped up in bed wearing a T-shirt and cotton shorts, Sage looked the picture of relaxation. *Not like a lump of dough at all.*

Inhaling deeply, Olivia was ready to pounce on the conversation. Before she spoke, she gulped. *Instead of peppering Sage with unwanted questions, I'll wait. This is not my conversation to initiate.*

"I'm off to gather groceries, see you in a bit," she told Sage.

Once in her car, Olivia drove the short distance to town.

She parked in front of the Lily Rock Marketplace. Determined to ignore the constabulary, she averted her gaze as she walked into the library. Meadow stood behind the counter. "Sage just called. She said you're her new doula."

Olivia walked closer. "I'm not a professional, but I can be a good sister and keep my eye on her for the next few months."

Meadow walked around the counter, her arms open for a hug. "Thank you, dear, for being who you are and taking care of Sage. She won't listen to me but she will pay attention to you." Enveloped in her ample bosom, Olivia felt tears come to her eyes.

She pulled away and smiled at Meadow. "So I came by to ask you about pregnancy and herbal tea. I googled the answer this morning but I figure you are the resident expert."

Meadow adjusted her glasses to give Olivia a stare. "That's very thoughtful of you, dear. Sounds like you're embracing the concept of 'it takes a village'." Meadow used air quotes, hiding a smile. At that moment loud voices came from the reference section.

"You have to get a job," said a familiar voice, crackling with animosity.

"You get the job. I don't feel like it. I'm the youngest. It's not up to me to support this family."

"Stop complaining, I'm trying to read," mumbled a lower voice.

Olivia looked across the room. Bella and Blair sat next to each other on the library sofa. Brandon was wedged between them.

Meadow handed her a scrap of paper with notes. "I'll order books from the branch library for you and Sage to read. They should be here in a day or two."

Meadow looked at the source of the voices. "They deliberately disregard the library rules," Meadow noted. "I'll give them one more chance and then I'll tell them to leave. Unless you want to..." She looked hopefully at Olivia.

Olivia snatched the scrap paper. "I am no longer in the business of monitoring the Grey family. You heard about their mother?"

Meadow leaned over the counter, speaking softly. "You found the body, you and Michael?"

"When I told Sage, she fainted."

Meadow shook her head. "She's very sensitive right now."

"That's why I want to stay away from that family. I feel terrible that they've lost both their mother and their father in the same month, but I can't help that. I can help Sage."

Meadow patted her arm. "We both have Sage to worry about." Meadow's head jerked up. Bella had turned to Blair and given her a shove.

"That does it!" Meadow said. Stomping her way around the counter, Olivia watched Meadow move determinedly toward the reading area.

"We will find the money," claimed Bella. "We just have to look."

"We'll never find it now that she's dead," whined Blair.

"That's enough," Meadow's voice thundered. Brandon ducked his head, looking at the comic book on his lap. "Young man, why don't you take some responsibility for your sisters? I won't have people arguing in my library."

Brandon rolled his eyes. He flung the book down on the low table in front of the sofa. "They never listen to me anyway," he said. Then he turned to Bella and Blair. "Come on. Let's get going."

The girls paid no attention to him, continuing to glare at each other. Brandon stood up from the sofa and began to walk away. Bella's shoulders dropped. "Oh okay, I'm coming."

"Well, I'm not," shouted Blair. "I don't have to go just because you are." She remained on the sofa.

Meadow spoke again. "I said that's enough. Keep your voice down. No one wants to be a part of your little family squabbles."

Olivia felt a smirk coming on. *That may not be true. Nearly everyone in Lily Rock likes butting into the business of other people. But I get what she's trying to say.*

Blair rolled her eyes at Meadow. With a sigh she stood and followed her siblings toward the exit. At first none of them acknowledged Olivia, who stood at the front desk.

Once Brandon and Bella left the library, Blair circled back around. She faced Olivia. "I want to talk to you," she said in a demanding voice.

"About what?"

"You got a chance to talk to Ashley, you and your boyfriend were the first on the scene. Do you think she's crazy, you know, crazy like put-her-in-a-hospital kind of crazy?"

Olivia looked more closely at Blair. She had circles under her eyes and her skin had broken out along her chin. Even her clothes appeared rumpled.

"You must be in shock," Olivia said kindly. "I can't really help with Ashley; I didn't know her very well. But I do know what it feels like to lose a mother and not have a father."

"I'm an orphan," Blair sniffed.

"You do have a brother and a sister," Olivia reminded her.

Blair blinked and wiped her nose with her sleeve. Her eyes considered Olivia. *I feel like she's seeing me for the first time.*

"Could we talk later?" Blair asked. "I feel like you'd help me, you know, figure out what to do. You seem like a person who knows stuff."

"I may tell you just what your sister did. You need to start looking for a job."

Blair's chin jutted out.

Olivia added, "Everyone heard you two arguing. Give me your phone. I'll put my number in. You can text me when you want to talk. I also have some experience finding employment in Lily Rock." Olivia turned to look at Meadow behind the reception desk. "And if you know what's good for you, you'll stop annoying the town librarian. She's the best source for job openings. If you get on her good side, she'll keep you in mind and let you know as soon as she hears when something opens up."

Blair took her phone out of her pocket. She tapped in her ID and handed it to Olivia, who quickly added her number to the contacts and gave the phone back. "Just text me and I'll give you some ideas about how to find work."

Blair nodded. She turned around, walking toward the exit without saying thank you or even goodbye.

Olivia watched out the window as Blair ran to catch up with her siblings. The three of them crossed the street, side by side. They climbed into the lime-green VW, with Bella behind the wheel and Brandon in the back seat. Blair stared out the window of the passenger side as the car pulled away from the curb.

CHAPTER TWENTY-TWO

Olivia put her purse down and immediately went to check on Sage. Peeking into the main bedroom, she found her sitting in the overstuffed chair, looking out the big window that faced the front of the house. "I'm back. Would you like a cup of tea?"

Sage spun the chair around. "Sounds good, and maybe some lunch soon. I'm hungry again."

Olivia chuckled. "Give me a minute. I'll put on the kettle and then make us a grilled cheese. Does that sound good?"

"Yum."

In the kitchen Olivia checked her phone. Janis Jets had called five times and texted twice.

Call me, the text said, followed by NOW in capital letters. After that Janis had tried on her phone.

She must be frustrated if she's using caps. I'd really like to know what she has to say... The kettle began to sing as Olivia pondered her texts. She put the phone down, pushing the possibility of returning the messages out of her mind.

Back in Sage's room, she laid the tray with the teapot and cups on the table next to the bed. Sage sat with her back against the headboard. Then she brushed her hair into a low ponytail on the back of her neck.

"I ran into the Greys at the library," Olivia commented. She watched Sage's face carefully. Sage's eyes widened slightly. *Just their name makes her unhappy.*

Sage held her cup in a tight grip with both hands. When she raised her eyes, Olivia saw apprehension. *Is she going to faint again?* Before she could express any concern, Sage said, "I haven't seen Bella since our gig at the pub the other night." She sipped her tea, then put her cup back on the tray, lifting the cozy off of the pot. She tested the handle. "Not too hot," she commented. Sage nodded to Olivia. "Want a refill?"

Olivia held her empty cup closer for her sister to refill.

"Blair is looking for a job," Olivia said.

"Bella makes me uncomfortable. I'm not sure she's a good fit for Sweet Four O'Clock." Sage patted her belly and closed her eyes, taking a deep breath. "Maybe we can audition some other people."

"How does this plan sound? We can stop rehearsing Sweet Four O'Clock while you're on bed rest. I'll let Paul know that he can take other gigs. Then after the baby comes we can organize possible dates and then we can audition another percussionist."

"Sounds good," Sage said absentmindedly. She looked out the window again.

Olivia cleared her throat. "What are your plans for the afternoon, post-grilled cheese?" She felt relieved as she slid the conversation to a safer topic.

"I have paint chips from the hardware store. I thought we could talk about colors for the nursery."

"It would be easier if we knew the gender," mused Olivia.

"I may ask the doctor when I check in at the end of the week."

"I'm sure he'd like that," Olivia said dryly. "He seemed to be very concerned about your health."

Instead of denying Dr. Martinez's interest, Sage merely nodded. "He did seem interested in me. I know he has a lot of patients, but his bedside manner reminds me of..."

"Doc," Olivia finished her sentence. "I didn't know Doc all that well but I wondered if you felt the same way I did. When did you first meet Martinez anyway?"

"I suspected that I might be pregnant late in April, because I felt tired all of the time and hadn't had my period. I did a home test and then waited for a few weeks and did another one. I wanted to get a medical confirmation before telling Meadow. I didn't want to get her involved until I knew for sure. So that's when I made the appointment and met Dr. Martinez." She sounded breathless. Sage leaned against the headboard and closed her eyes.

Even talking makes her tired. But now I guess I can eliminate the handsome doctor as a potential baby daddy. The timing isn't right.

A pounding sound came from the front door. "I'm going to see who's there," she told Sage. Stepping across the room, she peeked outside through a window.

Janis Jets raised her fist and kept pounding on the door.

Olivia walked back to give Sage a report. She stood at the foot of the bed.

"Looks like Janis is paying a visit."

"Go ahead and answer. I'm good just sitting here," Sage said.

"I don't want to talk to Janis right now. If I ignore her then I won't be tempted to interfere." She smiled brightly. "I'm going to be your temporary doula, at least until you can hire an official one."

Sage sighed. "You can take care of me and still help Janis. Go answer the door."

Feeling ambivalent, Olivia left Sage. Drawing closer, she heard Janis's loud voice. "I know you're in there, Nancy Drew. Open the door!"

She opened the door slowly, feeling the rush of Jets's irritation sweep past, followed by Janis herself.

"Oh hello, Officer Jets," she said, producing a smile.

"What are you playing at?" demanded Jets, spinning to face Olivia.

"I'm taking care of my sister today."

"Oh, is Sage okay?" Janis's genuine tone of concern caught Olivia off guard.

"She's better today. She fainted and hit her head. Then I had to take her to the doctor."

"Fainted?"

"I told her about finding Ashley and Bianca and she just passed out. Fortunately she only got a small bump on her head, but it frightened me a lot."

"And that's why I'd never get pregnant. It would be too humiliating. Imagine me fainting. Cooks would laugh so hard."

"Why do you think that? Cookie loves you and would be concerned."

Jets's eyes narrowed. "In case you haven't noticed by now, I'm not good with being vulnerable, and when you become a baby-making machine, it's all about weakness." She pointed to the kitchen. "Can we sit down for a minute? I wanted talk to you about my interview with Ashley Tennant and catch you up on the investigation and see if you have any insights."

"I would invite you in, but I'm making lunch for Sage. Then we're going to start planning the nursery, you know, pick out paint colors and see if we need new furniture. I don't have time to discuss your investigation."

Jets's jaw dropped. Her shocked face nearly made Olivia laugh. "So you're giving up your Nancy Drew amateur sleuth identity and becoming the doting auntie instead? When were you going to let me know?"

Olivia shrugged. "My priorities changed," she admitted.

Jets's mouth settled into a frown. Her face held many emotions, but the most dominant one was disappointment. "Okay then, I'll take my investigation somewhere else." Janis opened the door. "It's funny how I spent so much time pushing you out of my business and now that you voluntarily left, I feel disappointed, like something's been taken from me."

Before Olivia could respond, Janis walked through the door, closing it behind her.

She wanted to chase after her and say it had all been a mistake. But she stopped herself by gripping the door handle. *Don't undo what just happened. You were honest with Janis. You can't be responsible for how she reacted.*

Olivia released her grip. She stood in the great room, inhaling deeply. Instead of feeling relieved, she felt uncertain. Despite what she'd said to Janis about her best intentions, her thoughts about the investigation kept coming. *I wonder what Janis was going to tell me about Ashley?*

Olivia walked into the kitchen. *Think about lunch,* she told herself firmly. Head in the refrigerator, her mind kept running. *Did Ashley get an attorney? And I wonder if she's locked up in the Lily Rock jail or if she got out on bail...*

Olivia selected three different cheeses for the sandwiches. Gouda, aged sharp cheddar, and jack cheese from Oregon. She pulled out a frying pan and some butter before another thought about Ashley made her pause. *Would any of those Greys hurt Ashley? Maybe she's safer in jail?*

Stop it, Olivia. You made the right choice. Sage is the priority, not some murder investigation. Just let it go!

Once finished, she cut the grilled cheese sandwiches in two. As she placed them on plates, her mind finally settled. She entered Sage's bedroom with her tray of sandwiches. *They look yummy*, she thought, admiring the melted cheese dripping over the edges of the thick homemade bread.

Then Olivia felt her brain shift. *The cheese reminds me of...*

And once again her thoughts about the investigation took over. She pictured the last time she had seen Bianca. Lying on the ground, blood oozing from the back of her head. Her eyes stared straight ahead, the first indication of her death. *Blunt force trauma from a skateboard.*

I wonder what possessed Ashley to kill Bianca in that moment. I mean, there must have been a reason for her to react in such a violent way.

Olivia shook her head back into the present. She handed Sage a plate. "Here you go, just like Meadow would make it."

Sage looked down at the sandwich. "Are you okay? You seem preoccupied."

"Just thinking about paint colors." Olivia deflected Sage's observation by speaking brightly. She sat down in her chair, picking up a sandwich half for herself. "Let's eat and then talk about your ideas for the baby." She took a bite, watching the cheese ooze over the bread crust. Instead of enjoying the sandwich, she felt slightly nauseous. A vision of Bianca's face in the dirt with Ashley holding her skateboard, blood dripping off the front, made her want to gag.

She put the sandwich back, leaving it on a napkin next to the serving plate. "I'm not as hungry as I thought," she explained. "Please eat as much as you want. I'll have some more tea."

"This tastes amazing." Sage took another half of the sandwich. The quizzical expression on her face did not escape Olivia. *We're so busy dancing around each other's feelings. Even sharing a grilled cheese sandwich feels awkward.*

Olivia reached for the teapot. It felt cold to her touch. She poured the rest into her cup and then returned the empty pot.

Sage munched her sandwich without speaking.

Olivia held the cup of cold tea, telling herself, *Stop thinking about Bianca's blood. Stop thinking about Ashley and just stop thinking about how they got into that situation. No more questions; none of my business.*

Her stomach turned over as she swallowed the last sip of cold tea.

CHAPTER TWENTY-THREE

Olivia held up the paint swatches for Sage. One was a pale pink and the other the softest shade of green. "So what do you think? This one is called evergreen fog."

Sage raised one, then the other to get a good look. "They're so small and the wall is so big. I'm just not sure. I like both colors," she added hopefully.

Olivia sighed. They'd spent at least two hours looking through paint strips and samples that morning, trying to figure out which one would work for the nursery. "Might I suggest that knowing the baby's gender would make this decision easier?" She used her most hopeful voice, watching Sage's expression closely for clues. *She's in some kind of fog when it comes to making a decision.*

"You don't have to stare at me," mumbled Sage, "I'm not going to faint over a paint color."

A half smile appeared on Olivia's lips. "Okay, so you caught me. I've been reading you like my favorite novel for days, just to make sure I don't say anything to upset you."

Sage nodded. "I know I'm being overly sensitive. But I'm

fine now. I haven't passed out since last Sunday. Yay me!" She smiled ruefully at Olivia, who grinned in response.

"Yep, yay you. But what about the color?" Olivia nodded toward the closet. "Let's go into the room and hold the paint samples against the wall."

Located right off the main suite, the walk-in closet was large enough to be its own bedroom. Shelves lined one side. Sage had removed her clothing from the closet, leaving empty poles. Light streamed from the window, casting shadows on the wood flooring.

Along with the rest of the house, this private space had been carefully constructed by Michael Bellemare. The window faced the gravel driveway at the front of the house. The woods and mountains lay beyond, as far as the eye could see. Olivia felt safe in the space because she knew the window could not be detected from the outside. That was Michael's specialty—hidden spaces with lots of light.

She thought about the new house Michael was constructing for them. *He's so good at what he does. I can't wait until our house is ready to move into.*

"What are you thinking about?" Sage sat in the upholstered rocking chair that looked out to the breathtaking view.

"Oh, nothing," Olivia said absentmindedly. She watched as Sage bounced on the seat cushion, placing one arm then the other on the chair as if testing for comfort. "I think this would make a great nursing chair," she said, settling back into the cushion.

The chair gently rocked as Sage pushed her feet against the floor. She rested her elbows on the chair arms. "The perfect height for nursing baby," she commented.

"The chair is blue," Olivia noted. "If baby is a girl, will you have it recovered?"

"Stop it! I'm not that gender obsessed." Sage brought her arms back, folding her hands in her lap.

Olivia grabbed Scotch Tape from the changing table, which served as a work area. She secured the samples to the wall above her head. "So does this help?"

"That's not quite the right green." Sage stood up and peeled the sample from the wall. She replaced it with another sample and then stood back.

Since I've taken over as temporary doula, she's spent most of the morning relaxing and reading. I'll do some errands this afternoon while she naps.

Sage took the paint chip and set it back on the table. Then she sat back in rocking chair, closing her eyes. "I smell pot roast."

"I put the crock pot on this morning," Olivia said proudly.

"Sounds delicious," came a tired reply.

"Time for a cup of tea?" Olivia asked.

"Good idea. I'm tired all the time. Now that I'm not going to work, I can't imagine what I was thinking these past weeks. So let's have tea...because I've exhausted myself picking paint colors." Sage grinned.

Olivia giggled. "How about I meet you outside on the deck? The weather is beautiful and being outside is good for us both."

When Sage nodded an affirmation, Olivia walked through the large closet doorway to the main bedroom. She stopped to straighten the sheets and plump the pillows on the bed.

To her delight, Mayor Maguire lay on the floor in a sun spot. *I didn't know he was here.*

"Hey, buddy," she called to him.

He lifted his head, his tail thumping against the wood floor.

"We're going outside, want to come?"

The dog dropped his head and heaved a big sigh. His eyes closed.

"I bet you'll change your mind when you smell the coffee cake," she teased.

Once in the kitchen, Olivia slid her finger under the Thyme Out sticker that sealed the cake Cookie had dropped off earlier that morning.

"I brought sustenance," he'd said, standing on their doorstep.

"Come on in." She held the door for him. "Aren't you supposed to be in the kitchen baking your little heart out?"

"I got up an hour early to get the bread rising. I wanted to bring you two something before going back to Thyme Out. I have an interview set up, need someone to replace Bianca."

Olivia drew a deep breath. "She left you high and dry."

"Not her fault." Cookie shook his head.

"Being murdered isn't her fault," Olivia admitted, "but the circumstances still leave me with a lot of questions. I mean, why would Ashley just bring that skateboard down on Bianca's head?"

"That's what Janis is trying to figure out, but she's having trouble getting the girl to talk. Even Ashley's lawyer isn't having much luck. She sits in her cell and says nothing. Since the girl is so uncooperative, Janis finally had to call in a court-appointed therapist." Then he added, "Too bad she can't ask for your help."

Olivia felt indignant. "Just stop it! I can't get involved with Janis's investigation, not with Sage needing me."

"I never thought I'd say this, but you do have a gift. People just trust you and they open up. Maybe you could not mention it to Sage and just drop in to the constabulary and have a word?" Cookie looked hopefully at her.

"I can't do it. I just can't. The minute I put my toe in the water, I become consumed. Then I'll neglect Sage, and she really needs me."

With a shrug, Cookie stepped closer. He put his arm around her shoulders. "I get it. You don't have to explain again. Just know Janis misses you and wishes she had you to bounce ideas off of."

Olivia leaned into his side. "You mean Officer Janis Jets actually needs someone?"

He dropped his arm. "Surely you don't believe that tough woman facade. She's as vulnerable as the next, even more so. That's why she's so prickly."

Before Cookie left, Olivia had one more question. "So what do we actually know about Ashley? She's an athlete and does spectacular tricks on her skateboard. And then I heard she doesn't have parents or a family." *You just told him you didn't want to be involved in the investigation and now you're asking more questions!*

Cookie looked at her quizzically. "All I know is that Janis said Ashley and Brandon started hanging out when the they lived in LA. After a while she basically moved in."

"So they didn't meet in Lily Rock," Olivia mused.

"They all moved to Lily Rock together, nearly two months ago."

"Do we know why the Greys ended up here on our hill?"

Cookie grinned. "You see? You ask the right questions. Most people aren't that curious. They make judgements and then try to find evidence to back up what they already believe. In answer to your question, Janis isn't sure why they moved up here."

Olivia rolled her eyes. "You're right. I'm my own worst enemy." As he'd turned to go, she called him back.

"So who are you interviewing today?"

A slight smile came to the corner of his mouth. "Blair is the first and only applicant."

Olivia's heart raced. "I spoke to her yesterday."

"People in their young twenties need jobs," Cookie added curtly. "How else will they grow into being adults if they don't get out in the world and make a living?"

She felt a nudge to her knee. *Back to the present.*

Mayor Maguire yipped, his black eyes gleaming in anticipation. "So you want a bite of coffee cake?" she said.

When he didn't drop his gaze, she patted his head. "Follow me outside. You can hang out and I bet you'll get a few bites." She placed plates, cups, and the teapot carefully on a tray, picked it up, and carried it through the back door Sage had left open.

After leaving the tray on a table, Olivia sat down, propping her feet on the railing. Mayor Maguire sat between them, looking at the coffee cake.

Sage laughed. "He's impossible." She reached over to pick up a plate and placed a piece of coffee cake in her palm, offering it to the attentive dog. "Here you go. One bite and no more. You have to watch your figure."

"That's right," Olivia added. "You're the mayor of Lily Rock and you have to keep fit for all of those photo ops." He licked Sage's hand, turning toward Olivia. Then he leaned closer to sniff her lap, looking for another bite. Olivia shoved his nose aside, reaching past him for her plate.

The sisters ate in companionable silence, looking out to the woods beyond the deck. "Did you pick a color?" asked Olivia, willing her voice to sound interested.

"I think I want to see more green paint samples. Green is gender neutral and a trending color, or so I heard."

"Since when do you care about trending colors?"

"Since I got pregnant. It's the one thing I can think about

that doesn't make me anxious," admitted Sage. She reached out to pat Olivia's arm. "You're the best sister I could imagine. You'd rather be hunting down suspects," Sage's voice caught, "but you're staying with me. I want you to know it's working. I'm already feeling a lot better."

"Oh honey, I'm so happy to hear you're feeling better. And it's only been since Monday that I've become your self-proclaimed pregnancy doula. Just think how you'll be feeling by Friday."

Sage burst out laughing. "Okay, I know you've been a temp at a lot of jobs, but it just occurred to me you're now a temp doula."

"But what you need to know is that I am not a temp sister. I am full-on, totally committed, engaged, and at your service." She faced Sage to make sure her sister understood.

"I get it," Sage said quietly.

Olivia reached for the teapot, her thoughts swirling around her head. *I talk a good game, but my mind keeps coming back to Ashley Tennant. She needs to tell her side of the story, why she killed Bianca. Otherwise she'll end up in a women's prison for who knows how long.*

Once she finished the tea, Olivia looked over at Sage. Her eyes had closed, her hand dangling loosely from the chair over Mayor Maguire's back. Olivia placed her teacup on the table and quietly stood up. Returning from the house with a blanket, she carefully spread it over Sage's lap, tucking it around her sister's legs. Mayor Maguire opened one eye and then closed it again.

Olivia's heart filled with love just seeing them together. *Look at those two.*

With a start she realized she had errands to run. *I can go to the market. I'll leave her a note just in case she wakes up and wonders where I've gone. I can stop by the hardware store for more paint samples. I'll pick up foam brushes and paint the wall with strips of each color so that she can make her decision.*

Olivia picked up the tray filled with plates and cups to take them to the kitchen.

On the drive to town her thoughts settled over her shopping list. As she pulled into town, her mind traveled back to the investigation. *Poor Ashley. If only she'd confide in someone.*

CHAPTER TWENTY-FOUR

Michael brushed off the bench for her to sit down right next to him. He put his arm around her shoulders. "So how's Sage today, did you start painting the nursery?"

Adjusting her sunglasses to block out the midday glare, Olivia moved closer to pat his knee. "All is well with Sage. I got her more paint samples from the hardware store yesterday. She's taking a deep dive into making a selection."

He kissed the top of her head. "No confessions about the baby's father?"

"Not even close to a confession," Olivia admitted. "I think I've lost my super power."

"I know you want to know," he said, nodding, "but does it really matter? I mean Sage didn't know her biological father until two years ago. She turned out just fine."

"You're right. Plus I didn't know my dad either. My mom didn't consider it a problem. She never said anything bad about him."

"How did she explain your father's absence?"

"When I asked, she told me that he was a boy she'd met a long time ago. When I got older she added to the story, depending on what she thought I would understand. She also said that I shouldn't ever blame him for not being in my life, that it wasn't meant to be."

"Wasn't meant to be covers a lot of territory. But from a man's point of view, I'd want to know if I had a child out there."

"I know you would."

Michael eyed the basket she'd brought. "Is that our lunch?"

"I sliced the ham thick, like you prefer. Added Swiss cheese, lettuce and tomato." She lifted the lid off the hamper, placing it beside her on the bench. "One large ham sandwich for the gentleman," she said, handing it over with a smile. "When you're done with that, you can have my other half."

He nodded as he unwrapped the waxed paper.

Olivia looked more closely at the construction site. "So you're framing. I can see rooms shaping up before my very eyes."

Michael swallowed and then took a swig from his water bottle. "I also hired a guy to do construction cleanup. He'll be coming along any minute."

"Anyone I know?"

"He's right from your favorite Lily Rock family, none other than Brandon Grey."

"He put his comic book down and asked for a job?"

"He came by yesterday. After some hemming and hawing he mentioned he needed a job. He was a bit surprised that I required references and experience. After some back and forth, I explained that he could get experience and a good reference if he'd start as our construction cleanup guy."

Michael took another bite of sandwich. After he swallowed, he continued, "Then I told him if he impressed me, I'd let him work with one of our more experienced construction guys to see if he'd work out as an apprentice." Michael brushed crumbs from his lap. "He really thought he could just show up and get a job."

Olivia heard the sound of a car engine coming from behind and turned to look. The familiar lime-green VW Beetle had pulled up next to her car. "And speak of the devil," she said.

Michael glanced quickly and then turned back to her. "I'm hoping for some cookies after this sandwich..."

She shot him a radiant smile. "I've become a doula and Betty Crocker this week. Here are homemade white chocolate chip cookies with macadamia nuts for your pleasure." She reached inside the hamper, pulling up a plastic bag.

"All for me?"

"All for you." She placed the bag in his lap.

A car door slammed. Footsteps approach. Brandon stood in front of them. He hung his head, as if waiting to be noticed. A Comic Con T-shirt was tucked snugly into his high-rise jeans. A worn brown belt circled his waist. A baseball cap sat on his unruly hair.

Michael looked him up and down. When Brandon failed to say a word, Michael finally broke the impasse. "You ready to work?"

Brandon nodded.

"Use your words, man," Michael insisted.

"What do I do?" Brandon mumbled.

"Not play dumb. I told you earlier exactly who to report to and what you'd be doing. Bring the gloves?"

Brandon looked at his bare hands and then back to Michael. When he didn't answer the question, Michael sighed. "So far this isn't going too well. Think about what I told you to do and then do it. If you need another reminder, I'll tell you one more time, but then no more reminders for the rest of this week. I don't hand out my instructions lightly and I expect them to be heard the first time."

Olivia watched Brandon's fists clench. He turned abruptly, walking toward the construction site, disappearing behind the building.

"You're kind of a tough boss," Olivia commented dryly.

"I'm not nearly as tough as most contractors," he defended himself. "Plus the kid has no previous work experience. I know the type—not my first rodeo with oppositional personalities. He thinks by getting me to keep explaining, he'll get out of work."

"So that's how you sum up Brandon?"

"Got it in one." Michael took a big bite of cookie. "Plus he doesn't get to interrupt a lunch with my lady because he forgot his gloves. His poor planning is not my emergency."

"I see," she said, nodding. "There's no mercy from Michael Bellemare."

"I treat him just like the rest of my crew," came his reply.

"But you're very nice to your girlfriend." She touched his cheek.

Michael smiled. "You are not an employee. Plus I'm giving him a chance."

"But remember Ashley used to do all the talking for him. She even explained to me he has Asperger's."

"Maybe he does and maybe he doesn't, but he still has to try harder and make a living. Otherwise he'll turn out to be a deadbeat like his father."

She felt a tingle up her spine. "You've heard that too, how Beats was a deadbeat dad?"

"I heard it from you and from the horse's mouth. When I asked him about himself, Brandon launched into all kinds of excuses about not having a father figure growing up and how Dad was a deadbeat."

Olivia watched Brandon reappear from behind the construction site with gloves on. He dragged a trash can in the dirt. Stepping closer to them, he asked, "When's my break?"

Michael chuckled. "Show me some work and I'll tell you when to take a break."

Brandon's eyes glared, but Michael did not relent. He disconnected from Brandon by turning to Olivia. "Boy, these cookies are good. I love the macadamia nuts too." He slid his hand into the bag, removing the last cookie. Brandon stared at him without moving.

Michael darted a glance his way. "Get to work!" He broke off a bit of cookie, handing it to Olivia.

The boy huffed away, the trash can thumping against his leg. As soon as he was out of earshot, Olivia laughed. "I love mean Michael. I had no idea you had that in you."

He crossed a leg, taking her hand in his. "I'm just an onion waiting to be peeled," he said jokingly. "And maybe tonight we could go for the next layer..."

"Only if you promise me that mean Michael stays at work," she joked.

"I'm not your boss," he assured her. "I don't need to light any fires under you."

After she kissed him goodbye, she grabbed the hamper and walked to her car. Driving down the hill, she opened her window. The smells of summer wafted inside, the warm odor of earth and pine needles. The hot dry air brushed against her cheek.

"I am an orphan on God's highway," she began to hum. *That was the song on Ashley's video. The way she kicked her skateboard into the air and then hopped back on as if she knew right where it would land. Defying gravity and any logical explanation for how she could stay upright on the bolt of lightning with four wheels.* Olivia continued to hum. *That young woman on the skateboard had little to no resemblance to the frightened woman who stood over Bianca's body.*

What are the rest of the words to that song? Something about brothers and sisters with no ties of kinship...

One turn from the main highway and the sound of crunching gravel brought her back to the present. An unfamiliar car had parked at the farthest end of the lot next to her house. *Does Sage have a visitor?* She got out of her car quickly. Grabbing the hamper from the back seat, she slammed the car door to walk toward the front.

Once inside she heard voices coming from the kitchen.

"How long are you here for?" Sage was asking.

"I've got until next Monday," came a man's reply.

"So you can stay for dinner if you'd like," Sage interjected.

"How about I take you out?"

Olivia walked into the kitchen. She found her sister and a man chatting at the table. Sage looked up, her eyes bright and a smile on her face. Olivia recognized Jeff Grossman as soon as he turned his head her way.

He stood up to greet her. "Good to see you again," he offered, an easy smile on his handsome face. She put down the empty hamper to shake his outstretched hand. He dropped her hand and turned away, his eyes lingering on Sage.

"Good to see you too," she mumbled. Olivia stepped toward the pantry as she listened to Sage and Jeff.

"I'd like to go out," Sage said.

"I'll make us a reservation," replied Jeff promptly.

Olivia walked out of the pantry. Standing at the counter, she made herself busy filling the kettle. "I'll put on a kettle," she called out over her shoulder.

While the tea brewed, she brought three mugs to the table. "So what brings you to Lily Rock?" Olivia asked Jeff.

"Sage and I met last spring on the Colorado hike," he explained. He looked over at Sage with a quick tender look on his face. "I live in LA and thought I'd drive up to see how she's doing."

"She's pregnant," Olivia bluntly announced, waiting for his reaction.

"So I noticed," he said dryly.

Sage smiled. "Not exactly a secret." She patted her baby bump.

Olivia darted a glance at Sage, who glared back.

"We're going out to dinner," Sage announced. "So you and Mike can have some time to yourselves."

"Or I could make dinner for all of us," Olivia suggested. *If he's my niece or nephew's father, I want to know.*

"I've got this," Jeff assured Olivia. "But maybe another time?"

So that does it. They want to be alone and I'm not supposed to ask too many questions. She took her mug from the table without sitting down. "I've got things to do. See you guys later."

Once in the great room she felt her frustration more clearly. *I'm supposed to be the good sister, but she's not giving me any of the important information.* Olivia's jaw clenched. *It won't be good for her if I keep acting mad.*

Her eyes traveled around the room, stopping on her autoharp, which she'd left propped against the fireplace. *I haven't played since our last gig. Too busy picking paint colors. I'm going to tune and see if I can remember that orphan song. Maybe my bad mood will lift.*

Placing her mug of tea on the mantle, she grabbed her autoharp. "Going outside," she hollered to the room. The first deep inhale of pine-scented air made her feel less annoyed. *Self-talk,* she insisted to herself. *Just chill, Olivia. Sage is doing so much better. After the baby comes you can claim your own life again.*

Olivia sat down, shifting her autoharp to her lap. One strum across the strings proved it had held its tune. She pressed the G chord bar and strummed. The words to "Orphan Girl" came quickly.

Olivia began to quietly sing, "I am an orphan on God's highway." By the end of the first verse another phrase popped into her head. "I know no mother, no sister, no brother." To her surprise, her voice caught in her throat as her eyes filled with tears. Then it hit her.

This song tells my story about not belonging and having no family. I was that person before I arrived in Lily Rock. Maybe that's what Ashley's feeling too. Maybe something snapped inside of her and that's why she killed Bianca, something to do with being an orphan and feeling terribly alone.

Olivia stopped singing, knowing she'd stumbled onto something important. *There's a connection between Ashley, that video, and the song. But one thing I know for sure, that video was a cry for help.*

CHAPTER TWENTY-FIVE

Olivia felt the heat of the bright sunshine streaming through the bedroom window. She snuggled into Michael's warm body, feeling his arm wrap around her shoulders. He pulled her closer. She inched her hand up his chest to touch his mouth and then his eye. "You're awake," she said calmly.

"My eyes are open," he mumbled. "You can stop poking them now."

"I'm an orphan on God's highway," she said. "The song 'Orphan Girl' is running through my mind over and over. I can't shake it. My first thought this morning was on that lyric."

"I remember that one. Didn't Gillian Welch sing it a while back?"

"She did and it was brilliant," Olivia said. "I knew the song from before."

"So you sang it with the band?"

"Not with Sweet Four O'Clock. Right before I gave up gigging, I sang it a lot. Do you think the ear worm is trying to tell me to perform the song again?"

"Could be."

She waited for him to say more, but when his body softened, she realized he'd fallen back to sleep. She lifted his arm from around her shoulders, then slid out of the bed.

Olivia paused to listen to Michael's gentle breathing and the sound of birds calling to each other outdoors. *Finally I can push away the orphan...oh no, here it comes again.* The ear worm filled her thoughts. The repeating sound and voice singing, "I am an orphan too."

Walking across the room, she pushed aside the curtain to look outside.

"Did you hear the thumping and bumping last night?" Michael asked from across the room. Olivia smiled. Michael did that. He'd doze off and then when he woke up, he'd just start talking as if he'd never been asleep.

"I assume you mean noises coming from the guest room?" She turned around.

He shoved himself into a sitting position. Hair ruffled from sleep, he leaned his back against the headboard. "Last night you fell asleep and I stayed up a little longer. I listened for noises, you know, out of curiosity."

"I was curious too," Olivia said. "I mean, Sage assured me that she and Jeff weren't a couple. But he may have other plans, at least from what I could see yesterday. He can't keep his eyes off of her."

"Well that's the thing." Michael reached his arms above his head to stretch. She admired the toned muscles on both arms and sighed. He continued, "I didn't hear anyone in the guest room. It's right down the hall from us and I'm pretty sure no one slept there last night."

"Intriguing." Olivia nodded. "So you think Jeff and Sage might have, you know, slept together in her room..."

"Why do I feel so curious?" he moaned, plunging his fist into the pillow next to him. "Normally I don't care about what other people are up to."

"Living together in the same house sure brings up a lot of curiosity," Olivia admitted.

"Speaking of curiosity..." Michael's eyebrows lifted. "Do you want to explore your feelings this morning? I have a nice warm spot for you to share with me." He flipped the covers back with a sly grin.

Olivia pretended to examine her fingernails. "As a temp doula, I have early morning responsibilities. But today I think I can say yes to your invitation and then fix you breakfast afterward."

Michael ducked back under the covers. Then he poked his head out. "What's taking you so long?"

* * *

"Sage and Jeff aren't up yet," he commented, rinsing his breakfast plate in the sink.

"It's really weird, after getting used to just the three of us cohabitating, another person changes everything."

He grabbed a dish towel to dry his hands. "Remember how long it took me to admit I felt like a third wheel living with you and Sage?"

"I was thinking of that. Now I feel like the old married couple, as if we are Sage's parents and she's missed curfew."

He grinned. "I'm not going gently into that good night. I want to be the young romantic couple. It has nothing to do with age really."

Olivia chuckled. "I'm miffed. I became her doula and now she's moved on. Am I just the person who helps pick out paint colors and makes peppermint tea?"

"I think you may have done your job so well that Sage is feeling much better. Then Jeff walks in and maybe we have our baby daddy right in our own midst. Isn't that what you'd hoped for?"

"I suppose." Olivia nodded. "Sage with a partner and a healthy baby. That's exactly what I'd hoped for. I'm just surprised it all turned around in one week. Kind of mind-boggling."

He leaned down to whisper, "Thanks for this morning." Then he gave her ear a quick kiss. "I better get to the construction site. I have a boy-man coming to clean up. I need to keep my eye on him."

"So you didn't fire Brandon on day one. That surprises me, he wasn't exactly impressing you at lunch."

"He's a challenge. I'll tell you everything tonight. Gotta go." Walking out of the kitchen, he whistled a tune she didn't recognize. She turned to the sink.

When the truck started up outside, she picked up her cell phone to check recent messages. No texts and no calls. *Janis has given up.* She tossed the phone on the table. *I am so crabby.*

By the time Olivia had showered and dressed, she could hear the sound of Sage's happy laughter followed by Jeff's low response. *Apparently the lovebirds have woken up. And why am I not happier for them?*

Picking up her phone off the bathroom counter, she looked at the screen. *No messages. I wonder what Janis is up to today and if she's still holding Ashley...*

Olivia was irritated as she yanked her hair back into a ponytail, securing it with a black band. *Eavesdropping on my sister isn't helping my attitude. She has Jeff. Time for me to shake this bad mood. I'll drive into town and give them some privacy.*

Olivia walked upstairs, trying to make as little noise as possible. She grabbed her purse from the table by the front door. Closing the door softly behind her, she walked to the car, forcing herself not to look back. *I'm half hoping Sage will come running after me. How needy is that?*

The Ford puttered along the winding road to town, giving her time to explore her bad mood. *Like Michael said, Sage is much better. I'm doing my doula job.*

Thyme Out looked busy; she could see people in line as she drove past. Olivia found a space for her car on the other side of the park. Once the car was locked, she paused by the railing to inhale and admire the giant sequoia. *What ever happened to the knife Mayor Maguire found buried in the dirt? I wonder what forensics had to say and if Janis got any clues about Beats's killer.* This time she didn't push the thoughts away.

If Janis has evidence from the knife, then she may have the weapon that killed Beats. She was probably trying to talk to me about that a couple of days ago.

Again Olivia inhaled, aware of her thoughts. When she didn't resist the direction of her mind, she felt herself involuntarily take a breath. After she exhaled, all of the crabby edginess disappeared.

Making her way through the park and across the street, she stood in front of Thyme Out. The bell over the door rang as Olivia stepped inside. Most of the earlier crowd had left the bakery; only a few people occupied tables. The aroma of cinnamon drew her to the counter. Blair Grey appeared from the kitchen wearing a crisp white apron tied behind her neck.

She looks just like her mother in that apron.

"Coffee of the day," Olivia told the young woman, "and two lemon thyme cookies."

"I'll bring it to your table," Blair said crisply.

"And I'll be on the patio," Olivia said, leaving cash on the counter. "Keep the change."

Once outside she spotted an empty table. As soon as she sat down, Blair appeared with a mug and a plate. She left them on the table without a comment. Olivia took a sip of the strong coffee and then glanced around the patio. Her eyes stopped on Janis and Cookie. Their heads huddled together.

Olivia's heart thudded. For the umpteenth time that morning, she inhaled deeply. *I wish they'd say hi.* Glancing at her phone, she pretended she didn't care. *If no one wants to talk to me, that's just fine.* She yanked her purse from under the table to shove the phone inside. She dropped the purse and kicked it under her chair. *Sometimes that cell feels like an anchor.*

Olivia sipped coffee while she observed the people on the patio. Cookie and Janis were still talking. Her eyes stopped at the arbor that led to the alley behind the bakery.

Three roses bloomed, the last hangers-on in the heat of summer. One tenacious flower was yellow with a touch of pink on the edges. Beyond the arbor, her eyes rested on the grove of trees. Inhaling, her lungs filled with fresh mountain air and then her mind released the tension. *That's better, Olivia. Let that mood pass through you and go away. Keeping looking at those trees...*

A squirrel headed up a tree trunk. Chattering away, the small feet clutched onto the bark. *He's got a nut in his mouth. I feel like that sometimes, full of thoughts and trying so hard.*

A siren in the distance caught her attention. She reached for her phone to check on a local website. They often posted Lily Rock emergencies. She also had an app for weather reports and all of the up-to-the-minute traffic alerts. *I'm not going to look. Checking my phone every two minutes is putting me in a bad mood. Just sit here and be calm,* she told herself.

Other people on the patio had the same idea as they scrolled on their cell phones. *They want an explanation for the sirens.* Olivia finished the last sip of coffee. *It's hard not to look,* she admitted to herself. Then her head jerked up when she heard her name being called.

"Olivia," came a voice from the cafe doorway. She turned to see Michael scanning the crowd. Once he caught sight of her, he rushed over to the table.

"You've got to come." He grabbed her elbow, helping her to her feet. "Something's happened to Sage—they're taking her to the hospital down the hill. Come on, I'll drive."

Heart beating wildly, Olivia followed Michael toward the exit. Before she could walk through the doorway, she felt someone at her elbow. Janis, her face looking grim, said, "I got a text from Meadow. She couldn't get ahold of you."

"I turned my alerts off," she admitted.

Cookie came up right behind her. "Why don't you drive Olivia? I'll take Michael. We'll meet you at the hospital."

Janis Jets took Olivia's elbow with authority. "Come on," she said in her low voice. Quips and sarcasm had been replaced by quick action.

Olivia felt a rush in her ears. She leaned into Janis for support.

"You can sit in the front with me," Janis said firmly. "You can fill me in on Sage."

Olivia nodded. "Thank you," she said quietly.

Michael didn't argue. He leaned over to kiss her on the cheek. "I'll see you at Memorial Hospital. Call me on your cell."

"I will," she said in a daze. Turning her phone back on, messages from Sage and Meadow appeared on her screen.

On the way across the street, she held the phone to her cheek to listen to Sage's message: "I have a horrible headache. Came on out of nowhere. Jeff called the paramedics." Sage's voice sounded frightened, sending a chill down Olivia's spine. She blinked back tears.

"I only left her for an hour," she mumbled to Janis.

"Let's get moving." She unlocked her truck with a click. "Get in," she said, gesturing to the passenger side. Olivia hiked herself into the seat as Janis came around the back to climb behind the wheel.

"It feels like your niece or nephew may have decided to arrive early," Janis's calm voice stated.

But baby isn't due for another four months. I should have been with her.

Stop it, Olivia. Sitting in a pool of your own recriminations won't help.

CHAPTER TWENTY-SIX

Olivia sat next to Michael in the waiting room of the Memorial Hospital. Janis Jets and Cookie sat across from them, a low table piled with outdated magazines in between. Every time a voice came over the loudspeaker, Olivia felt her stomach drop. *Not about Sage, not about Sage,* she kept repeating in her mind.

She felt certain that a mention of Sage's name over the loudspeaker would only be bad news. She squeezed Michael's hand. He squeezed back.

Jeff Grossman sat away from the others in the corner of the room. Olivia watched him scroll on his phone. When he looked up, she smiled at him. He nodded and then continued to read. *He could tell me what happened with Sage. I should be curious but I don't think I'm ready to hear right now.*

Her eyes drifted to the people occupying the seats across the room. Janis sat with her arms folded, her eyes closed. Cookie's face looked stern as he stared at the nurse's station. The only one missing was Meadow, who'd been called back to Sage's room.

"You should be there," Olivia had said. "Text me if she wakes up or you get any information from the doctor."

"I most certainly will. As her sister, I think you need to be on the emergency contact list right next to me." Meadow was unable to hide the quaver in her voice.

Olivia opened her arms to give Meadow a quick hug. "I love you," she whispered in her ear.

"I know you do, dear. You're my daughter now and I want you to know you did everything you could. This past week you kept an eye on our girl and I am so grateful."

Olivia heard someone clear their throat behind her back, breaking her from her memory of earlier. She turned around to find Dr. Martinez standing in front of the elevators. He paused as if waiting to be noticed. A stethoscope wrapped around his neck, lying against a white lab coat. He walked closer to Olivia. "I'm happy I caught you," he said gently.

"How is Sage?" Olivia asked instantly. "Do you know what happened? Can we take her home?

"That's what I came to tell you. She's stable now. My diagnosis is preeclampsia. The baby is fine and she's fine, but we have to make plans for the next months until she delivers."

Before Olivia could register the doctor's diagnosis, the elevator doors swung open, and Meadow exited. Catching Olivia's eye, she came closer and spoke to the doctor. "Is my daughter okay? Will the baby be premature? Sage was, you know, only three pounds."

The doctor flipped pages on his clipboard. "I have her history and she mentions prematurity at birth and that you are her adoptive mother."

"And Olivia is Sage's sister, they had the same biological mother, so she can give you more of a health history."

"Not really," Olivia spoke up. "My mom didn't talk much

about her pregnancy. I was a couple of weeks early, but not like Sage. That's about all I can give you."

The doctor's face settled into concentration mode. "I see. I'm not concerned with a more detailed health history about your mother at this point. We know what to do to help Sage." He spoke directly to Olivia. "Did you call any of the people I recommended in my office?"

Olivia shook her head. "I didn't call because, well, Sage picked me. I thought I could help Sage by staying home during her week off of work."

Dr. Martinez looked grim. "I may have underestimated the severity of her condition. But now she requires more than a week off of work. We want to keep her and baby gestating for as long as possible. Every day matters. For now I'd like you to work on hiring a nurse practitioner or a doula. I have another patient to see. I'll check in after that."

As Dr. Martinez walked away, Olivia reached to squeeze Meadow's hand. "I assume you're going back to her room. I'm going to update Michael. Text me when I can come see her."

Before she could turn to go, Michael appeared at her shoulder.

"The doc said Sage will be okay."

Relief showed on his face.

"Meadow will text when I can go see her," she explained.

"Okay then, that's very good news. Can I get you a drink of water or a snack? There must be a vending machine around here somewhere."

"I saw a coffee cart on the first level. Maybe a bottle of water would help."

"You wait here. I'll ask the others if they want something and make a run. Be back soon." Michael walked toward Janis and Cookie just as Olivia's phone pinged.

A text from Meadow. She's awake. Your turn.

"I'm going to see her now," she said across the room to Janis and Cookie. Jets nodded. And then Olivia's eyes stopped on Jeff. When she nodded to him, he stood to his feet, coming closer.

"I didn't want to interfere," he explained. "How is she and when can I see her?"

"Dr. Martinez says she has preeclampsia. They're letting in family members one at a time."

"I don't know what that is, but it sounds bad. But she's okay, I mean for now?"

Olivia patted his arm. "As far as I know. As soon as I talk to her, I'll get your number and text. Would that help?"

"Yeah. It would. I think I'll get outside for some fresh air. But my phone will be on." He walked away, toward the doors leading outside.

Before entering the elevator, Olivia stopped to explain to the nurse, "I'm Sage McCloud's sister. Can you tell me what room she's in?"

"Her mother told me you'd be the next visitor. Take the elevator to the second floor, then take a left and go down the hall. Room 259 is at the end of the corridor." The nurse spoke crisply, her eyes returning back to the computer screen.

Stepping off the elevator, the smell of antiseptic gave her stomach a turn. She looked at the bulletin boards, filled with photos of healthy babies and mothers, that lined the halls to push back the nausea as she walked quickly down the corridor.

The door to room 259 stood ajar. Olivia poked her head in. There was only one bed near the window where she saw Sage lying down, her hair spread out over the pillow.

Olivia walked around the bed to sit in the chair closest to Sage's head. She reached over to touch the hand with an IV line attached. Sage's eyes opened, a slight smile curving her lips.

"Hey," she said. She turned her hand over, cool fingers intertwined with Olivia's.

"Hey yourself," Olivia responded, feeling her eyes fill with tears.

"I've never been in a hospital before." Sage maneuvered her other arm as she struggled to sit up.

"Just stay put," Olivia urged. "I can do the adjusting." She pushed her chair a few inches closer so that they could see each other without Sage having to raise her head.

"Did you speak to Dr. Martinez?" Sage asked.

"He said he'd be here to talk to us after he's finished with his next patient."

"He's awfully handsome," Sage smiled. "See, I'm not that sick."

Olivia chuckled. "How are you feeling now?"

"I'm okay. Still kind of woozy."

"Did the doctor have any information about why the headaches?

"He called it preeclampsia. I'll be on bed rest. He said he had a pamphlet?" Sage smiled.

Olivia nodded. "I see. There's always a pamphlet, right?" Then, because she couldn't help herself, she added, "Your other boyfriend just stepped outside. Do you want to see him?"

Sage looked confused. "Oh, you mean Jeff? He's not family so I don't think they'll let him in."

"He isn't family. I thought he might be the baby's..."

Sage's eyes grew wide. "Oh no, not Jeff. He's just a friend."

"A friend who spends the night?"

"We didn't do anything," Sage explained. "He slept on the

sofa in my room. He's just a great guy and he wanted to hang out."

Heat ran up her face. Olivia blurted, "So are you going to tell me...who is baby's father? I thought it must be Jeff when he showed up and spent the night. He said you'd met on the hike in Colorado. I just figured..."

Sage's head sank further into the pillow. She closed her eyes. "I guess it doesn't take a detective to figure out when I got pregnant." Then she opened her eyes, a look of fierceness penetrating Olivia's gaze.

The door opened, and Olivia expected to see Dr. Martinez, but to her surprise it was none other than Officer Janis Jets. She shifted awkwardly from foot to foot before speaking.

"I hate hospitals," she announced, stepping closer to the bed. Bending over to stare at Sage, she said, "You're looking pretty good." Then she stepped back.

"Why are you here?" Olivia asked.

"None of your business," Jets snapped at her. "I want to talk to the patient right now. You can go."

"I'm her sister. You can't just dismiss me!"

"This is police business." Jets looked at her. "So git..."

"She can stay," Sage said, her voice sounding tired.

Olivia stood to her feet. "You can sit here," she told Jets, walking around to stand on the other side of the bed.

"I'm not sitting," Jets groaned. "I don't want to stay that long. I just want to ask Sage a couple of questions for my investigation."

Olivia's heart quickened. Despite her earlier protestations, she wanted to know how the case was going, and now she could hear without having to admit she made a mistake when she'd disengaged.

"So I've been looking at phone records, mostly those of

Beats Malone. And I see that he called you, not just once but several times. You two talked a lot, sometimes for an hour or more."

Sage didn't smile an acknowledgement. Olivia waited for her to deny talking to Beats, but she didn't do that either.

Janis continued, "In fact, I got into his email and I see you'd sent him your address and that he was coming up to Lily Rock to hang out with you."

Sage closed her eyes, her bottom lip trembling.

"The day he came to meet Olivia was also the day he was supposed to meet you. Am I right?"

Sage nodded, her eyes still closed.

"For the past two weeks I thought Beats was here for Olivia, but it turns out he had other ideas. Olivia wasn't the only band member of Sweet Four O'Clock that mattered to him."

As tears slipped down Sage's face, Olivia's heart beat faster. *Is she implying what I think she's implying?*

"So on that hike in Colorado..." Olivia began.

Sage opened her eyes. She sniffed and then looked at Olivia. When Olivia didn't ask further, Sage whispered, "I promised I wouldn't..."

"So on that hike," Olivia said slowly, "you met Jeff but you also got to know Beats. He was there too."

Sage spoke quickly. "We hit it off right away. After each hike we'd sit in with other musicians and then one thing led to another."

Olivia felt her heart jump to her throat. *And that could only mean one thing.* She watched Sage as she said, "Beats Malone is the father of your child."

Tears filled Sage's eyes. "Yes, that's right."

Jets intervened. "I don't care about the baby daddy. I care that Beats came up here to visit Sage and that I don't have her alibi for the time in question." Her jaw tightened. "Did you kill Beats because you were angry at him and because he didn't want the baby?"

Sage shook her head, her eyes wide and cheeks flushed. "Beats was going to move to Lily Rock to be with me and the baby. That was our plan. He was supposed to meet Olivia that day and explain. He hoped she'd realize how great he'd be with Sweet Four O'Clock, and that he was thrilled about the baby."

Jets leaned over the bed. "It's the timing I want to know about. So when Beats was found dead, you hadn't seen him yet. Is that right?"

"I was supposed to see him after he met Olivia. We were going to surprise her together. But then it all fell apart." Sage's eyes welled with tears. "When Olivia told me she discovered a dead body and that Beats had not shown up, well, that's when I suspected it was over, that I'd be raising baby on my own."

Jets's face softened. "You don't have to cry," she said. "I just wanted an explanation, that's all. It's obvious you had every interest in keeping Beats Malone alive. I get it. I suppose you were working that afternoon and that people can verify seeing you?"

Sage sniffed. "I was in my office that afternoon. You can ask the academy administrator."

"By the time I came up for our morning chat, you already knew about Beats."

"A student stopped me in the parking lot that morning to say the drummer Beats Malone was found dead in the pub parking lot."

"That's why you were so upset when I showed up." Olivia looked flabbergasted. "I thought it was because you were pregnant and a little hormonal. Why didn't you tell me then about Beats and the baby?"

"I would have, but I couldn't," Sage admitted. "He told me not to tell anyone, at least until he'd made the move to Lily Rock. He didn't want his ex-wife or children to know about our baby."

"Is that right..." Jets mumbled.

Olivia shook her head in disbelief. "I don't understand why it had to be a big secret. Everyone who knows you would have been thrilled to hear about a baby and would have welcomed Beats with open arms."

Sage's fingers began to knead the sheet. Olivia watched as her bottom lip trembled, her eyes glistening with tears. Finally she said, "Our baby wasn't good news for everyone. As soon as Bianca heard about Beats starting a new family, she cut ties in LA and moved up to Lily Rock. That's what he told me, and I believed him. His ex never got over their divorce and she made his life a living hell ever since. When he turned up dead, I knew I had to keep my baby safe by not saying a word."

CHAPTER TWENTY-SEVEN

Exhausted from phone calls and getting things ready, Olivia sighed. She'd gotten up before dawn with one purpose in mind: making her home compatible for Sage's recovery.

"What's preeclampsia again?" Michael asked.

"I am now a self-proclaimed resident expert," Olivia explained. "Not that I want to be, but for Sage's sake, someone has to take charge."

"Okay then, resident expert, explain why we've created a daybed on the deck and have rearranged her room with nearly everything within reach."

"I did all of that because Sage needs to remain in a reclined position until the baby is born. Kind of like a Victorian lady." Olivia reached for her cell phone. "And because I now dub you the co-resident expert, I will forward you all the information that Dr. Martinez sent me about her condition."

Michael pulled out his cell and waited. He opened the document and read while Olivia looked toward the woods, her eyes finally stopping at Lily Rock. She remembered the doctor's orders quite clearly. Luis Martinez had made Sage's next few months sound quite grim.

"Sage needs to keep the baby in utero for as long as possible. No stress and no walking around for long periods of time. A prone position is preferred to an upright one. Include nutritious food and lots of sleep. She has become the living incubator for her child. If the baby comes too early, lots of costly medical interventions will become necessary, along with ongoing lifetime consequences for the developmental health of the child. Every day she keeps the baby in her uterus counts."

"So Sage has mild preeclampsia." Michael concluded, turning off his cell.

"That's what Dr. Martinez said." Olivia nodded. "Otherwise he wouldn't send her home but keep her in the hospital for the next three to four months."

"Sage would hate that."

"Who wouldn't hate that? So we're setting up the house to accommodate her needs for now and then we'll adjust after baby arrives."

"I did read the cure for preeclampsia is to deliver the baby."

"That's right." Olivia nodded. "I have a list of ways to keep her occupied and I'm thinking her friend Jeff could help." She hesitated. "If Jeff needs a place to spend the night, could he use your old house? Is it ready for guests?"

"I cleaned out all of my stuff months ago." Michael nodded. "I aired the place, changed the sheets, dusted, and swished scum out of the toilet just last week."

"You are the man of my dreams, at least one who isn't afraid of a little housework." Olivia smiled at him.

"At your service, ma'am," he said. "And now full-service Bellemare will get some more coffee." He rose from his chair and made his way toward the house.

Olivia gazed into the woods again, thinking about Sage's

bedside confession the day before. She'd waited for Sage to fall asleep before catching up with Janis.

As soon as she stuck her head out of the hospital room, Jets snatched her elbow. "I need to talk to you."

They stood away from Sage's room, leaning against a wall. "I had no idea about Beats being the father," Olivia insisted.

"Anyone could see that by the look on your face." Janis shrugged. "But I hear Doc Martinez told you to hire a doula or a trained nurse until the baby comes. Are you going to do that?"

"I hope to have interviews lined up before they send her home tomorrow," Olivia said instantly.

"Then that means you can hang up the temp doula job and help me sort out this murder investigation." Jets did not meet her eyes. Her voice sounded hopeful.

"It's been on my mind the entire week. I tried to be there for Sage, but I was preoccupied with the investigation. That Grey family and the dead parents just activate my curiosity. I guess I am a big snoop and there's no getting around it." When Janis didn't disagree, she added, "And now my niece or nephew will be related to those horrible young people."

"Not exactly the family connection one would hope for," Jets agreed. "But now you'll help me, right? I don't have to grovel or pretend I missed you or any of that. We'll just pick right up like nothing happened. I'm the boss and you're not. Simple as that."

Look at Janis all conciliatory. Should I milk this situation or just get on with it? She glanced at Jets, who still looked at her shoes. "I'm dying to know. Whatever happened with the knife and the DNA?"

"None of your business," Jets insisted. Then she grinned. "Boy, that felt good to say."

Olivia sighed, her thoughts returning to the present. She

closed her eyes to inhale the late summer air. It felt dry and combustible, a warning of potential fire danger, not unfamiliar to southern Californians.

By the time Michael returned she was ready for more coffee. "So I'm meeting up with Janis right after we get Sage settled and fed."

Michael refilled both their mugs, placing the empty pot on the table. He sat down. "I'm happy you can go back to the investigation. On the other hand, all of this preparation makes Sage sound more like a prize racehorse than a person."

Olivia's eyes grew wide. "You're right. We have a new paddock, wholesome food, and a comfort animal named Jeff. I cannot deny your implication." She laughed and then stopped abruptly. "I don't think that was the most compassionate thing to say."

"I think a healthy bit of laughter over Sage's situation may be the most compassionate way to be," he said.

"I guess what I'm trying to say is that taking care of sick people may not be instinctual for me. Better to admit that right now than to think I'll be a good nurse."

"I never wanted you to be a nurse," Michael mumbled. "I prefer independent, constantly inquiring Olivia."

Though she hadn't admitted to herself that his opinion mattered, she felt relieved. "Do you now..."

"Not everyone is a born caregiver," he added. "Leave that to the Meadows and the doulas of the world. Did you find one, by the way?"

"I have three potential doulas arriving at the house this afternoon. One is also a licensed registered nurse."

"Good job of multi-tasking."

"I arranged the interviews. Sage will pick the doula." She looked at her cell phone. "Time to drive to the hospital. Our prize racehorse, aka mother-to-be, requires transportation."

Michael chuckled. "Are you going to tell Sage about being a racehorse?"

"The first chance I get," Olivia insisted with a grin.

A few minutes later Michael opened the front door. Olivia looked down, nearly stumbling over Mayor Maguire.

He stood up instantly, his tongue hanging out the side of his mouth.

She edged her way around the labradoodle as Michael followed. When the dog didn't come with them, she called, "Let's go, M&M!"

He bounded toward the truck, his feet tapping against the gravel.

As soon as Olivia opened the back door, he hopped inside. Turning around with his back to the cushion, he faced front, his tail wrapped under his body.

"The mayor is ready," she announced to Michael.

On the way down the hill, Olivia looked out the window. She closed her eyes for a minute, feeling the truck slide into the winding curves. Music from Michael's playlist made her hum. The drum beat caught her attention. *Just over a week ago I was waiting at the pub to meet Beats Malone. Those four young people sat together. They were laughing. Arlo brought them a beer. They ordered some food and then...*

Her memory stopped. She opened her eyes as Michael drove into the hospital parking lot. *There's a detail that I know but don't remember. It may help with the investigation.*

* * *

Once she got Sage settled against the mound of pillows on her bed, Olivia left for town to do some errands. Entering the library, she found Meadow in her usual spot behind the reference desk.

Meadow saw her and smiled. "Did she get home?"

"She's already taking a nap," Olivia said, feeling proud of herself. "Michael and I arranged her room and an outside daybed in case she wants to get some fresh air and look at Lily Rock."

Meadow's eyes lit up. "I would have done exactly the same. It's so good to know she's in the right hands and that I don't have to smother her unnecessarily."

"There's one thing I'd like to consult you about." Olivia rested her hands on the counter. "I've arranged for three doula interviews this afternoon. That will be enough for Sage in one day. But I'd like to plan for tomorrow. Is there a chance you would be available for dinner? Until the official doula shows up, I'd like to keep her occupied."

"Of course, dear. I already made a vegetarian lasagna that I can bring over, so you don't have to fix dinner. And I've been putting a few new mystery books under the counter to bring for her to read."

"I'll just toss a salad then."

"And I'll bring a loaf of sourdough with the casserole. Done and done." Meadow's eyes brightened.

But then her smile vanished as she glanced toward the door. She leaned across the counter to whisper, "I think someone is listening in on our conversation." She gestured with her head. "Turn around slowly and you can see for yourself."

Olivia patted the counter with one hand, pivoting gradually toward the place where Meadow had indicated. As soon as Bella Grey caught her watching, she glanced down at her phone.

"How are you?" Olivia said in a loud voice.

"Just fine," mumbled Bella. She headed toward the sofa,

plopping herself down in the middle. She stared across the room at Olivia and then looked away.

Olivia turned back to Meadow. "So only one Grey sibling today. They usually travel in packs. What's going on?"

"That one has been here off and on for the past three days. She sits on the sofa and looks at her phone, then she heads back across the street."

Olivia felt a tingle at the back of her neck. "Does she work at the computers?"

"No, but she may be using our WiFi connection on her smart phone."

"That's true. So why does she hang out here? Any ideas?"

Meadow leaned over the counter, lowering her voice. "I'm thinking she's supposed to be looking for a job but hides here instead. I've seen many teenagers over the years avoid lots of work by going to the library. No one ever questions their reason."

Makes some sense. Blair and Brandon are working. It's Bella's turn. "Keep an eye on that one," she told Meadow. "In the meanwhile I'm heading over to the constabulary."

"Officer Jets has not found Beats Malone's killer." Meadow nodded, her eyes looking serious. "Two weeks is her usual window for figuring things out and bringing a culprit to justice."

Olivia smiled. "Maybe I can give her a hand. See you later."

Once outside the library, she stopped before taking steps toward the constabulary. The lime-green VW was parked next to the curb. Blair Grey sat behind the wheel. Olivia hurried across the street to tap on the driver's side window.

"What do you want?" Blair asked. "I'm going home; I've been working since six o'clock."

Olivia blurted out, "I was wondering if you're planning a

memorial for your father and mother. Some of us would like to pay our respects."

Blair's jaw dropped and her eyes widened with surprise. *She didn't know I figured out that Beats was her father.*

Olivia plunged right in with more information. "When I googled Beats Malone, I saw in his bio that he had three children. Then you told me your ages and I put things together. I was not completely convinced at first, but that day at the library, I heard you tell Meadow about the name on your driver's license. Then it all became clear. Your last name isn't Grey, it's Malone."

"I am not a Malone!" Blair slammed her fist on the steering wheel. She rolled up her window, shoving a key into the ignition.

Olivia stepped back as the engine started up. The VW lurched out of the parking space. *So I pushed her button. Can't wait to tell Janis.*

CHAPTER TWENTY-EIGHT

Brad sat at his place behind the desk. "Hey, Brad," she greeted him.

"Hey, Olivia," he responded, not looking away from the computer.

I'm not going to make idle chitchat.

Waving her entry card in the air like a conquering hero, she slapped it against the pad by the door, which instantly slid open.

She shoved the card key in her purse with a shrug.

Olivia stood at Janis's open office door.

"Have a seat," Janis said as soon as she looked up.

Olivia sat in her usual place, the chair across the desk.

Janis scowled at Olivia. "Why are you grinning?" She shook her head. "Actually I don't care." She shoved her iPad across the desk. "Check out the forensics on the knife."

Olivia read the notes quickly and then looked back up at Janis. "Are you surprised at any of the findings?"

"I had hoped they'd find fingerprints," admitted Jets.

"But they picked up Beats's DNA from the blood caught under the wood handle."

"So even if the evidence doesn't point to the killer, we did find the weapon we were looking for. There's something about that knife that puzzles me," Jets added.

"What's that?"

"When we searched the Grey home, I saw a set of knives that looked exactly like the one we found buried under the sequoia. They were all lined up in one of those wooden blocks that people set on their counters. The block had the name of a fancy kitchen shop stamped on the side, one of those places in Beverly Hills." Janis shook her head. "Anyway, I digress, the expensive knives looked sharp and dangerous, with long blades." Jets shuddered. "Not your average steak knife, I can tell you."

"I didn't think more about the knives because all of the slots were filled." She glared at Olivia. "Not one missing," she added. When Olivia didn't respond, she kept talking. "I stopped looking for the weapon after that, until the mayor found it under the sequoia. Anyway, the knife we did find was wiped down." She took a breath, continuing to think out loud.

"Everything in me says one of those Grey kids killed Beats. But they have a clear alibi in the pub; I mean, you were an eye witness along with Arlo. So I have nothing that will stick." Jets grimaced. "I hate it when that happens."

"Remember that night when you and Cookie saw Blair Grey sitting on a bench at two in the morning?" Olivia asked.

"Go on..."

"She was playing catch with Mayor Maguire, at least that's what you told me."

"And playing fetch with a dog means what exactly?" Jets's forehead wrinkled.

"Blair must be familiar with the park at night. Maybe she buried that knife when he was watching." Olivia took a deep breath and kept talking. "He watched her and thought it was a new game of fetch."

When Jets looked skeptical, Olivia continued to explain her theory. "Sometimes he does that with me. I bury a ball in a pile of leaves and he fetches it the next day, when he's ready to have another round of play. I think M&M sees his life as one long game of fetch. A ball, a frisbee, a knife; I've buried eggplants that he's dug up and brought back. He's not picky about what he fetches."

Olivia paused, then finished her explanation. "Don't you see, that's what he did with me. When I watched him in the park, he remembered something was buried, so he dug it up."

Jets leaned back in her chair, her arms behind her head. "On the one hand, relying on the antics of a labradoodle may not be the grounds for a good investigation." Her eyes narrowed. "But on the other hand, you can't discount the mayor of Lily Rock just because he's a dog. He's brought us many a clue in the past. Remember that boot?"

Olivia grinned. "M&M pointed out the clue that changed the course of the investigation. We solved the case."

"You mean the Lily Rock constabulary solved the case. I'm not giving Mayor Maguire credit for our bust. He's already too popular."

Olivia suppressed a grin. Janis stared at the corner over her head, not speaking. So Olivia took the lead. "I asked Blair Grey when the memorial service would be."

"You did what?" Her arms came down as she leaned over the desk. "Just when I count you out as a wimp, you do something like this. Step up to that spoiled entitled young woman and make her squirm. How did she respond to your inquiry?"

"Oh, she got really angry." Olivia smiled. "In fact, she drove away so fast she nearly ran over my foot. Let's just say she was surprised. Very surprised. Probably because I knew she was a Malone not a Grey."

"Yeah, poor her. But you've given me an idea." Jets grabbed the iPad. "Assuming she isn't planning a service for Beats or her mother, I think we could go ahead and plan one ourselves. There's nothing stopping us. Both Beats and Bianca died in Lily Rock. We can spin this as a good-for-the-town kind of event—even if the family doesn't want to honor the dead, the town does. I'll get Cooks on a reception and have my assistant plan a program."

"Bulletin," Olivia interrupted, "they call them bulletins for memorial services. Maybe we need someone to preside too, just to make everything official."

"Whatever," Jets growled. "We can pin up invitations around town and post it on the Lily Rock Facebook page. Done and done. We'll get a few people. There's always someone who just loves a good send-off memorial."

"I'll let Hello Age know," offered Olivia. "In fact, we may be able to use their chapel for the service. I can also ask if they have an officiant on call. Want me to check?"

"I do not," Jets commanded. "I have my assistant Brad to do those tasks. You go home and wait for my next direction." She tapped her fingers nervously on the desk. "This is finally going to get interesting."

"So what do you hope to accomplish by holding your own memorial service?"

"That's the thing, Nancy Drew. Those kids have not seen their parents in the same room for many years. They have their stories about Dad, how he's a deadbeat and all. Frankly I'm tired of hearing their woe-is-me-I'm-a-poor-kid-whose-father-abandoned-me stories.

Jets shrugged. "The Malone aka Grey family feels more like *Lord of the Flies* than *The Three Musketeers* to me. If I'm lucky, they will turn on each other and we'll find the one who killed the deadbeat dad."

"Putting emotional pressure on them may work," Olivia mused. "But you're forgetting they all had alibis."

"Alibis maybe, but with more facts we can break that wide open."

Olivia took a minute to consider Janis's plan. "How about I take your idea, putting pressure on the Grey family, and raise you one? Can we get Ashley a day pass to attend the memorial?"

"She's not at summer camp," Jets snorted. "She's in a minimum-security prison until her trial comes up. But I'll see what I can do. How about I arrange an interview with just the two of you, one-to-one? You can sing her songs and work your magic. Maybe she'll spill more information. I know she's holding back."

"She did kill Bianca," Olivia said. "That's a foregone conclusion because she confessed."

"But she never explained her reason."

"She admitted to being angry," Olivia said.

"I'm angry all the time." Jets shrugged. "That doesn't explain why a woman would bash another person over the head with a skateboard."

Olivia nodded.

Jets rubbed her hands together. "Okay then, back to planning the memorial. I'll get Brad to call Hello Age. I'll call the office over at the jail in the desert and see about getting Ashley a pass to hang out for an interview with you and to attend the service."

Satisfied that the conversation was over, Olivia stood up. "See you later." Then she added, "I have to practice a song on the autoharp."

Relishing the sound of Janis Jets's guffaw, Olivia made her way out of the office.

* * *

Sage smiled at Olivia. "So I'm your fancy racehorse." Her back rested against the nest of pillows. A pink flush had returned to her cheeks. "I think I'm going to like this treatment." She sighed as Olivia handed her a glass of cool lemonade.

"Okay, that's enough, Seabiscuit," mumbled Janis Jets. "I came by to see how you are, not to wait on you hand and foot."

Sage fluttered her fingers in the air. "Oh, I don't need you," she said contentedly. "I have Olivia and Michael and a parade of women wanting to be my doula. Maybe I'd better get ready for the interviews." She mocked Jets with a flutter of eyelashes. "Do my nails need polish? A new color for fall, perhaps..."

Olivia laughed. *Sage hasn't been this playful in months.* "It's good to see you're adapting to this new way of being," Olivia said dryly.

Sage held up her hand. "Does that mean you'll be doing my nails soon? The cuticles are very dry." She pretended to pout.

"Oh, give me a break," grumbled Janis. "I've had enough of you, Seabiscuit. I'm outta here." She turned to Olivia. "Be sure to let me know who you hire to be the nurse to Miss Fancy Pants here. I want to do a quick background check on your choice."

The mood in the room shifted. Olivia glanced at Sage to see her reaction.

"Why are you so worried about my doula?" Sage said immediately, her voice sounding anxious.

"Let's just say I don't trust any strangers to Lily Rock, so long as I have this open investigation."

Sage's eyes clouded over.

Olivia stepped in. "None of that!" she insisted. "Keep your investigation away from my thoroughbred racehorse from now on. I'm handling this and will do my own background check. She's training for a big race and you can't distract her with the trivial details of your work problems."

Jets heaved a sigh. "I think we've about exhausted this metaphor. See you people later. I have work to do." Janis headed to the front, her footsteps clomping against the wood floor. The doorbell rang.

Olivia left her chair to chase after Janis. She found her standing in front of their open door.

"What are you doing here?" Jets's body blocked the unexpected visitor.

Once Olivia walked closer she saw Blair Grey standing outside. Blair had changed clothes since she last saw her outside the library. Black slacks, a crisp white blouse, and her hair pulled back into a bun.

"I'm here to interview for the doula job," Blair said.

"Don't you already have a job at Thyme Out?" Olivia asked.

"Are you a qualified nurse?" Jets said, scowling. "What makes you think you can interview to be a doula?"

Olivia stood to the right of Janis.

"I heard they were hiring so I thought I'd just show up and apply," came Blair's snippy response.

"And I'm telling you, they've already filled the position," lied Jets.

Olivia faced Blair. "Where did you hear we were hiring?"

A flush ran up the young woman's neck. "I overheard you talking to the librarian."

"I assume you have a doula's certification and a list of references?" Jets interjected.

"I don't need references. This is Lily Rock. Everybody just does as they want here. At least that's what everyone tells me. So you're going to turn me away?"

Olivia cleared her throat. *She seems convinced that wanting a job is the same as qualifying for one.* Instead of confronting Blair's false assumption, Olivia explained as patiently as she could. "I have people interviewing for the position with references, credentials, and years of experience. Some are even registered nurses as well as doulas. I'll interview them and then if I don't find someone who is suitable, I'll give you a call."

Blair glared at Olivia.

She's so convinced that she's right. It's alarming!

"Never mind," Blair said sharply. "I'll find something better." She turned and stomped toward her car.

"It's hard to feel sorry for her when she's so nasty," Jets said. "That's coming from a woman who has her own share of bitter and resentful opinions."

Jets continued her evaluation. "All three of the Greys act like a well-oiled team of self-righteous individuals with no patience for anyone who disagrees."

"Have you heard of body dysmorphia?" Olivia asked.

"What does that have to do with the Greys?"

"Take the same idea and apply it more broadly. The Greys have a dysmorphic image of themselves, starting with who they really are. They act like a close-knit family who have nothing but time and money on their hands. But the reality of the situation is they are a dysfunctional family living in a rundown rental house, unemployed, with no real plans for the future."

She watched as the VW Beetle drove up the driveway toward the main road.

"And that, Nancy Drew, may be the crux of our investigation," Jets agreed. "Who the Grey family is as opposed to who they think they are. I gotta go now."

"I have to check up on the patient and get ready for the interviews," added Olivia.

Jets smiled. "Tell Seabiscuit I want to do background checks before she hires anyone."

CHAPTER TWENTY-NINE

The following morning Sage sat against her nest of pillows, a cup of tea on the table next to her bed. Olivia sat in the easy chair close by, a mug of coffee in her hand. "So which one of the women felt like the perfect choice of doula?"

"I liked the last one. She's also a nurse and she lives in Lily Rock."

"That would be Pearl Overman," Olivia said. "I liked her too. She seemed calm and well mannered."

Sage burst out laughing. "A good fit for a nervous show pony like me."

Olivia chuckled. *She's a lot less jumpy since she confessed.* "So do you want to handle Pearl's employment details? I'll get a contract from the internet that she can sign since she doesn't work for an agency. Then I'll run it past Janis for a quick background check."

"All right..." Sage conceded, putting down her cup. "With that settled, or nearly so, I have another question. About Beats. Maybe you can help me figure out the one thing I never got to ask him."

Olivia's heart quickened. *Finally we can talk.* "What was that?"

"He never said how Bianca found out about his move to Lily Rock. I mean, she got the jump on him and brought her beehive here before he could get a job, let alone find a place to live."

"That is curious. Did he post something on social media that he was interested in moving to Lily Rock or that he met someone from here?"

"I never looked." Sage's mouth closed in a tight line. "I suppose he had accounts. They're probably managed professionally. He was kind of a big name in music circles."

"Arlo told me the same. On the day I was waiting for Beats to show up at the pub, I googled him out of curiosity. I didn't see anything about a family in Lily Rock, even on his Facebook. I had to dig deeper, into a ten-year-old article, before I found out he had three children. He could have taken personal information down. I know people who hire professionals to keep their accounts really clean and up to date."

"Maybe he did the social media cleanup after it was too late," Sage suggested. "When Bianca moved up here, he may have realized his mistake and taken his post down right away."

"One post about his future plans turned out to be a horrible mistake. I mean, he's dead and so is she." Olivia watched as Sage's eyes filled with tears.

"Nothing we can do about all of that," Olivia said briskly. "Your job is to rest and eat and get ready..."

"For the big race," Sage finished her sentence. Then she added, "Being pampered was fun for the first day, but now I'm feeling a bit sorry for myself."

Olivia picked up Sage's empty cup. "Nothing a nice afternoon nap won't cure. Plus Meadow's coming for dinner. She's bringing some books from the library."

"Mom is coming to dinner?"

She wants her mom. Of course she does.

"She's bringing her vegetarian lasagna and a fresh loaf of sourdough."

Sage smiled. "Okay then, that sounds like something I can look forward to." She looked around the room, her gaze coming back to Olivia. "I'm so grateful to you and Michael. I'm sorry I'm crying at the drop of a hat. I suppose it's gonna be like this for a while, a bit up and down."

"Of course it is, honey. You're making a baby. A mysterious form woven into the depth of your being. Plus you've been thrown an emotional curveball with Beats."

She looked closely at Sage's face, then continued to chat. "Here's my plan. I think one special visitor a day may be great for your spirits."

Sage smoothed her hands over the comforter. *Considering she's been given bed rest for the next few months, she's handling it quite well. And then she's grieving Beats's death, maybe more than his entire family put together. Even though she only knew him for a short time.*

"I forgot to tell you," Olivia kept talking, hoping to fill the silence, "Janis and I think that Beats and Bianca deserve a memorial service as a decent send-off. It looks like their children aren't interested in making the plans, so we're going to arrange a town event. You can watch on your laptop."

Sage tilted her head to one side. "That would be good," she finally said. "I am collecting stories to tell baby when they are old enough to ask about their father. If I could say I knew him a short time and then say that Lily Rock threw him a memorial service to say goodbye, well that would give baby something to remember." She patted the covers over her belly.

"You can leave out the part about Beats's ex-wife," added Olivia.

"I can improvise with that part of the story," mused Sage. "It bothers me that I don't feel safe talking to his kids; they will be baby's half siblings. They're just so angry."

"Janis and I did some research," Olivia admitted. "She got the court documents for the dissolution of his marriage to Bianca. He was awarded joint custody. According to the court-appointed arbitration documents, Beats was very consistent. Every other week the children lived with him."

Sage's jaw set. "He was such a kind person and genuinely excited about our baby. That deadbeat things sounds off to me."

Olivia shrugged. "It's as if they want to stay mad at him." She looked closely at Sage's tired expression. *Time for my little pony to have a nap.*

"How about you get a nap," Olivia prompted. "I'll take these cups away and leave you for a bit. If I go anywhere, I'll let you know."

Sage needed no more urging. Snuggling into her pillow, her hand pulled the comforter close to her chin. Olivia walked quietly out of the room, closing the door from behind.

"You're napping too?" She found Mayor Maguire stretched out on the sofa, his paws in the air, his head back. His lips fluttered as he emitted short woofs, eyes shut tight.

The snoring stopped as he flipped onto his belly. He leaned his chin on the sofa cushion, his tail wagged a greeting. "Good boy," she told him, walking toward the kitchen.

Once she rinsed the dishes, she dried her hands and reached for her cell phone to call Janis Jets.

"Hello," came a gruff reply.

"It's me."

"I can see my screen ID. What do you want? It's my day off."

"Something Sage and I talked about this morning, about

Beats and his children. It's bothering me." When Janis didn't express any interest, Olivia continued to explain. "The discrepancy in stories seems really off. The court doesn't describe a deadbeat dad. Could that be a clue, the discrepancy, that we're not looking at more closely?"

"Are you done?" A yawning sound filled her ear.

She insisted again, "So you don't think that matters, that the stories are different?"

Jets giggled. "Get it? Beats is a deadbeat dad? Nice one."

"Have you been listening to me? This isn't funny. You were there. Blair showed up on our doorstep asking for a job. What if she knows about Sage's baby? She may try something, to hurt Sage. She's angry and mean. I wouldn't put it past her."

"You think I haven't considered that?" Jets's voice grew serious. "I've got your house under surveillance. Plus Cooks and I are watching the three Bs from Cayenne and Arlo's deck."

Olivia heard a voice in the background. "More coffee?" It sounded like Arlo.

"Who's on surveillance at our house?"

"My capable assistant. I'm paying him overtime, so don't go out and offer him a sandwich or something. He's working for another couple of hours."

"Brad's our surveillance?" Olivia couldn't keep the indignation from her voice. "The mayor is sleeping on my sofa. He's more capable. I bet Brad is right outside now smoking weed behind the house."

"Stay with your girl, okay? I put Brad there for some insurance. Goodbye," Janis said in a clipped voice.

Olivia sat down at the kitchen table to consider her situation. *I'm here with Sage and the mayor. Michael is up at the construction site, hopefully his eye is on Brandon. Janis and Cookie are on the lookout for the Greys at their house.*

DEADBEAT DAD

Everything sounds normal, so why am I feeling so jumpy?

A brisk knock came from the kitchen door. Through the glass she could see Brad standing outside.

When he saw her, he smiled and tried the doorknob. Finding it locked, he called out, "Hey, Olivia."

"Hey, Brad." She came closer to open the door and let him inside.

He walked past her into the kitchen. "Why's the door locked?"

"I'm taking every precaution to keep Sage safe."

"Okay then, you should know I've been staking out your house." He ran his hand through his hair.

"So I just heard," she said. "Want some coffee?"

"Sure, that would be good." He pulled out a chair and sat down.

She filled a clean mug and set it in front of him on the table.

"Thanks," Brad said in a happy voice. He took a sip and then put down the mug abruptly. "Oh, I almost forgot. Janis says I'm supposed to keep an eye out for a lime-green VW Beetle."

Olivia nodded. "Aren't you supposed to keep the Grey family away from our house?"

"I guess." He scratched his head. "Why is that exactly?"

Maybe Janis doesn't tell her capable assistant everything. Maybe she just gives him orders to keep him busy and out of her hair.

"You'll have to ask your boss," Olivia said. "Anything else? I have work to do."

"Kind of." He took another sip. "I saw that VW Bug yesterday at the dump."

Her impatience slipped away. She leaned forward. "What did you see exactly?"

"I didn't tell Janis because I didn't know she was interested in that particular vehicle until this morning."

"Tell me what you saw at the dump."

"Okay, so the older Grey girl, she's pretty hot you know, she had a box in the back seat of her car. I went over to ask her if she needed help. She smiled at me and so one thing led to another and I spent the next half hour chatting her up. And then I helped her with the box."

"Did you look inside?"

"I kinda did. I peeked 'cause I was curious. You know, the boss taught me to keep my eyes and ears open just in case I want to be a police investigator one day."

I can't believe I'm keeping a straight face. Brad an investigator. Come on, Janis!

She inhaled deeply to keep from biting Brad's head off.

"So there were old papers and lots of photos," he said, looked pretty pleased with himself.

Olivia's head jerked up. "Photos?"

"Yeah, old bent-up ones. My mom has a drawerful at home just like that." He beamed. "Some of me and my old girlfriends." Brad blushed. "I guess you don't want to see those."

You guessed that right, buddy.

"So Brad," she softened her voice, "do you know how often the trash company picks up the full bins and replaces them with empty ones?"

"First and third Tuesday of the month," he said with certainty. "I know that because my garage has a connection with the dump. We have a lot of recyclables and we need to get them dropped off on certain days."

Before Olivia could digest Brad's information, her cell phone pinged.

A text from Janis Jets.

VW on the move. We're following. Headed your way.

She dropped the phone on the table, her heart beating fast. "Janis says the VW is coming our way. Do you want to stay in the house or go outside?"

Brad glanced nervously out the window over the sink. He shoved his chair under the table. "Don't tell Officer Jets that I stopped in. She'll be mad."

He rushed out of the door, forgetting to close it behind him. She checked the lock on the doorknob and then shoved the door closed, testing it one more time.

She walked back to the sink. Staring out the window, she saw Brad drive away. *I guess his surveillance is over for now.*

Olivia heard voices coming from the front of the house.

"Bork, bork, bork."

The mayor's incessant barks raised the hair on her neck. *I wonder who's out there? Do I answer the door or just pretend I'm not home...*

She walked from the kitchen toward Mayor Maguire. He stood on the sofa, head over the back, his nose pointing to the front door. "I got this," she said quietly in his ear.

He looked at her and shook his head as if to say *no you don't*. Then, turning his head aside, he issued a series of low growls.

Olivia walked closer to the door. She looked through the peephole. Bella Grey stood outside, looking grim and impatient. She held a cell phone in her hand.

"Bork, bork, bork!"

"Shush, Mayor," she told the dog. He jumped over the back of the sofa, landing on all four paws.

"I know you're in there," shouted Bella. "Open the door!"

CHAPTER THIRTY

Olivia opened the door cautiously. Her eyes rested on the agitated face of Bella Grey.

"Where is she?" Bella pushed past her, walking inside the house.

"Bork, bork, bork." *The mayor doesn't like her tone of voice either.* He stood next to Olivia, the "grrrr" coming from the back of his throat.

Bella froze, alarm on her face.

The mayor moved closer. His tail did not wave. He stood between Olivia and Bella, issuing a continuous stream of warning barks.

Olivia held out her arm. "Maguire. I've got this," she told the dog.

He gave a quick glance in her direction. He shook his head, the tags on his collar jingling. Then with a huff, he sat.

"No more barking," Olivia added.

The dog glared at her, turning away to look at Bella.

Bella spoke to the dog. "It's okay, doggie. I'm looking for my sister." Her singsong voice irritated Olivia even more.

The mayor growled from the back of his throat. He stood on all fours.

"Sit," Olivia told him.

He stopped growling but stayed standing.

Olivia turned to face Bella. "If you step outside, he will feel less protective."

Bella took backward steps, without turning her back on Mayor Maguire. She stepped through the open door.

"Bork," he said. Olivia stepped alongside Bella. A moment passed. Shaking his head, the tags jingled and Mayor Maguire lay in the house, facing the open doorway.

Bella did not meet Olivia's stare. She scrolled on her cell phone, eyes darting from message to message.

"Who are you looking for?" Olivia asked.

The phone disappeared into Bella's back pocket. Her eyes narrowed. "I'm looking for my sister, Blair. She said she was coming by here because she got a job as a doula."

"I thought she had a job at Thyme Out."

"She hates it there. Reminds her of Mom. So she's looking for other work, at least that's what she told me."

"When did she tell you that?"

"This morning."

"So she failed to report that we already lined up viable candidates with experience and that she wasn't one of them?"

Bella stepped closer, her face an inch away from Olivia's.

Okay, I'm done with this!

Olivia stepped aside as Mayor Maguire lunged past her. "Bork, bork, bork, bork, bork," came his warning.

The dog shoved his way between Olivia and Bella.

"Sit," Olivia tried again.

Bella, wide-eyed, turned and ran. Mayor Maguire took off right behind.

"If you stop, he won't chase you," Olivia shouted.

Bella took one last step. Maguire sat. "Bork, bork," he added.

"She can't do this to me," Bella wailed.

Olivia used the palm of her hand as a signal. She walked around the dog to stand in front of Bella. "Who can't do this to you?"

"My stupid sister!" Bella shouted.

Mayor Maguire cocked his head to the side.

Olivia cleared her throat. "Blair could be anywhere, but I know she's not here."

"You don't know anything. She's playing hard to get. Not the first time she's ghosted me."

"How long has it been since you last spoke?"

"Since this morning," Bella spat.

Olivia tried again. "Ghosting doesn't mean for two hours."

"Don't get technical with me. That's what my family does. We're very close." Bella pulled out her phone and stared at her screen again.

During the interaction, Mayor Maguire stood on all fours. Feeling a nudge at her knee, she looked down. "No treats, buddy."

His tail drooped with disappointment.

"Are you holding my sister hostage?" Bella said in a harsh accusatory tone.

"I'm not holding anyone hostage. I'm at home not because of your sister but because of mine. She's not feeling well and I don't want her upset."

"You have a sister?"

The girl's eyes darted from her screen to Mayor Maguire and back again. *She doesn't know that I have a sister... Maybe Sage isn't in any danger.*

Bella's jaw stuck out. "Did Blair say where she was going when she left your house?"

A familiar truck rumbled down the driveway before Olivia could speak. Gravel spit out from under the tires. Janis Jets jumped from the passenger side. She slammed the door shut as Cookie sat behind the wheel. Janis's eyes took in the scene.

"What's going on here?" Jets demanded.

Bella didn't respond.

Mayor Maguire wagged his tail.

"Bella is looking for Blair," Olivia explained.

Jets raised her eyebrows.

Bella held up her cell phone. "I'm afraid something's happened to her."

Jets cleared her throat. "Maybe she's getting her nails done or is having coffee with a friend..."

"She doesn't have any friends. Just her family!" Bella shouted.

"Doesn't she ever leave the house or go away for a few days?"

"Not without me, she doesn't. We do everything together."

"You need to calm down," Jets said. "Give me that phone." She grabbed it from Bella, taking advantage of her surprise. Jets stepped back to look at the screen.

"Give me that!" cried Bella. She lunged toward Janis, her hand raised.

"Back off," Jets warned. "Remember the last time you lost your temper."

Bella dropped her arm, screaming at the top of her voice, "Give me my property now!"

Janis carefully scrolled with her thumb, looking intently at the screen. "You have a tracker installed," Jets said quietly.

"My mother insisted. She wanted to know where we were all the time and she had to do that because of Beats. He could turn up and try something."

"What kind of something?" Olivia asked. Had Beats tried to abduct them?

"Beats Malone was a deadbeat, a horrible person. He did everything he could to turn us against our mom. He made so much money and never gave us a dime. He cheated on us and hooked up with other women." Her singsong voice sounded as if she'd memorized it for a play. Bella's face hardened into a look of disdain.

Jets handed the phone back to the distraught Bella. "Sounds like your sister wants some me time," she commented dryly. "That's not an offense which requires police assistance."

"She can't do that. We're sisters." Bella shrugged with frustration.

"I can look in town for her, on an unofficial basis," Jet offered. "You have the tracker. It looks like Blair's phone has been turned off. But we can drive through Lily Rock and have a look. It's Sunday so the library is closed. Thyme Out is open. Have you tried there?"

"She doesn't like going there. It reminds her of Mom."

"That doesn't mean Blair won't get herself a cup of coffee on Sunday as she adjusts to her loss."

As Janis continued to reason with Bella, Olivia reached down to pat Mayor Maguire's head. She waited for a pause in the conversation to say, "I have to go inside now."

"You do that," Jets said. "I'll help Bella find Blair."

Mayor Maguire accompanied her, walking to the front door.

She overheard Janis ask, "What about your brother? Could Blair be with him?"

Once the door had been closed, the dog followed her into the kitchen. Turning to the cupboard, she found a can of tuna and some sweet pickles. She placed both on the counter.

Michael's name flashed on her phone screen.

DEADBEAT DAD

She put down a knife to answer. "Hello."

"I don't suppose you could bring lunch up to the house," he asked.

"I'm making Sage tuna sandwiches right now. I'll make some more but I can't leave her."

"Is everything okay?"

"I've had a visit from both Grey sisters. One wanted a job and the other wanted to talk to her sister. Those girls are strangely attached at the hip."

"It's the cell phone," commented Michael sardonically. "I'd call you every fifteen minutes except you'd think I was a clingy boyfriend."

"Can't have that." Olivia smiled.

"You don't, do you? Think I'm clingy?"

She thought of his broad shoulders and keen intellect. The easy way he gave her space when she needed it, and the calm way he pulled her close when she'd had enough of her own whirling thoughts. "I never think you're clingy. Clingy is another word for control. I've had that and I know what it feels like. You're not that guy."

"And here I thought we were teasing," he said dryly.

"I've had a very odd morning," she admitted.

"Don't worry. I've got the other Grey kid up here at the site."

Olivia's heart quickened. "Brandon's with you?"

"I'd have come home earlier but he's here with a bottle of vodka, fast asleep in our almost drywalled dining room."

"Did you try to wake him?"

"Oh I tried but got nowhere."

"You don't sound very worried."

"This isn't my first drunk guy hiding out at a construction site. I didn't want to leave him alone. He apparently walked up here. I don't see the VW. So I'll just hang around until he

239

makes some noise. I'll give him a ride home and then be there for that tuna sandwich."

"Janis is with Bella. They're looking for Blair. Maybe you could text her and she'll pick up Brandon."

"These three orphans are becoming Lily Rock's problem," Michael commented.

"They have no coping skills and panic when they're not connected to each other," she observed. Olivia stopped abruptly. "I think Sage may be awake. Love you, gotta go."

"Love you," Michael said. Then the phone clicked off.

When Olivia brought in the tray of sandwiches and lemonade, Sage wasn't in her bed. The sound of running water came from the bathroom. Olivia placed the tray on the table and then straightened the sheets. By the time she'd plumped all the pillows, Sage returned.

"You look more rested."

Sage had changed her pajamas and brushed her hair, which fell softly over her shoulders. Her eyes looked large and calm, the dark circles nearly gone. She sat on the edge of the bed, looking toward the tray of sandwiches. "I'm hungry," she admitted.

Olivia felt a surge of relief. *It's working. The bed rest is helping her and that makes me happy.* She waited for Sage to sit back against the pillows before pulling up the comforter. "Your back okay?" she asked.

"Just fine. Stop fussing." Sage whinnied like a horse, letting her lips flap. "This racehorse is hungry. What's for lunch?"

"Your favorite, tuna and sweet pickles." She set the tray on the bed so that Sage could easily reach for the food.

Do I tell her about Blair and Bella...

Sage took a bite of sandwich and then reached for the

other half. Olivia lifted a sandwich for herself, sitting back in the chair. "More lemonade?" she asked as Sage swallowed.

"I'm good with this." She held up her half-full glass. "I thought I heard people out front."

Olivia avoided her gaze. "It was nothing. Janis and Cookie came by. They're gone now. Michael will be home soon."

"Does he always work on Sundays?"

"He likes to check in at the construction site every day. Usually he doesn't stay this long, but something must have come up." Olivia looked up at her sister, hoping she'd successfully avoided what could have been an emotionally charged conversation with half-truths.

"I hear gravel crunching," Sage said, nodding toward the window facing the front of the house.

"I'll be right back." Leaving Sage's door ajar, she walked toward the front.

Olivia opened the door quickly expecting to see Michael. To her surprise he wasn't alone. He grinned, nodding to the man standing next to him.

A disheveled Brandon dropped his chin to his chest. Wobbling from side to side, he fell limply against Michael's shoulder for support.

"Are there enough sandwiches?" Michael asked. He gripped Brandon by the shoulders, ushering him into the house.

Olivia closed the door and locked it securely.

All three Greys at my front door in one day. How have I gone from keeping them away from Sage to fixing Brandon a sandwich?

CHAPTER THIRTY-ONE

Michael ushered Brandon through the great room into the kitchen. He used his foot to pull out a chair at the table. Brandon fell into the seat, nearly toppling to the floor. "Take it easy," Michael told him. He propped Brandon's feet in front of his body for balance. "How about some coffee and then..."

Brandon stopped to raise his nose into the air. "I smell fish. Not tuna fish! It makes me want to..." He began to cough at the back of his throat.

"Okay, no tuna, not a problem." Olivia turned away, feeling her stomach clench. *I'm going to reflex vomit if he keeps this up.*

Her cell phone pinged.

Sage had texted. What's going on out there?

Olivia texted back.

Michael came home with one of his employees who isn't feeling well. Do you need something?

Nope. Just curious.

Olivia put the phone on the counter and then filled a glass with water. She turned around to face Brandon. Propped close to the table, he rested his head on his arms. Michael smiled at her. "Is that for me?"

"No." She placed the glass in front of Brandon. "Drink this water and I'll make some coffee." When he didn't raise his head, she glared at Michael. "You brought him here. Why don't you make the coffee? I'm going to check on Sage."

She left the room feeling frustrated. *He knows I'm trying to keep that family away from her. Why did he bring Brandon home?*

Olivia found Sage reading a book.

"Michael's making coffee and I thought I'd hang out with you for a bit. How are you feeling?"

Sage looked over her reading glasses. "I'm fine so long as I stay in bed. I don't even feel queasy."

"You look good."

"I'm really enjoying this book." Sage's eyes went back to the pages.

Olivia took the hint. She gathered the lunch dishes before leaving the room. Michael's voice floating in from the kitchen. "You drank that entire bottle of vodka?"

"My sister helped," came the sullen reply.

Olivia put the dishes on the counter. She stood beside the table looking at the two men. She moved the glass of water closer to Brandon's hand. "Drink this. I'll get some crackers. Which sister did you party with?"

"Not a party exactly. More like we were bored." His hand bumped against the glass, nearly spilling water over the side. He did not take a drink. "Blair drank most of the bottle," he said as an afterthought.

"Bella was here looking for her," Olivia said. "She was worried."

"Bella worries about everything. She thinks she's taken the

place of our mother and gets to boss us around." Brandon viewed the glass of water skeptically. He finally reached out to pick up the glass and took a sip.

Olivia waited to see if he'd throw up. When he took another drink, she walked to the cupboard. "Coffee's ready," she told Michael over her shoulder.

She slid a package of saltine crackers toward Brandon. "Here, try these."

He looked away.

"So I figured," Michael said, "Brandon could take a shower and get some rest at my house. Then we can call Janis and see if she's found Blair."

Olivia glared at him. She shook her head vehemently.

Michael rubbed his chin. "Or I could take Brandon back to his place," he said brightly.

Olivia nodded.

"Can I have a beer?" Brandon asked.

"You've got to be kidding." Olivia frowned at him. "No more booze. Get some of those crackers down and off you go." She heard the flare in her voice. *I'm overreacting.*

It's about protecting Sage, but there's another reason. She looked from Michael to Brandon and cleared her throat. "I don't tolerate alcohol abuse in my home. I'm not a free zone where you can just drop in and get sober. I'm a recovering alcoholic."

"Oh damn," Michael exclaimed.

He didn't think about that, Olivia realized.

"Come on, Brandon. Out you go. This is Olivia's house and she isn't in the mood."

Michael mouthed, "I'm sorry," as he stood and then yanked Brandon to his feet.

"It's not my fault that I drink," Brandon wailed. "Beats

DEADBEAT DAD

Malone was a deadbeat, a horrible person. He did everything he could to turn us against our mom. He made so much money and never gave us a dime. He cheated on us and hooked up with other women."

Olivia's jaw dropped. *Word for word what Bella told me earlier.*

Attempting to gain balance, Brandon stumbled, nearly falling into Michael.

Michael took him by the shoulders. "Okay, buddy, stay in an upright position. I'm going to drive you home right now."

Brandon looked around the kitchen. "You could make me some eggs," he suggested. "I'd eat those with some toast."

"I am not your cook," Olivia said firmly.

Brandon's chin began to quiver. *He's lost his mother, father, and his girlfriend's in jail. Now comes the part where he feels remorse for his behavior.* She sighed deeply, looking toward Michael.

"Okay, you take him to your place and clean him up. I'll make some eggs and toast. When you get back he can eat, but then he's got to go."

Michael didn't waste time. "Come on, we're heading that way." He gestured with his head toward the back door. "Give us half an hour."

Once outside, Michael moved Brandon down the path toward his old house. Arm around the younger man's shoulders, they took slow steps.

Olivia picked up the phone to text Janis Jets.

I have Brandon here. Found Blair yet?

When Jets didn't answer, she walked to the refrigerator to pull out a carton of eggs. By the time she'd warmed a frying pan her phone pinged.

No Blair.

Olivia cracked the first egg.

* * *

As promised, Michael and Brandon returned in half an hour. Brandon smelled like patchouli soap, his hair slickly combed. Michael looked grim.

As Brandon slumped into a kitchen chair, Michael walked to the sink. He spoke in a low voice. "Sorry about that. He's cleaned up and not slurring his words. I hope that helps." He looked to the frying pan filled with scrambled eggs. "I can take care of feeding him if you want to leave us."

Olivia half smiled. "I actually am curious about a few things. Maybe I can get him to talk while he eats."

Michael reached for a plate.

Olivia sat down at the table. She looked closely at Brandon, who shifted his gaze. "I'm sorry if I sounded angry earlier," Olivia began. "I know you've had a terrible couple of weeks. Plus you must be worried about your girlfriend."

"Not really," he said. "She's not my girlfriend."

"So you and Ashley weren't, you know, dating?"

"I just did her videos. She liked Lily Rock at night, the empty streets and the hometown vibe. She liked assaulting that vibe, riding the streets in the dark like a dangerous intruder."

Olivia nodded. "So Ashley is a performance artist?"

A slight smile came to the corner of his mouth. "You could say that. She needed me to video, an outsider-looking-in kind of thing."

"How did you and Ashley meet?"

"Comic Con."

"Oh really..." When he didn't say more, Olivia felt flustered. *He's so awkward to talk to.* Fortunately Michael interrupted with a plate of eggs and two slices of dry toast.

"Here you go." He put the plate and a fork in front of Brandon.

While he ate, Michael sat down next to Olivia. They both watched Brandon devour the eggs. "Any butter?" the boy asked.

"Probably not good for an upset stomach," Olivia said. "See how the food settles and then we can make more toast with butter."

As Brandon took the last forkful of eggs, she turned to Michael. "Janis has not found Blair yet." She glanced at Brandon to see if he looked concerned. When he didn't react, she plunged in again.

"I'm so sorry about your mother."

His face froze, a small bit of scrambled egg stuck to the corner of his mouth. "My mom..." His voice sounded dreamy. He didn't finish his thought.

He knows she's dead, right? She pointed to the egg on his lip and then wiped the corner of her own mouth. He nodded, and wiped both corners of his. "She's dead," he said, as if it had just occurred to him. Then he added, "Ashley killed her for no reason."

Brandon finished his toast. He licked his lips. Eyes still bloodshot, but he sat up straighter in his chair.

"So you don't miss Ashley?" Olivia started again.

"Should I...miss her?"

He's asking me if he should miss Ashley. Like I'm supposed to tell him how to feel.

"You seem uncomfortable with expressing your feelings." Olivia knew this might draw a defensive response from him but she continued anyway. "Is that why she did all the talking for you?"

"You mean Ashley?"

"That day in the coffee shop, she spoke for you."

"Oh right, I forgot about that. I guess she did talk for me. My sisters do too. I'm not that great at communicating." He looked at Olivia, his gaze direct. "Can I have the buttered toast now?"

Michael answered instead. "Some more toast and then off you go. I'm taking you back to your house. Olivia has enough to do."

Once Brandon finished eating, Michael ushered him to his feet. They walked together from the kitchen, leaving Olivia alone to think. *Maybe I got the relationship between Ashley and Brandon all wrong. He did say she killed his mother, but the words had no emotion behind them. It's as if he has no feelings. Not surprising he drinks.*

Olivia picked up her cell phone from the counter and called Janis.

"Hello," came the stern voice.

"Any news on Blair?"

"Oh yeah, we found her. I'm furious. I got all upset because Bella was in such a tizzy. It took me a foot massage from Cookie and two beers to realize I overreacted. Do you believe it? I'm a seasoned police officer and that child in a woman's body got me so agitated I spent hours trying to find her sister who, by the way, wasn't even missing."

"Where was she?"

"Taking a nap in the shed behind their house. Now that Ashley no longer sleeps there, Blair decided she'd use it as her den. She turned off her phone and slept the entire day just to annoy her brother and sister."

Olivia broke in. "They're joined at the hip with their cell phones and living conditions. So when one of them disconnects, they imagine the worst has happened. Don't be so hard on yourself. They lost both parents in a matter of two weeks. You had every right to be worried."

"But that's what's annoying me! I think one of them killed their father. I don't know how that connects to Ashley killing Bianca, but I'm gonna figure that out if it's the death of me."

"Don't say that," Olivia warned. "We have enough dead people on our hands. Tell Cookie you need another massage. Then you'll feel much better." She clicked off the phone.

By the time Michael returned, Olivia had fixed Sage a light supper. She scrambled the rest of the eggs and added a fruit salad with buttered toast and fresh strawberry preserves.

He walked in as she was tiding up the sink. "Eggs for dinner okay?" she asked. "I have enough for the two of us."

"He's reunited with the sisters," Michael told her. He walked to the refrigerator. "I'll make you a fruit spritzer if you'd like to take a minute outside before dinner."

"Eggs?" she repeated.

"How about we save them for tomorrow morning's breakfast? I'll take you out."

She shook her head. "We can't go anywhere because someone has to stay with Sage."

He sighed. "I forgot. It seems like I'm forgetting a lot of things lately."

"It's kind of tense, with the unsolved murder, Sage on bed rest, and you in the middle of a construction project."

"That must be it." Michael smiled at her. "How about this? I'll call over to Refuge and have them bring us a meal. We can save the eggs and still be close at hand if Sage needs something."

Olivia didn't hesitate. "Great idea. I'll go tell Sage we'll be outside. She can text me if she needs something."

"It beats ringing a bell from the other room. Now that would get really old, really fast."

Really old, really fast. Maybe that's what happened with the Grey family. As the kids got older, they may have resented Bianca's control over them. It must have felt smothering. Did they push back? How did Bianca react?

CHAPTER THIRTY-TWO

By Monday morning Olivia knew what she had to do. *I'm going to sit down and talk to Janis and then insist that we bring the Grey siblings together to talk. We can use the memorial service as a ploy if necessary.*

Listening to the lively voices coming from Sage's bedroom, Olivia poured herself a mug of coffee. Pearl Overmann was already at work. Hired immediately after Janis Jets's background check. "She's squeaky clean. Go ahead," Jets had reported.

"I have a list of groceries," Overmann stated calmly. "I start off with healthy choices as soon as I take over." She handed Olivia her cell phone. "If you put your contact information in here, I can send the grocery list."

Though short in stature, Pearl exuded authority. Dressed in black slacks with a tucked-in white button-up shirt, she looked professional and efficient. Her white sneakers appeared worn and very clean. The most interesting part of her appearance was her auburn-red hair. She wore it styled in a pageboy with bangs cut evenly over her forehead.

Once they'd exchanged contact information, Pearl

nodded. "I'll leave you to it then." With that, she turned and headed back to Sage's room.

Olivia's confidence soared. She felt more energy than she had for days, knowing Sage was in professional hands.

Olivia leaned in the doorway to listen from the other room. "A pregnancy is a team effort. Baby and mother work together for the sake of a good birth. Doulas help the entire family, including making a birth plan. Who in your immediate family..."

Olivia smiled. *I guess I'm no longer needed here.* She assessed the grocery list left in her text messages. *I'll drop in at the constabulary and pick up the groceries on the way back home.* Coffee mug rinsed and in the sink, Olivia made her way to the front door.

On the winding road into town, she realized, *I've been so focused on alibis of the siblings, I feel like I've missed something right in front of me. Maybe Janis and I can figure this out together. Something about the pub that night...*

Once in town she parked and made her way toward the constabulary.

"Hey, Brad," she called, giving him a quick wave of her hand. Using her pass for the inner door, she stepped into the hallway where she could hear Janis Jets speaking from interview room one.

"So you're to stay here for a couple of days while we close this case."

I wonder who she's talking to?

Janis continued to speak. "We're planning a memorial service for Beats and Bianca on Wednesday. I want to bring you along, not in handcuffs of course, but because I think your presence will loosen the lips of that Grey family. They don't know what you have or have not told me."

Olivia stepped inside the room. Ashley Tennant sat opposite Jets, the boardroom-sized interview table between them. Janis looked up when she entered and then looked back to Ashley.

"And now Olivia Greer will have a few words with you while I get some coffee."

When Ashley didn't turn around, Olivia came forward. Jets nodded to her chair and then left the room.

"Hello, Ashley," Olivia said calmly.

Ashley's clear blue eyes met her gaze. Olivia noted her stringy straight hair. The girl looked as if she hadn't taken a shower in days. The color of the Riverside County Correctional Facility jumpsuit gave her skin a sallow cast.

Jets popped back into the office. "Can I bring either of you anything?"

Ashley shook her head no.

Olivia answered, "The usual."

Jets hurried from the room. Olivia took her time. *I don't think I've ever sat on this side of the table before. The seat of power.*

Olivia embraced her inner Janis Jets, opening with a direct question. "So what I want to know is why you killed Bianca." Her voice sounded full of authority and distant to her own ears.

To her surprise, Ashley didn't hesitate. She spoke clearly without any further prodding. "It's pretty obvious that Bianca was a horrible woman. She ruled her children and held them captive."

Olivia felt a niggle of suspicion. "Did you tell Officer Jets the same thing?"

"I'm not telling her anything," muttered Ashley. "I confessed and that should be enough."

"But why are you telling me this, because Janis has left the room?"

"Because you get me. I just feel it somehow. When I saw you at the pub the night Beats was killed, you kept looking over at us. Just like me. You're somebody who stands away from the crowd and who notices everything."

"We have something else in common," Olivia added in a soft voice. "We are both orphans on God's highway. I watched your video over and over. When you added the soundtrack, I realized. I came to Lily Rock just like you, with no parents and no family. I thought I'd only be here for a weekend and look at me now. I belong."

Ashley's eyes flooded with tears as she nodded. Olivia looked around the room for a tissue just as Janis walked in, both hands holding coffee mugs. "I see you two are getting along," she said dryly, placing the mugs on the desk. She reached into her back pocket, coming up with a wad of paper napkins.

"Here, use these," she told Ashley, flinging them into her lap.

Jets didn't reclaim her chair. Instead she took two steps backward, giving Olivia and Ashley some space. "You go ahead and keep talking. Just pretend I'm not here."

Olivia had the distinct impression that the coffee was Janis's excuse to sit behind the two-way mirror and listen in. She watched Ashley dab her face with the napkins. "You said Bianca was a horrible person. You don't seem sorry for killing her."

"I'm not one bit sorry. She polluted everything she touched. She tried to use me and I'd just had enough. I didn't plan on killing her but I'm not sorry she's dead."

"Okay then." Jets stepped out from the corner. "I think I've got the picture here. I want you to have an attorney present before you say more." She looked at Olivia. "I think Ashley needs to get a shower and some fresh clothes. We have facilities in the back, I'll take her down the hall."

Ashley nodded, standing to her feet.

Jets looked at Olivia with a meaningful glance. "Be right back."

Once the two left, Olivia returned to her side of the table. *I wish I had time to ask a few more questions about her relationship with Brandon.*

Jets returned shortly. "I sent Ashley to the showers. Apparently they don't keep a careful eye on hygiene down the hill. Probably understaffed." She sat in her chair behind the desk.

"So I know what she told you, but what did you hear in all that mumbo jumbo about orphans and highways?"

"We did connect." Olivia squinted. "Ashley had some kind of connection with that family that I'm thinking was not reciprocated. Brandon was eating eggs with us yesterday and he shed some light on a few things."

"Brandon was at your house?" came Jets's startled response.

"Anyway, he said that Ashley wasn't even his girlfriend. They met at Comic Con."

"I'm surprised Bianca even let her son have a friend at all," Jets said.

"I was thinking the same. Maybe Ashley felt more for Brandon than anyone realized. I do think he has some kind of disorder, maybe Asperger's maybe not, that makes him awkward and uncomfortable with other people. He's not in sync with his feelings at all."

"Thank you, Madame Freud. Any other half-baked opinions for me this morning?" Jets tapped her fingers on the desk.

"That's it," Olivia snapped back. "How about the memorial; did you reserve the space at Hello Age?"

"Brad arranged for Wednesday at four o'clock. He'll be putting up flyers all over town. Do you want to play some music?"

"Sage can't play and we still don't have a drummer. I could do a couple of songs with the autoharp."

"Practice singing, I want to see everyone crying and hugging again. Makes me feel all gooey inside." Jets smirked.

"Yes, boss," replied Olivia.

"I'll call Meadow and if she can get the Old Rockers to pitch in some casseroles and a little cash. Cooks will bring desserts."

"Remind me again, what do you hope to accomplish by having a memorial?"

"My gut tells me it's one of them who killed Beats. The problem is I can't get one alone long enough to get any traction on my suspicions."

"What about Ashley? She may have killed them both. She's already shown us her fierce temper."

"People have patterns. I don't think Ashley would confess outright about Bianca. And then keep Beats a big secret."

"Don't forget they were all in full sight at the pub while Beats died downstairs."

"I haven't forgotten," mumbled Jets.

"And their mother was making dinner at home," added Olivia.

"I didn't doubt Bianca's alibi. I mean, she was the kind of mother who would cook dinner and expect everyone to turn up when she said so. Plus we found evidence in the refrigerator." Jets grimaced. "Maybe this is a first. Alibied by a meatloaf with a side dish of mac and cheese."

"Not to change the subject but your assistant came by yesterday to talk to me."

Jets looked annoyed. "I instructed Brad to keep a lookout from a distance. He wasn't supposed to drop in for coffee."

"Anyway, he told me he'd followed Bella to the dump. He helped her lift a cardboard box into the bin. He said the box was full of old photos and papers. That got me to thinking..."

Jets looked interested. "He told me he followed the VW Beetle but he didn't mention helping out one of the suspects at the dump."

"I think he has a thing for Bella," Olivia commented.

"Stop it!" Jets slapped her hand on the desk. She picked up her cell. "Get in here now," she said.

A knock came from the hallway.

"In," roared Jets. The door slowly opened, revealing Brad May wearing a sheepish smile.

"Can I get you anything?"

"Olivia told me you ran into one of our suspects. A couple of days ago at the dump?"

Brad scratched his head. "She's hot and I helped her out. You told me to follow the VW so I did."

"I didn't tell you to flirt with one of our suspects," barked Janis. "So you saw photos in the box?"

"I did."

"Do you think the box is still there?"

More scratching and then, "Riverside County will pick up tomorrow."

"Then get yourself over there and find that box. Put it in your truck and drive it back here. I want to know why Bella Grey suddenly decided to clean house."

"Do I have to?"

"Get outta here," roared Janis. "Don't make me ask again."

Brad closed the door as Janis leaned back in her chair. "Stop smirking," she told Olivia. "You could have told me this sooner."

"He's your assistant. I thought he'd already told you." Olivia's smirk remained.

Jets ignored her jab. "I saw their house during the search. Stuff everywhere, upstairs and down. So then Bella gets a sudden urge to tidy and sort? Not likely."

A thought suddenly occurred to Olivia. "You never told me what you saw from Cayenne and Arlo's deck. Did Cay have any insights? She's been watching the family for weeks."

"Not really." Janis paused, her face growing thoughtful. "I hung out with Cay and Arlo because their deck gave me a great view of the Grey house. But now that you mention it, Cayenne did say something funny. About that lime-green VW Beetle."

Olivia leaned forward.

CHAPTER THIRTY-THREE

Olivia's heart beat faster. "What exactly did Cayenne say?"

Jets frowned. "That's just it. Cay was interested in that VW. She told me that the Grey family didn't have a car. At least not until we found Beats dead. I didn't realize the significance of the timing, otherwise I'd have gotten a warrant to search it along with their house."

Olivia stared at Janis, who stared back. Jets broke the silence. "Okay then, I'm going to figure out a way to get a warrant to search that car. And I'd like you to accompany my worthy assistant to the dump. Let's see if we can find that box."

"Ick." Olivia's nose wrinkled in disgust. "I don't want to dig in a dumpster."

"The work of the constabulary has no end of glamour. Even when things get dirty and smell bad, we hold our heads high," Jets replied with a smirk.

"And our noses too," muttered Olivia. "I'd better hurry and catch up with Brad."

She found him at his desk, looking at the computer.

"Hey, Olivia," he greeted her.

"Janis wants me to go with you to the dump," she muttered.

"That's cool," he said. "I'll go later. I'm into something else right now."

She looked at his computer screen. "Online dating doesn't count as work," she said flatly. "I'll follow you. I'm parked right outside. I have to get back to check on Sage. Don't dillydally."

Brad grinned. "You sound like my grandma. Dillydally, that's funny." He turned off the computer, still chuckling. "I'll drive around front."

Olivia sat behind the wheel waiting for Brad. She heard the truck rumbling slowly down Main Street. Backing her car from the space, she pulled out behind him, driving toward the road leading out of town.

She followed Brad's truck down the gravel road, past the entry point, to where the dumpsters were located. Signs had been posted for sorting purposes. Each one, carefully labeled, encouraged the specific recycling of trash.

Brad leaned out the driver's window. "Over there." He pointed to the paper recycling sign. She pulled her car up next to him and groaned. The dumpster was full, overflowing boxes tumbling from the top.

"It's twice as full as it was the other day," Brad commented. "There are a lot of boxes on top of the ones I dropped inside."

She looked down at the work gloves he held in his hand. "How about you toss stuff out and I'll look inside?"

He pulled on one glove, then the other. "This is a man's work for sure. I'm on it." In one mighty tug he pulled himself up over the edge of the dumpster, disappearing from sight.

"You okay in there?" she called out.

When he didn't respond she grew worried. Coming closer, she rose to her tiptoes to peer over the ledge.

"Outta my way," came Brad's voice. Hands gripped the side of the dumpster. His body followed, boots landing on the gravel.

"What's wrong?"

"There's bugs in there," exclaimed Brad. "And it smells really bad."

"Paper recycling shouldn't be that terrible," she said encouragingly. "Just move faster than the bugs and I think you'll be okay." *I am not going to jump in there after you.*

Brad grimaced. He turned to face the bin and then hoisted himself back over the top again. She heard a muffled voice call out, "Hey, Olivia, I found some beer cans."

Does he think this is some kind of treasure hunt?

"Toss them out," she called in an encouraging voice." Two cans whizzed past her head. She ducked to avoid the third. Banging came from inside the bin. *What's he doing in there now?*

"Is everything okay?" she called out.

"Got some cool hiking boots here. They're dirty but can be worn. My size!" Brad's head emerged from the bin, his hand holding up a worn pair of boots. He dropped them over the side.

His head disappeared again. Finally she heard the sweet sound of success. "I've got it," he called. Thumping accompanied by a large cardboard box, shoved over the side. It fell to the dirt, papers and photographs floating in the air.

Olivia rushed to pick up the stray papers. Then she sat in the dirt next to the box and reached inside. Under old bills and receipts she found a stack of photographs buried at the bottom. A rubber band bound them together.

The first photo showed a young couple standing with their three young children. The man was tall and lean, his arm around a small blond woman. A boy and two girls stood in front of them—the girls frowned, while the boy's face held a smirk. Bunny ears poked up over one girl's head. Olivia looked at the next photo.

Brad stared at the photos over her shoulder. "So is that the box Janis was looking for?" He bent over to get a closer look.

She held up the photo. "It is. Look at this picture. What do you see?"

He took it from her hand. "It's the Malone family. I'd know them anywhere. Bella was cute even then."

"So that's Beats and Bianca?" Olivia wanted to make sure.

"Yeah, I'd say that's them. I didn't know Beats, but that sure looks like Bianca, with the blond hair.

She nodded, taking the photo back.

"So I did a good thing, right? I found the box..." Brad stammered, eyes begging for approval.

"You did great," Olivia assured him. "These photos are exactly what we needed." She wound the rubber band around the stack and then shoved them in her purse.

She stood up. "You saw the car, right?"

He picked up the box. "You can't miss that thing. That lime-green classic Beetle is in that one photo. I bet it's the same one they drive around Lily Rock."

"I assume there aren't a lot of those classic VWs around."

"I'm a mechanic, remember. I know my cars. I've never seen one that color."

She moved ahead to open the passenger door of his truck. He hoisted the box onto the seat. "Thanks for helping," he told her. "I'll make sure Officer Jets gets this. See ya later." He walked around the tailgate.

As she reached to open her car door, he called out, "Don't you want to give me those photos? I'll put them back in the box."

"I'll take them to her," she called after him.

DEADBEAT DAD

Olivia drove home, processing the photo. *It must have been taken when Brandon was seven or eight, which makes Bella four or five, and Blair just a toddler. But what about that old car? If they had it back then, why did it just suddenly appear in Lily Rock?*

As she drove the winding road toward her house, she realized, *I forgot the groceries!* Her thoughts immediately flipped back to the investigation. *On the night Beats was found, Janis said something about checking on Beats's car, but I don't remember if they found it.*

Olivia parked in the shade in front of her house and turned off the ignition. As soon as she got out of the car she saw Pearl Overmann coming toward her.

"Hey, Pearl," she called out. They stood face-to-face.

"You never brought back the groceries I specifically asked for."

"I completely forgot. I am so sorry. Were you able to have lunch without them?"

"I found the vegetable garden out back. I picked some greens for a salad and we ate tomato soup. But next time I'd like to make soup fresh, not from a can."

"Sage loves tomato soup," she said brightly.

"See you tomorrow," Pearl said crisply.

Olivia waved and made her way toward the house. *Maybe Michael can pick them up.* Once inside she went to check on Sage.

Asleep in her room, resting in the nest of plumped pillows, Sage looked at peace with her world. Backing out quietly, Olivia closed the door before she heard fists pounding on the front door.

"What took you so long?" Jets pushed her way past Olivia. "How's Sage?"

"She's sleeping, keep your voice down."

"Brad said you have some photos for me."

"You won't believe what I found!" Olivia snatched her purse. "Follow me," she told Janis over her shoulder. Unwinding the rubber band, photos spilled onto the table, some turned upside down. Janis leaned over to quickly sort them right side up.

Pointing, she said, "See here. This is what I was saying. We have happy dad taking kids to the zoo. And there? Dad with three children playing in the snow laughing. And how about this one?" Janis pointed to a larger photo. "Dad talking to little kids at school. I think that's a young Brandon in the front row. Looks like one of those days when you bring your dad to school to talk about his work things."

She turned to Olivia. "So I want to know why those Grey people keep calling him a deadbeat dad. It's obvious that he was a part of their lives." She turned to the table again.

"Look here, Beats toweling off a kid at the swimming pool. And how about this one? Beats teaching Bella to play drums." The photo showed a man leaning over the back of a young girl, adjusting her fingers around a drumstick. Both were smiling.

Janis turned back to Olivia. "Am I crazy or do you see it too? The Grey family complained about Beats abandoning them, but these photos show something entirely different."

"I heard them call Beats a deadbeat dad over and over. Bianca wasn't any better. She had nothing to say that sounded remotely favorable toward her ex. But then most exes don't have glowing accounts of their divorced spouse, unless they're movie stars."

"It's the discrepancy that makes me think it's important. I mean, on the one hand, kids bad-mouth parents. I get that. But on the other hand, I can't deny the photographic

DEADBEAT DAD

evidence." She pointed to the photos. "We have a happy father relating to young children in positive ways."

She turned over one picture showing Beats and three children at the beach, a date stamp clearly marked in the corner. "Look, this one dates after the divorce. I know from our research that Beats had half custody. He had the kids at his house and took them places on the weekends.

"We also know that Bella made a special trip to the dump to get rid of these photos. What was her purpose and did the other siblings know?"

Olivia pushed the photos around until she found the right one. "Just to add to your inquiry, I found this photo of the Malone family. See what you think."

Janis snatched the picture. She stared at the images, her eyes narrowing. "They're standing in front of that damned lime-green VW." She looked up at Olivia. "I thought Beats got a ride to Lily Rock, an Uber maybe or with a friend. We never found his vehicle. No one came forward so I let that part of the investigation go."

"I wondered about that on my way home from the dump. But in your defense, we didn't know the Greys had any connection with Beats Malone until recently."

"You can make excuses for me, but I should have seen that. It's not like a lime-green VW Beetle is invisible."

Janis Jets stared at the photo, a grim look on her face.

"So what's next, Officer Jets? Surely you have a plan."

CHAPTER THIRTY-FOUR

Jets continued to stare at the photo, biting her bottom lip. Olivia waited for her to speak. "I can't think right now," she admitted. "I'm too angry with myself. Why don't we just sleep on this and get together tomorrow?

"Even if the photo is considered circumstantial, it points us in a new direction. I did the paperwork for a search warrant on the VW. In the meantime, hang out with your sister. At least she's doing something productive."

On the doorstep Olivia watched Janis walk to her truck. *First time I've seen Janis so down on herself.* She closed the door, wondering how she could help.

"Olivia?" Sage called from the bedroom.

"On my way," she answered back. Walking briskly through the great room, she cautioned herself. *Let go of the investigation. Don't let it spill over onto Sage. Janis will find her way.* She inhaled deeply before opening the door.

"What a day I had today," she said, a big smile on her face.

Sage lifted herself up on the pillows. "Do you come bearing healthy fruits and nuts? My doula wasn't happy with you." Sage grinned at Olivia, who sat on the edge of the bed.

"Pearl Overmann is a handful. She reminds me of your mom."

Sage chuckled. "I think you may be right. Pearl and Meadow, two know-it-alls. Let's get them together soon and watch the fur fly."

"Oh, good idea!" Olivia rubbed her hands together. She exaggerated a concerned look on her face. "But only if you think you are up for it, I mean in your delicate condition and all."

Sage patted her belly. "We're ready and able. I'm already getting bored just lying here and I have months to go."

"Okay then, first we have the memorial for Beats and Bianca. And then after that a little lunch with Pearl and Meadow. That should be a hoot!"

Olivia watched Sage's expression carefully. Her eyes briefly dimmed and then cleared. Sage smiled tentatively and then nodded.

Appreciating Sage's effort, Olivia felt herself relax. *So long as I leave out the murder investigation, she'll be okay.*

* * *

The next morning she felt warm lips on her ear. "Wake up," Michael whispered. "Janis wants to talk to you."

"I'm sleeping," she groaned.

"Jets called my phone because you didn't answer yours," he explained. "She's giving you ten minutes to wake up before she calls back. I'll make coffee. You get showered and ready. The constabulary needs your expertise."

"Ugh," groaned Olivia. "I don't want to be a constabulary consultant. I want to sleep." She heard his laughter echo down the hallway.

Knowing better than to keep Janis waiting, Olivia slid out of bed and got ready.

Once in the kitchen she reached for the mug of coffee as Michael handed over her cell.

She took a sip and then hit redial. On the first ring Janis answered, "I'm coming to pick you up. Be ready outside." She hung up.

Olivia held up her half-full coffee mug. "Can I have mine to go?" she asked Michael.

"Yes, ma'am." He pulled a travel mug off the shelf. "Jets is in a temper. You're going to need all the help you can get." He poured coffee to the top.

"I'm happy she rebounded from yesterday." She screwed the lid down tightly. "Sage's doula should be here soon. Can you wait just a bit and let her in?"

"I would be happy to help. See you later," he replied.

She opened the door just as Jets's truck roared down the driveway. Gravel spit out from the tires as the truck stopped. Then the passenger side window rolled down. "Get in," Jets commanded. Olivia opened the door, hopping onto the seat. She placed her mug in the holder. A warm nuzzle at the back of her neck made her smile.

She reached her hand over the seat to pet Mayor Maguire's fuzzy neck. "This must be important if she invited you along." With one last pat she settled back into her seat, securing the belt.

"Where's mine?" Jets grumbled, nodding to her coffee mug.

"Thought you'd already had enough by this time in the morning." Olivia turned toward the open window, leaning closer so that the air would dry her hair.

Jets put both hands on the steering wheel. She pressed the

gas as the tires spun on the gravel, then headed toward the main road.

"Where are we going?"

"To talk to Cay. She's been watching the Greys' house since last night. It seems they've decided to pack up and leave Lily Rock."

"Is that so?" Olivia said with surprise.

Janis leaned down to grab a paper out of her backpack. "I've got a warrant to search the VW. I hope to get there before they hit the road. I don't have enough evidence to take them into custody, but I'm hoping to find something in that car that will point to the killer."

Jets pushed her foot on the accelerator, tires screeching into the curve.

Olivia gulped, glancing in the back seat. Mayor Maguire had curled himself into a ball, apparently not worried about Janis's driving. "Did you bring the mayor along for the ride?"

"He invited himself." Jets bit her bottom lip, bearing down on the next curve. In a few feet she turned left, her truck bumping along the uneven dirt road toward the Greys' house.

Cayenne and Arlo shared a driveway with the Greys. Instead of turning right, she turned left.

"There it is," Olivia noted. The lime-green VW Beetle sat in front of the house with the trunk wide open.

"Got 'em," claimed Jets. She pulled the truck to a halt. Yanking the keys from the ignition, she reached for her cell phone. "I'm here," she barked. "I'll stall them until you get here." She shoved the phone into her backpack and opened the truck door.

"Okay, here's the plan," she told Olivia. "The slower we move, the more anxious the Greys will become. Just go along with me. I'm hoping they will obstruct justice, which will give me cause to bring them in for questioning while we look over the car."

Mayor Maguire yipped from the back. Olivia opened her side and his back door. In one leap the dog ran ahead to keep up with Janis.

Jets stood on the porch and knocked with authority. "Lily Rock police." When no one answered she pounded again. "Don't make me break the door down."

Olivia saw a curtain move in the window, and finally someone opened the door. Bella peeked out. "What do you want?"

Jets did not hesitate. "I have a warrant to search your car. My people will tow it to the lab or you can hand over the keys and cooperate. Either way works for me, though I must say if you go along, things will go better for you later."

The door flung open. "What do you mean better for me later? I'm not a suspect and neither are my siblings. You're just trying to make us look bad."

Olivia gulped, feeling a tingle of anticipation. She noted Jets's slight smile and her hand at the back of her blazer. *Look out, girlie, you don't know who you're dealing with.*

"Bring me my backpack," Jets barked toward Olivia, "I left it behind."

Olivia looked around. *That's what she meant by stalling.* She walked slowly toward the truck.

Lifting the bag from the car, she took her time walking back to Jets. Bella glared at her, her eyes furtively darting, as if she felt trapped. As Olivia held the backpack out to Jets, Bella's face froze.

"Just get the phone out and hand it to me." Jets did not drop her eye contact from Bella.

Olivia did as she was told.

Once Jets took out the phone, she pushed a button and

spoke loudly. "Tell the forensic team to bring their best equipment." She stared at Bella and then clicked the phone off.

Whether it was the timing or Jets's intensity, either way the girl began to cry. "I didn't do anything. We were just going on vacation for a few days. We weren't running away."

Olivia blocked out the girl's excuses, realizing that Janis had taken complete charge of the situation using time to her advantage. *And look, she didn't even need to pull out a gun.*

"Stop the whining," Jets ordered. When the girl only cried harder, she added, "Stop crying and stand out here where I can keep an eye on you." Jets gave Bella a slight shove.

She turned to Olivia. "You watch her and let me know if the other siblings show up. My team will be here shortly. We can take them to the constabulary in cuffs if they continue to obstruct my investigation."

Olivia nodded at Bella. "You'd better do as she says. For some reason she's taken a dislike to you and that won't go well if you don't cooperate."

"I didn't do anything," Bella cried.

Two unmarked cars came down the dirt road. The first one stopped behind Janis's truck, followed by the other. A uniformed police officer popped out. He walked toward the porch. Nodding at Olivia, he pulled a paper from his front pocket, handing it over to Jets.

"Right this way, miss. You can sit in the back seat of our car until Officer Jets gives us further directions."

Bella ducked her head. The tears had stopped, replaced by an angry scowl. She stepped off the porch as the officer took her elbow. "Watch your step, miss," he told her politely.

"What's going on?" Blair stepped outside looking disheveled, her hair a mass of tangles. "I was sleeping." She rubbed her eyes, staring toward the back of the officer who took her sister away.

"I wouldn't say anything more," Olivia warned.

Jets interrupted. "What Olivia is trying to tell you is that you may need an attorney."

"But we were getting ready to leave," Blair said, pointing to the car. "We're packed and everything."

"Where were you planning to go?"

"Down the hill and as far away from Lily Rock as possible," she admitted.

She didn't bother to link stories with her sister.

"What about the memorial for your parents?" Jets asked.

"That's just some stupid Lily Rock idea," she scoffed. "We're not religious. Plus we have the ashes." She reached down her rumpled T-shirt to pull out a necklace. "We're all wearing a bit of mom around our necks." She dangled the locket from the chain for them to see.

Olivia felt puzzled. "You wear your mother's ashes around your neck as jewelry?"

Blair looked shocked. "Why not? She was our one and only parent, and that's how we're grieving her death."

Olivia shut her mouth. *Okay, so the locket thing may be more common than I thought. But what about Beats? He's still at the morgue with no one to pick him up and Mother has already been cremated and hung around the kids' necks...*

Blair put the ash locket back under her shirt as Mayor Maguire trotted up. He nudged her knee. She bent over to give him a pat. "Nice doggie," she said. The mayor leaned into her leg.

I guess M&M feels sorry for her...

Olivia heard an engine turn over. She watched as the police car drove up the driveway toward the main road, the back of Bella's head visible through the window.

"Where are they taking my sister?" Blair demanded. She bent over to put her arms around Mayor Maguire's neck.

"To the constabulary," Olivia told the girl. "Do you want to go with me? I can walk to town with you. Mayor Maguire will come along."

Blair kept the dog in her embrace. "I'll get my shoes." She stood, heading back into the house.

CHAPTER THIRTY-FIVE

"Let's walk across the street to the constabulary. I want to warn you, Officer Jets may have some uncomfortable questions, not just for your sister."

"I'm down with that," Blair said. "She can ask me anything she wants."

"Even about the death of your father?"

Blair's eyes narrowed. "I never knew my dad, not really. He was always touring. My mom was the only person I ever needed. Deadbeat meant nothing to me."

There it is, that deadbeat thing again.

"I'm just curious." Olivia paused, then asked, "When did you see your dad last?"

"I told you he meant nothing to me." Blair sprinted across the street. A loud honk penetrated the air as a large SUV came to a skidding halt. The car behind the SUV barely avoided a rear-end collision.

Olivia shook her head. *Blair lives on the edge. Impulsive and dangerous. She didn't even look for traffic. Self-destructive.* She hurried across the street to catch up with Blair. "That was a close call."

DEADBEAT DAD

"What do you mean?" Blair looked genuinely puzzled.

"You almost got hit by a car."

"Oh that. People will stop. They always do." She turned the knob of the constabulary door. Olivia followed her inside.

Instead of breezing past Brad, Olivia stopped in front of his desk. "This is Blair Grey. You've met her sister Bella."

"Hey, Blair," he said, his eyes smiling first, followed by a grin. "What's up..."

"Hello," she said, ducking her head.

"We want to talk to Officer Jets," Olivia explained. "I'll open the door." She moved around the desk to slap her key card on the panel, gesturing for Blair to follow.

Once in the hallway, Olivia explained, "The jail cells are over here." She stopped at the first one. "Hi, Ashley, how are you doing?"

Ashley's hair hung softly around her face in curls. Her eyes had lost the glazed look. Not answering Olivia, Ashley stared at Blair. "So first Bella and now you."

Blair ducked her head.

When she didn't speak, Olivia intervened. "We're getting to the bottom of the murder investigation. Did Janis tell you?"

"She didn't tell me," Ashley mumbled. "But I've been chatting with Brad. He's pretty cool actually. He's seen my skateboard videos on YouTube."

Blair raised her head. "Nobody cares about your skateboard videos. You're in jail because you murdered my mother!"

The accusation sent a chill up Olivia's spine. She touched Blair's shoulder. "Never mind that. We're going to speak to Officer Jets." With a quick glance of goodbye to Ashley, she escorted Blair down the hall.

"Over here," called Jets. She stood in the doorway of interview room one. Olivia nodded, taking Blair by the elbow. The girl shook her off. "I can see where to go."

To Olivia's surprise another woman sat behind the interview table. *She looks vaguely familiar.*

Blair sat down in the only available chair, while Olivia tried to remember. "Do I know you?"

The woman stood, her hand reaching out to Olivia. "I'm Zoe Brewer, a court-appointed advocate for underaged minors."

"I remember now! You helped a student at the music academy."

"Officer Jets mentioned that you helped her on that investigation too."

Olivia glanced back at Janis when Brad popped into the room, interrupting the conversation. He dragged an extra chair behind him. "Be right back," he said.

Once seated, Olivia asked, "So far as I know there are no minors in this investigation."

Janis Jets cleared her throat to explain. By then Brad appeared with another chair. Jets sighed. "Olivia, come over to this side." She dragged two chairs, pointing to one. "I'd like Blair and Bella here, backs to the door. I want you on this side with Dr. Brewer and me."

"Where's Bella? I need my sister," cried Blair.

"I'll go get her," Brad said.

"Grab one more chair," Jets hollered down the hall. "It's a party in here."

Brad returned with a chair in one hand and Bella's elbow in the other. She glanced at Blair and then at Jets. "Do I get to sit down?"

"Right here," Brad said, shoving the chair next to Blair. He rolled his eyes at Olivia.

"That's all I need for now," Jets told him. "If you want to

stay close by, hang out in the media room, just in case I have trouble with videos."

Bella's eyes opened wide. "What video?" she asked suspiciously.

Janis sat in between Olivia and Zoe Brewer. "I'm happy you asked that," she said casually. "We have one video with Ashley skateboarding. We know Brandon was the videographer."

"Where is Brandon?" Blair asked.

"We can get him if we need him later. I want to get a few details straight." Janis turned to her computer. "Brad taught me to do this. Look up on the wall. I'm projecting the video."

She clicked on her computer and "Orphan Girl" began to play. All eyes watched the video of Ashley Tennant, her hoodie pulled over her head, executing tricks on her skateboard. Jumping from the bench back to the boardwalk, and then up a wall and down again. Olivia watched Bella's and Blair's amazed expressions. *I don't think they've ever seen Ashley skate.*

Bella's jaw dropped while Blair's eyes grew wide. When the video finished, Bella spoke first. "So what? Ashley rides a skateboard. What's that got to do with us?"

Jets smiled. "Not much with you, but it has everything to do with Ashley. This tells us who she is. It's an artistic expression of loneliness, pushed by speed and talent. It's performance art, executing skateboard tricks in the dark in a place where skateboards are not supposed to be. It tells me she has a streak of defiance."

Blair spoke up. "I don't care if Ashley is some kind of artist. She killed our mother. She needs to be punished."

"We're not denying the fact that she killed your mother, but we do wonder about her motivation. Ashley won't tell us what was on her mind, but I think I've figured it all out. This leads me to our next video. It's CCTV of the night your father was killed, from the Lily Rock Pub."

Jets clicked another button on her computer. A fuzzy picture came up on the wall. The camera caught the parking lot at the front of the pub. "Now you can see that the camera takes in most of the parking lot, but not all of it. There's a blind spot back there by the stairway." Jets stopped the video. "At first I didn't see any evidence that would help me with my investigation. But now that I know more, I see what I missed the first time." She continued to run the video, pausing it again.

The fuzzy black and white video caught a car shaped like a VW Beetle. Two people sat in the front seat. The passenger was slumped over, his face smushed against the window glass.

Jets cleared her throat. "So that's your mom and dad, driving in the VW Beetle together. That's your dad, slumped over in the seat."

She pressed another button, fast-forwarding quickly, then stopping. She pressed the button again. This time the VW Beetle was leaving the parking lot, ten minutes later according to the time stamp. Jets said, "This is the same car leaving the parking lot, heading in the opposite direction."

Olivia instantly realized what Janis was trying to say. "The passenger is gone," she said aloud.

"That's right. The passenger is gone." Jets stopped the video. She turned to Blair and Bella. "When did you two realize that your mother killed your father?"

Neither girl spoke. Bella folded her arms across her chest, while Blair ducked her head.

"No worries, I know exactly what happened," Jets said in a slightly triumphant voice. "Your mother drove to the far end of the parking lot, where no one could see from the outdoor patio. The camera lens doesn't reach that far either. We'd call that a blind spot," Janis added, as if it weren't already obvious.

"So it's clear to me that she drove up to the edge of the trees, got out and opened the door, and yanked your dead father out. She must have rolled him a foot or two into the woods, shut the passenger door and then drove away."

The girls remained silent.

"Was he already dead?" asked Olivia.

"From what we can tell, Bianca stabbed and killed him with a steak knife. We're going over the Greys' house and outdoors again with a fine-tooth comb. I bet my forensics team will come up with the place Beats was stabbed."

Jets faced Blair. "You buried the knife behind the sequoia in the park and then replaced the knife so that the block in the kitchen would look full. And that worked. When we searched your house, I dismissed the possibility of the knife belonging to your family out of hand. Until Mayor Maguire dug up the other one. I know you used to play fetch with Mayor Maguire in that exact spot. We've seen you in the park late at night. We have witnesses."

"Circumstantial," Blair said. "Won't stand up in court. I'm not stupid."

"We asked for CCTV of that night just to make sure. There are cameras in the park up in the tree branches."

Blair looked at her hands, her lips pressed closed.

"I'm going to take your silence for an affirmation. I think you both knew all along your mother killed your father. I think you not only knew, you may have sat in the pub all night, just so you'd be out of the way for her when he came up to give you the car."

Bella glared at Jets. "We had nothing to do with killing Deadbeat. It was all my mother's idea."

"Why did she kill him? I don't understand," Olivia interjected.

"He kept pestering us and wouldn't leave us alone. He brought us that stupid car like it was going to make a difference. My mom moved here to get away from him."

"Not what I heard," Olivia interjected.

"What do you mean?" Bella asked accusingly.

Her stomach clenched. Olivia knew right away she'd made a mistake. *Don't tell her about Beats's plan to move to Lily Rock and about Sage and the baby, you idiot. That's just one more thing for them to hate their father for.*

Jets glanced at her quickly and took the conversation back. "So you knew Bianca planned to kill him but did not interfere?"

"Deadbeat was bringing up a car for us to drive. My mother agreed to meet with him to talk about that and her spousal support."

"I thought your dad abandoned you and didn't pay her any money?"

"That's what she told us," Blair said. "But after she was dead, I looked at her papers. It turned out she'd been getting money from him every month, even after we turned eighteen."

"So your mother lied to you?" Jets shook her head.

"She did not! She was the perfect mother and the only parent we need...I mean needed." Bella stumbled over the words.

Jets turned toward her computer. "I have another video." She pointed to the wall. "And here we have the four of you, sitting inside the pub, talking and eating a burger."

Olivia's stomach clenched. She watched the familiar video again.

As the video paused, Jets spoke. "Your mother's alibi was

that she was making dinner for the family. Yet you're all eating burgers."

Olivia gulped. "I just noticed, none of you have a cell phone."

Bella explained. "Mom traced all of our phones and knew where we were every minute of every day. She had us texting her every hour to make sure we were safe. She always told us Beats would kidnap us and make us live with him."

"But you're all adults. Why would that threat make any sense once you'd grown up?"

"She's been telling us Beats would kidnap us since we were little," explained Blair. "Deadbeat tried to get to us, but we stopped answering his calls, texts, and emails. He was so pathetic."

"No one questioned my mom," explained Bella. "So we just went along with her."

"Until that night," Olivia pointed out. "Did you all agree not to text her and not to come home for dinner?"

"Not all of us, Ashley disagreed," Bella said, "until we threatened to lock her in the shed. Brandon just let her hang on because he felt sorry for her."

"We didn't even know him, not really," added Bella.

Olivia sat back, mystified by the Grey family dynamic.

Jets shut down the CCTV video. Silence filled the room. Olivia turned to Zoe Brewer, still unsure why she'd been invited to the interview. She felt Jets's eyes on her.

"I'll explain about Dr. Brewer in a few minutes," Janis told Olivia flatly.

"In the meantime, you two can go home. I'm not going to press charges today but I suggest you retain an attorney. I'm not sure, once everything is sorted out, that we won't charge you with accessories to the murder of Beats Malone. On the one hand, the evidence is circumstantial, but on the other hand, you turned your back on your mother, increasing her anxiety. If you hadn't done that, Bianca may not have felt so desperate. But in the end, she was the one who killed your father in cold blood."

Blair stood up quickly. "Let's go, Bella. We're free to go."

Blair and Bella left the interview room. Jets got up from her seat to close the door. Once she sat down, Olivia broke the silence.

"Their hatred for Beats gives me chills. Blair and Bella seem completely irrational and even delusional about their father," Olivia said.

Jets added, "Which explains to me that Bella got rid of the photos because they proved her father wasn't a deadbeat." She turned to Zoe Brewer. "Maybe now is the time for you to explain to Olivia about why you're here."

Dr. Brewer cleared her throat.

CHAPTER THIRTY-SIX

"I'm just devastated by this interview," Dr. Brewer began.

"I need some water," Olivia said, clearing her throat.

"The Greys turning on their own dad—that was pretty intense," agreed Jets. "I have to admit I won't mind seeing the backs of those two." She picked up her phone to text. Putting it back on the table, she added, "I told Brad to bring us refreshments. He's heading to the diner and will be back soon." She turned to Zoe Brewer. "Tell Olivia what you told me."

"It feels confusing, I know," the older woman explained. "What we have here is two people who could not manage to co-parent their children after a divorce."

"That seems pretty obvious," Olivia said, nodding. "You must be some kind of expert on families like this. That's why Janis called you in."

"I have a degree in marriage and family counseling," Zoe admitted. "Unfortunately the Grey family slid under the court's radar and they didn't get the help they needed when the children were younger."

"What do you mean?"

"I accessed their court records. It seems the divorce was acrimonious from the very beginning. The court knew Bianca Malone would be a problem because she undermined Beats at every turn, particularly around money and custody."

"I suppose they did arbitration?" Olivia asked.

"It took months for them to settle because Bianca kept changing her mind and then stonewalling, refusing to talk to anyone."

"Sounds like her kids," muttered Olivia. She shook her head. *That's it. That's what's been bothering me. None of them even looked at a cell phone that night at the pub. They must have been stonewalling Bianca.*

"Plus we can't dismiss the financial piece of the divorce. In California they add up the parent's income and use a formula to arrive at a reasonable child support rate. Every kid brought in more money for Bianca." Jets shook her head. "You might as well put a price on every head. Sounds stupid to me."

"That's true," Dr. Brewer said thoughtfully. "According to the records, it didn't take long for Bianca to see how more custody resulted in more money. Even after a couple of years, Bianca didn't change her ways. She kept taking Beats back to court to get more."

"A friend of mine had that kind of trouble," admitted Olivia. "But she eventually reached an agreement with her husband for the sake of the children."

"It's a flaw in our legal system," Dr. Brewer explained. "If you are rich you can buy your way out, but for most people the money matters. And then in this case, Bianca felt so much anger and resentment because it was Beats who ended the marriage. So she started to undermine Beats's relationship with his children from the very beginning."

"Bianca did a very thorough job. They were still

complaining about Beats even after Bianca was murdered," Olivia said.

"There's a name for this situation. It's called a syndrome," Dr. Brewer said matter-of-factly.

"Is it in that mental illness category?" Olivia asked.

"Not yet, but I see several families who are headed in the direction of parental alienation syndrome every year."

"So who's to blame for this?" Jets asked. "I want someone to arrest."

"The interesting part is that the seeds for this dysfunction are sowed right at the beginning of the couple's courting. One of them takes control over the other, while the other person gives in for the sake of keeping the peace."

"Do you mean Beats didn't push back?" Jets asked.

"He had his reasons, I'm sure. Bianca had a temper and she could be very nasty. Plus Beats more than likely went on road trips so that he didn't have to deal with her. Three kids later we have the makings of parental alienation, even if the parents stay together."

Olivia looked pensive. "I'm getting a better picture. Maybe Beats had enough and asked for a divorce, and then all hell broke loose."

"That's it," Dr. Brewer said, nodding. "The accusing parent uses the children as weapons against the other parent. They have any number of tactics, all based on lies and manipulation. The problem is that the children who turn against one parent end up turning against themselves."

"Maybe that's why none of the children ever launched," Olivia said. "And why Brandon, Bella, and Blair all act anxious and belligerent. They even have that weird sound they make together when they want to spook people."

"And Brandon barely talks to people outside the family. Plus I think he has a serious drinking problem. My boyfriend brought him to my house because he found Brandon drunk at his construction site." Her eyes grew wide. "And then don't forget Blair. She's impulsive. Just today she rushed into traffic."

"That Bella is a piece of work too," muttered Jets. "She's antagonistic and pushes the other two around. Just like her mother."

Dr. Brewer sighed. "I would have to do more individual evaluations and take a deeper case history, but everything you say points to parental alienation syndrome."

"Can they get help?"

"Now that both parents are dead, the chances of getting help are slim. But I will suggest good therapists for all three, even though they are too old to see me professionally and no longer fall under my jurisdiction."

Jets looked grim. "They still fall under my jurisdiction and I have the mind to put them all behind bars."

"Would you arrest them for helping their mother kill their father?" Olivia felt sad just saying those words.

"On the one hand, I don't have the evidence to support their involvement. But on the other hand, they did obstruct justice by pretending they didn't know. Blair did hide the weapon, after all." Jets tapped the table with her fingers.

Dr. Brewer spoke up. "This may be the time to focus on the victim."

She means Ashley.

"You're pretty smart for a shrink," Jets interjected. "So let's move on to see what we're going to do with the girl we have in cell number one. Here are my plans."

Jets opened a different page on her iPad. "The memorial is still on. Brad got some videos of Beats in concert to play for the service. He's made a montage of Beats hanging out with his children over the years. We're going to reinstate

Beats's reputation and celebrate his life right here in Lily Rock."

"Will we memorialize Bianca?" Olivia asked.

"I'm leaving that up to her children. Too bad I can't arrest a dead woman." Jets looked genuinely unhappy.

Dr. Brewer commented, "I think it's admirable for the town to hold a memorial for a man who never lived here, but I do find it odd. Is this common practice in Lily Rock?"

"He didn't live here but his youngest child will be one of us," Jets explained.

"Do you mean Blair?" Dr. Brewer looked puzzled.

Janis spoke hastily. "Not Blair. There's another child. A baby. On the way." Before Janis could explain further, Brad stuck his head in the door.

"I've got fries and milkshakes," he announced.

"Comfort food." Dr. Brewer smiled.

Jets lifted an eyebrow in her direction. "I like a woman with good culinary instincts."

* * *

By eleven o'clock the next day people gathered to celebrate the life of Beats Malone. In the front row Olivia sat on one side of Ashley, while Janis Jets sat on the other. The Old Rockers filled the row behind them. Olivia turned her head to count the people. She leaned in to Ashley. "Some thirty or so faces at the memorial."

Ashley shrugged. "I still don't know why I'm here."

"Because this town wants to honor Beats and they want to support you."

"That makes no sense." Ashley looked down at her new white sneakers. "They don't even know me. Plus I killed Bianca. What kind of a town honors a murderer..."

"There were extenuating circumstances," Olivia said quietly. "Even if you're not telling us everything, the court advocate is willing to make allowances. You're only seventeen. You didn't plan on killing Bianca. Plus you were surrounded by a very dysfunctional family."

"I still killed her," muttered Ashley.

"Dr. Brewer got in touch with a good attorney. The Old Rockers are footing the bill. You're in good hands."

"If you say so." Ashley looked around the room, as if searching for someone. "Is that Meadow woman an Old Rocker? She's right over there, the one with the ridiculous hat."

"Meadow McCloud is an Old Rocker. She's lived in Lily Rock for ages."

"Yah, well she visited me in jail. Brought me cookies and some kind of herbal teabags."

"She did the same for me when I first came to Lily Rock." Olivia smiled. *Meadow actually drugged me with her herbal teas, but I don't have to tell Ashley all the particular details.*

"Good morning," came a voice over the loudspeaker.

"Why is that woman running the memorial?" grumbled Ashley.

Olivia leaned closer to explain. "We found out that Dr. Brewer is a retired pastor. So she said she'd lead the service for Beats."

"That's just crazy," muttered Ashley. "Lily Rock is weird. I'm dragged out of my cell, dressed up in clean clothes, and trotted out to listen to a bunch of people talk about a dead guy I didn't even know."

"No one here knew him either," Olivia admitted. *The one who knew Beats the best is in her bed watching the service on Zoom; she's the mother of his unborn child.*

Olivia's eyes drifted to the podium where Zoe Brewer continued to speak. She felt an elbow in her side.

Ashley whispered, "What's that dog doing up there?"

Olivia explained. "He's the Lily Rock mayor."

Ashley sucked in her cheeks trying to hold back a laugh. "You're just as crazy as everyone else," Ashley said. "You drank the Lily Rock Kool-Aid."

Olivia sighed. She wanted to tell Ashley she'd felt the same when she'd first arrived in Lily Rock.

How do I explain that at first everyone looks crazy? And then one day they don't. Lily Rock gets under your skin. Then pretty soon the mayor becomes your best friend and you get adopted by an Old Rocker.

How do I tell her that Lily Rock champions the least likely people? How do I tell Ashley that everything's going to be okay and that Lily Rock will stand behind her for as long as she needs?

The next announcement interrupted her thoughts. "And now we have a slideshow with music about the life of Beats Malone. He was well known in his Los Angeles community of musicians and a good father to his three children. The video has been edited by Brad May. Olivia Greer will accompany with a song for the opening montage."

Olivia hurried to the front of the room. Earlier she'd left her autoharp on the piano bench, ready and tuned. She picked it up and sat on a stool in front of the podium. Smiling at Ashley, she strummed her first chord and then her clear voice began to sing.

"I am an orphan on God's highway." At that moment the lights dimmed as the video began. Brad had scanned the photos from the box. Beats Malone holding baby Blair came first, with his two older children looking on. His face glowed with joy as he held the swaddled baby.

Four minutes of photos gave Olivia the chance to sing all the verses. By the time Brad paused the video, she strummed her last chord. Placing her autoharp back on the piano bench, Olivia sat next to Ashley.

The girl's hand reached over to grasp Olivia's. "That's the song," she said, her voice sounding husky. "The one I dubbed over Brandon's video."

Olivia squeezed Ashley's hand and held it in hers. They both watched the video continue with photos of Beats drumming with his band, along with shots from the many gigs he played over the years.

After the video came to an end, everyone sat in silence. Finally Dr. Brewer stood behind the podium. "Sometimes the best way to honor a person's life is to hold the silence," she assured them. "Now that we've completed our service, I invite you for refreshments provided by Thyme Out. Walk through the lobby and into the atrium where the food and beverages will be served."

Ashley leaned over to whisper in Olivia's ear. "I didn't mean to kill her," she said in a quiet voice.

Olivia felt a tingle up her spine.

In a low voice Ashley kept explaining. "Bianca never liked me. She hated that I hung out with Brandon. She told me I was stupid all the time. She wouldn't even let me sleep inside their house. She kept all of their food locked away so I wouldn't eat any when she wasn't looking."

Olivia held her breath as Ashley kept talking.

"After Beats died, no one talked about him. I didn't know he was their father until it came out by accident one day. I asked how they got the car all of a sudden. And then they just unloaded all about Beats, how horrible he was to them. That day I killed Bianca? I just asked one question and she went ballistic."

"What was that?" Olivia said softly.

"I asked Bianca how Beats could be such a deadbeat dad if he brought that car all the way up to Lily Rock for his kids to drive."

Ashley's voice began to tremble. "She started screaming at me, telling me I was worthless and how no one could ever love me. Then she told me how Beats had no right to steal her children. She moved to Lily Rock to stop him from contacting the kids. She shoved me. I fell on the dirt. As I was getting up she kept screaming and then finally confessed that she killed Beats herself.

"Once I was on my feet, I kept asking her questions. I hoped once she told me she'd calm down. So Bianca agreed to let Beats drop off the car. She never told her kids. They were supposed to go together to surprise their kids at the pub. While he waited for her in the car, she pocketed a knife from her kitchen. She settled herself into the driver's seat and asked him for the key. When he turned to give it to her, she stabbed him in the chest. Then she waited. Once he stopped breathing, she drove to the pub and pushed him out.

"She told me she was proud of what she'd done, like it was a good thing!"

Olivia put her arm around Ashley's shoulders. There was no stopping her now, the words tumbled from her mouth.

"When she was screaming all of that to me, coming toward me, getting closer and closer, I felt like I'd be the next one. So I used my skateboard and swung it at her, just to keep her away. I didn't really think about it."

A sob escaped her lips. Olivia patted her shoulder. She heard someone clear their throat. Janis Jets waited nearby, as if she'd heard everything. Jets came closer, dangling a tissue from her fingers.

Olivia took the tissue, tucking it into Ashley's clenched hand.

"A first for me," Jets muttered. "I've never given a damn about someone I've arrested who confessed to murder. But this one," she pointed to Ashley, "she's different. A case of self-defense is what I'm thinking. I'm gonna be there at the hearing and make sure the judge gets the whole story."

Ashley looked up at Jets. Her face was puffy from crying. "You're just another Lily Rock weirdo," she muttered.

"On the one hand, you're exactly right," Jets agreed. "But on the other hand, an entire town of Lily Rock weirdos has decided to adopt you as their own. So cheer up, skateboard girl, you're going to live to shred another day."

Olivia looked confused.

"That's skateboard talk," Jets explained. She nodded to Ashley. "This one knows what I'm talking about."

Olivia took Ashley's elbow, encouraging her to stand. "It's time for the reception. Thyme Out cookies are the best. In case you didn't know, Janis and the owner of Thyme Out are a couple. I suspect you'll be getting care packages of cookies and muffins in jail while you await bail."

Ashley stood between Janis and Olivia as the three women walked down the aisle toward the exit. Her head swiveled from one side to the other, taking in the exchange.

"Have you told Ashley about the new baby?" asked Jets.

"Not yet," Olivia answered, "all in good time."

"She might as well know we're not done with Malone's offspring," Jets replied.

"What new baby?" Ashley asked. "You'd better tell me now, since I'll be going away for a while."

Olivia chuckled. "You won't be away for long. Not if Janis Jets has anything to do with it. She can be quite persuasive with higher-ups when given half a chance."

"I am very persuasive," Jets agreed. "And I don't need an autoharp to get a confession like some people."

Ashley looked at Olivia and then back at Janis. She shook her head. "You're both nuts."

"Welcome to Lily Rock," Jets said. "We're all nuts."

Olivia nodded. "Just think, you'll soon be one of us whether you like it or not."

GET A FREE SHORT STORY

Join my VIP newsletter to get the latest news of Lily Rock along with contests, discounts, events, and giveaways! I'll also send you *Meadow's Hat*, a short story set before book one :).

Sign up on bonniehardywrites.com/newsletter

ACKNOWLEDGMENTS

I hope you've enjoyed *Deadbeat Dad* and that your interest is piqued for the next book about Sage's baby and the Lily Rock gang.

I'd like to thank my readers for their continued support of this series and for all of your emails about your pets. It's such a delight to see photos of cats, dogs, iguanas and even a ferret. It seems Mayor Maguire has friends on the internet.

I'd also like to thank Christie Stratos and her team at Proof Positive. They remember my characters better than I do on some days.

Thanks to Kate Tilton and her finely tuned organizational approach. I've known that I was a story teller for a long time, but I never imagined myself an independent publisher until I met Kate.

And to my daughter, Emily: Thanks for taking the time to read aloud the feedback for my books. Hearing comments in your voice helps me to understand.

As always I am grateful to my husband who happens to have an excellent eye for detail. He took *Deadbeat* with him on our vacation, just so we could chat about Lily Rock. Bill, you're the best!

ABOUT THE AUTHOR

Born and raised in Los Angeles, Bonnie Hardy is a former teacher, choir director, and preacher. She lives with her husband and two dogs in Southern California.

Bonnie has published in *Christian Century*, *Presence: an International Journal for Spiritual Direction*, and with Pilgrim Press.

When not planting flowers and baking cookies, she can be found at her computer plotting her next Lily Rock mystery.

You can follow Bonnie at
bonniehardywrites.com
and on Instagram @bonniehardywrites.

- facebook.com/bonniehardywrites
- instagram.com/bonniehardywrites
- goodreads.com/bonniehardy
- bookbub.com/authors/bonnie-hardy
- amazon.com/author/bonniehardy